THE MURDERED MOLLS

Josef Slonský Investigations
Book Seven

Graham Brack

SAPERE
BOOKS

Also in the Josef Slonský Series
Lying and Dying
Slaughter and Forgetting
Death on Duty
Field of Death
A Second Death
Laid In Earth

THE MURDERED MOLLS

Published by Sapere Books.

224 Trafalgar Road, Ilkley, LS29 8HH,
United Kingdom

saperebooks.com

ISBN: 978-0-85495-145-1

CHAPTER 1

Prague, Czech Republic, 2008

When Josef Slonský asked for the bedpan, he did not really want a bedpan. What he really wanted was for the curtains around the bed to be drawn so that no-one would see him shuffle down the bed to unhook the clipboard at the far end.

Slonský, Josef, he read, *Date of Birth: 11.XI.1947.* He could hardly argue with any of that. There followed a couple of graphs demonstrating that his blood pressure and pulse were consistent. Unfortunately, they were consistently high, as the doctors kept telling him as if it represented a moral failure on his part not to keep them under control.

Beneath these there was a list of the medication to which he was being subjected, or would have been subjected if he had not hidden them inside his pillow, with the exception of the painkillers, of course. He glanced down at the offending knee, still bearing the yellow stain of the disinfectant with which it had been swabbed before the operation, and tutted.

The proximate cause of his enforced stay in hospital was one Pepa Mach, a slimy little cat burglar of some notoriety, who had devised a method of attacking upstairs rooms using an adapted rope ladder with grappling hooks at the top and a T-shaped support beneath so that they could be pushed into place. This enabled him to progress from balcony to balcony until he found an open window.

During the tourist season, Mach had been extremely successful. It was rarely possible to attribute a theft definitively to one or other burglar, but the scratches on the balcony rails and the speed of entry suggested that the same man was responsible.

Then came the day when, by pure chance, he was spotted. A woman working late happened to look out of an office block's rear windows and saw a small figure in black climbing the rear of the boutique hotel behind. The large empty backpack swinging from a shoulder suggested that he was not a late night window cleaner.

The police were summoned, and Slonský, as the on-call detective, was interrupted in the middle of his third glass of Pilsner. Being in no state to drive, and not having a car anyway, because he saw no point in having something that was so difficult to park in Prague and was often slower than public transport, Slonský caught a bus and arrived to find that a cordon had been thrown around the hotel while an officer had entered with a view to catching Mach in the act.

Mach had eluded the officer, but was still trapped in the hotel, and it was fairly certain that from whatever secret vantage point he had managed to find he was watching closely for the chance to slip away. At any event, that would explain why he decided that Slonský was the least athletic link in this human chain around the hotel, and at some point he simply hitched the rucksack on his back and ran towards the lane to Slonský's side.

Slonský attempted to push off the wet cobbles to block the exit and felt a sharp pain in his knee. Despite his sudden immobility he lunged to grab Mach by one ankle and held on until other officers arrived to pin Mach to the ground and complete the arrest. Such was the pain that he was unable to give Mach a proper kick in the ribs and had to settle for a nudge with his toe-cap.

When he was transferred to hospital the doctors had diagnosed a complex series of tears in various parts of the knee that Slonský did not know he had — having been shown a picture of what went on inside a knee, he remarked to Navrátil that it was a miracle that anyone ever mastered the complexities well enough to walk at all — and surgery had been undertaken.

Each day since then began with a ritual. The sister in charge of the ward would wish him a good morning, Slonský would retort that it was indeed a good morning, because he hoped it would be the last that he would spend there, to which she would reply that there was no prospect of his going home.

'But we keep being told that you need the beds,' he had protested on this particular morning.

'So we do, for the benefit of people like you who need them.'

'But I don't need one. Why can't I go home?'

The sister, not a woman who was easily intimidated even by a defiant Slonský, bent over so she could fix him eye to eye. 'Because, Mr Slonský, you are an older man who lives alone in a block of flats with no lift. It's not at all suitable for a man with a dodgy knee.'

'I'm a working man, not a senior citizen.'

'So you are, and need I remind you that you were injured at work. If it happened before, it could happen again, which is why we have to ensure that you make a full recovery.'

'It's not my fault I live alone. My wife left me.'

For a moment the sister had a response on the tip of her tongue, but decided it was probably inappropriate, so she chose another. 'I'm sorry to hear that, but without help it would be difficult for you to live independently. Perhaps we can get social services to consider installing a chairlift or some handrails.'

Slonský winced. Was he really to be reduced to that? He cast his mind back to his last work-related hospital stay, when he had a bullet removed after a warehouse raid went wrong. He had been living alone then but nobody told him he couldn't go home. That wound had been a lot harder for him to reach, too, being the result of a ricochet and not, as some maliciously implied, the outcome of his running away. He could still feel a twinge in his buttock in damp weather.

Slonský returned the clipboard to its rightful place and flopped back on his pillows.

'Are you done with the bedpan, Mr Slonský?' asked a young nurse from outside the curtains.

'False alarm,' he said.

'Never mind,' she said brightly. 'That happens in a lot of older men.'

Slonský was allowed two visitors every visiting time, and two visitors was precisely what he got, leading him to suppose that someone was drawing up a rota, and the prime candidate was sitting in front of him now.

Lieutenant Kristýna Peiperová was tall, blonde, athletic, ambitious and seemed to have a gift for remembering birthdays, name days, christenings, wedding anniversaries and other trivia that passed Slonský by. Things like his staff's first names, for example. Since she was off duty she was holding the hand of her new husband, Lieutenant Jan Navrátil, who looked greatly disturbed by the possibility that this display of rampant affection in a public place might be improper.

'Is there anything we can get for you, sir?' she asked.

'Yes,' said Slonský. 'A floor plan of the hospital so I can work out my escape route.'

'Everything is under control, sir. Lieutenant Dvorník has taken charge.'

'You tell me everything is under control, and in the same breath let slip that Dvorník is running the show?'

'There's very little crime, sir,' Navrátil chipped in. 'We're coping.'

'That's not the point, lad. The point is that I'm trapped in here with only a small selection of radio channels to keep me sane, and at least two of them are adding to the problem. What exactly is "house music", anyway?'

'I'm not the person to ask, sir,' Navrátil politely explained. 'But we want you to enjoy the break and recover fully.'

Slonský smelled a rat. 'Dvorník hasn't gone soft on leave applications, I hope?'

'You can ask him yourself tonight, sir,' Peiperová explained. 'He's coming after work with Sergeant Mucha.'

'Ah, Mucha! He won't let me down. Tell him to bring me a large screwdriver so I can remove a few window catches.'

CHAPTER 2

Navrátil first began to suspect that somebody up top did not like him very much at around ten minutes to five when the call came in. A woman had telephoned saying that she had heard a commotion in the neighbouring flat and had gone to investigate but nobody had answered the door, although she was sure her neighbour had been at home.

Since they both lived on the third floor of their block, looking in the window was not an option, but she had doggedly kept knocking for some time before deciding that there must be something wrong, because Katya went to work in the evening and there was no sound of her getting ready.

Navrátil inspected the address and sighed. Černý Most was not a select area of town. Sitting out to the north-east its main interest was the large shopping mall that had been built to entice Prague shoppers out of the city so that they could enjoy looking at gadgets they could not afford without being put to the trouble of touring the city in search of them. The apartments were largely *paneláky*, prefabricated concrete-sided blocks designed to remain standing at least until the builders got off the site. Navrátil always found them depressing, though he could understand that given a choice between a *panelák* and no house at all, plenty of young couples chose the *panelák*.

He drove out to Černý Most, parked the car at the mall and walked the rest of the way, thus giving himself the best possible chance of having a car to go back to. He found the address and climbed the urine-scented staircase to find the neighbour who had made the phone call waiting on the landing.

'Are you the police?' she asked.

Navrátil showed her his badge.

'They say you know when you're getting older if the policemen look younger,' she said. 'God, but I must be ancient.'

'I'm Lieutenant Navrátil,' explained the young policeman.

'A lieutenant? Already?'

Navrátil could think of no response that would not sound cocky, so he nodded towards the door. 'Still no sound?'

'No. And she would usually be gone by ten past five.'

'Perhaps it's her day off.'

'She doesn't really get days off. Not in her job.'

'What is her job?'

'I don't exactly know, but I think it's some sort of escort work. She doesn't bring men back.'

Navrátil looked around the landing.

'I know,' the woman said, 'I wouldn't bring anyone back either.'

'I was looking for something I could use to get in,' he replied.

'Aren't you going to kick the door in? That's what the police usually do here.'

'Then I have to get someone to make it secure again. There's nobody else who would have a key, I suppose?'

'There's a woman who comes over visiting now and again but I don't think she has a key. And she always comes in the morning.'

Navrátil inspected the lock. It looked quite elderly and basic, and he was sure that Slonský would have had it open in a few minutes with his little lock-picking set, but Navrátil had refused to learn to use it on the ground that it seemed rather underhand to him. At this moment he was regretting that choice.

There was nothing for it. He would have to smash the door down. Instructing the woman to stand aside he retreated across the landing and threw himself at the door.

The door in question was fully up to the general standard of 1970s *paneláky* doors and disintegrated at the first contact, leaving Navrátil sprawled on the floor of the hallway. He picked himself up and looked at his hands to see if they needed cleaning. They certainly did.

But it was not grime that had stained them, but fresh blood. Lots of fresh blood.

Ordering the neighbour to stay back, Navrátil fished in his pocket for some gloves and eased open the door to one of the rooms at the front. It proved to be a sitting room and so far as Navrátil could tell it was in good order. He turned to the room next to it, which was a bathroom with an old-fashioned tub raised on feet that looked as if they belonged to a lion or some similar animal. The kitchen was opposite this, and was a gory sight. A selection of knives lay haphazardly on the counter, and all of them were coated in blood.

The source of the blood was in the bedroom. The victim's silence was explained by a large strip of duct tape wrapped round her head just under her nose. That, and the fact that the head was on the windowsill. The remainder of the body was on the bed, secured to it by the wrists and ankles. There was a large cavity between the hips. While Navrátil was still very innocent on the matter of female anatomy he was fairly sure that he knew which bits were missing.

There was an old-fashioned radiator on one side and a chair on the other side of the bed with some folded clothes on it. Taking his mobile phone from his pocket he called for a pathologist, some technicians and some uniformed help to keep sightseers out, though who would want to see this particular sight was beyond him.

Slonský was disgusted. 'A simple request, and you let me down.'

Mucha was unabashed. 'It's for your own good.'

'Can't I be the arbiter of that?'

'Evidently not, because you don't know when something is for your own good.'

'If I can't have a screwdriver, what about that fancy penknife you always carry?'

'If I give that to you I won't always be carrying it, will I?'

'He's got a point there,' added Dvorník cheerfully.

Mucha decided another line of argument might be more fruitful. 'You remember the old days. Before the Wall came down, what would you have done in this position to get yourself let out?'

Slonský needed no time at all to come up with the answer. 'I'd have slipped a doctor a few crowns to sign the paperwork.'

'Exactly. So it won't surprise you to know that in the brave new world of today I'm having to refuse money from police officers who want me to bribe the doctors to keep you here. I could have made a couple of thousand this afternoon alone when people heard I was coming.'

'Name names.'

'My lips are sealed. Though I will say that Colonel Rajka wasn't one of them.'

Rajka was Director of Criminal Police and therefore Slonský's immediate superior. A former Olympic wrestler who still looked like he could rip his shirt any time he wanted by flexing his chest muscles, he was well able to pick Slonský up and return him bodily to the hospital if need be.

Slonský flopped back on his pillows. 'I'll go stir crazy in here,' he whined.

It was at this moment that an idea of such surpassing brilliance entered his head that he half expected to see a light bulb above him as in the old cartoons he watched as a boy. The fact that it had not previously occurred to him he attributed to his enforced abstinence from beer, the essential mental lubricant that kept his brain cogs purring.

'They won't let me go because I'd be on my own,' he said. 'But if a kindly soul were to let me lodge with them while I recuperate...'

'The wife's sister is staying with us,' blurted Mucha.

'No, she isn't,' Slonský snapped. 'You were far too happy when you arrived for the Evil Witch of Kutná Hora to be with you again.'

'I've got eight children and a small flat,' Dvorník chipped in.

'I could babysit so you and your wife could have a night out,' suggested Slonský half-heartedly.

'It was having nights out that led to the eight children,' Mucha observed, leading Dvorník to nod wistfully.

'Navrátil and Peiperová have two bedrooms in their new place,' mused Slonský.

'They're newly-weds,' said Mucha. 'They'll keep you up all night with the noise from their bedroom.'

Slonský shook his head. 'Navrátil has strong views on that kind of thing.'

'He had strong views before he was married,' Mucha replied. 'Once the ring is on the finger he'll be like any other young man. Besides, you wouldn't want to play gooseberry. Imagine what a wet blanket it would be for them to think that their boss is only ten metres away.'

'I don't actually have to stay there,' Slonský objected. 'They just need to sign to say I'm staying with them. Once I'm out I can get a taxi home.'

'That won't work,' said Dvorník mournfully. 'I think the welfare people have to come and visit to see how you're settling in, like when you're a new mum.'

'I wouldn't know,' Slonský growled, 'on account of never having been a new mother. But if it gets me out of here I'm prepared to try faking anything.'

'What happened to Slonský?' asked Dr Novák as he crouched by the bed to measure the blood splashes.

'He slipped on some wet cobbles trying to turn suddenly as he arrested a burglar,' Navrátil explained. 'It seems he's done quite a lot of damage to his knee ligaments.'

'Ouch!' exclaimed the pathologist. 'Knees can be tricky blighters, especially at his age. He'll probably never dance the tango again.'

Navrátil was tempted to ask if there was any evidence that Slonský had ever danced the tango before his injury, but decided to let it rest. He wasn't sure that he wanted to see it. 'Is there any extra information you can give me, Dr Novák?' he asked.

'You're a lot more polite than Slonský, aren't you? One or two things. You'll be pleased to hear that her head was cut off after her death. Not long after, but definitely after. Sadly, I don't think I can say the same about the missing uterus and associated organs. Roughly the top third of the vagina has been removed, with a fairly clean cut. And the internal female parts aren't here.'

'I was hoping they were under that blood,' confessed Navrátil.

'No, the bladder is still there but the rest has been spirited away.'

Novák strode purposefully into the hallway and up to the demolished door. 'I can't understand why nobody heard anything.'

'She was gagged with tape over her mouth.'

'Even so, you can make a lot of noise screaming, and I can't imagine that she didn't scream when this was done to her.'

'Let's hope she was at least unconscious.'

'We can hope,' agreed Novák, 'but having your belly ripped open is the kind of thing that would bring many people to their senses quite quickly. And there's no sign or smell of a volatile anaesthetic.'

'You mean like chloroform?'

'That sort of thing. Despite what you see in movies, chloroform is a very difficult thing to subdue someone with unless they co-operate, and you're likely to see burns on the lips and bruises where the pad has been held on. At first inspection I don't see any of that. No, Lieutenant, I think what we have here is perhaps the nastiest killer I've ever come across in the Czech Republic.'

CHAPTER 3

A council was taking place in the canteen. Dvorník and Mucha were briefing Navrátil, Peiperová and Peiperová's trainee, Officer Lucie Jerneková on their hospital visit of the previous evening.

'We ought to warn whoever is going today that Slonský may ask them to take him home with them,' said Dvorník.

'I'd love to help but unfortunately my sister-in-law is staying with us,' Mucha explained.

'And my house is a bit packed with us and the eight children,' Dvorník added.

'I'd be okay with it,' Jerneková sniffed, 'but I live in the barracks and they have rules about taking men back to your room.'

'I should think they would,' Navrátil exclaimed.

Jerneková shrugged. 'They tell you they want you to feel that it's your home,' she said, 'but then they make rules like that. Not that I'm fussed one way or the other about men, but it's the principle of the thing.'

Mucha felt he should intervene. 'Who is going today?' he asked.

Peiperová checked her diary. 'Colonel Rajka and Officer Krob this afternoon, Major Lukas and Officer Jerneková tonight.'

'I'll have a word with the Colonel and Major to put them on their guard,' said Mucha.

'Major Lukas is a good man,' Peiperová said. 'He could very easily be persuaded to help.'

'Not while I'm there,' said Jerneková. 'Anyway, didn't someone tell me his two daughters still live at home?'

'Eva and Eliška? That's right,' agreed Peiperová, the only one who could be guaranteed to have remembered their names.

'There can't be much space then,' Jerneková continued. 'Besides, a responsible father wouldn't want an older man under his roof if he's got two daughters.'

'In fairness to Captain Slonský,' Peiperová objected, 'I can't think of any man who would be less likely to behave improperly with a woman.'

Navrátil opened his mouth as if to object but thought better of it.

'I agree,' said Jerneková. 'But we know him, and they don't.'

'Where is Krob anyway?' Mucha enquired.

'At his physiotherapy session,' Navrátil explained.

A few months before Ivo Krob had been injured when a man to whom he was handcuffed had decided to end it all by jumping off a hillside. Krob had saved himself by grabbing a tree, but the result of dangling over a drop with around ninety kilos of murderer hanging from his other wrist had been to cause serious damage to his shoulder. Several operations and a lot of manipulation later, he was beginning to get some use back in the arm, but he could not drive, and since Jerneková had not yet obtained a driving licence, he had been paired with Rajka while Jerneková would travel with Major Lukas.

'I'll tell him what we've been saying when he gets back,' suggested Mucha.

'It's a shame Captain Slonský doesn't have any family to go to,' said Peiperová.

'If only the thing with Věra had worked out,' Navrátil added.

'Věra? Who's Věra?' asked Jerneková.

'Captain Slonský's wife,' Peiperová explained. 'Or almost ex-wife, I suppose. She left him not long after they got married, disappeared for thirty years, then reappeared a couple of years ago to explain that she had never actually filed the divorce papers he'd signed, so they were still married.'

'Forgetful, is she?' Jerneková commented.

'Who knows why she didn't go through with it? Anyway, it all went wrong when Captain Slonský took her out for a birthday dinner last October and a man came up and introduced himself as her ex-partner.'

'Jesus Maria!' exclaimed Jerneková. 'And people say *I'm* socially inept.'

'It seems that Mrs Slonská had been economical with the truth about her recent past,' Navrátil summed up. Peiperová knew that he was itching to tut at the end of his summary, but was holding back because he recognised it was actually none of his business.

'We're rather getting off the point,' Mucha reminded them. 'We mustn't weaken. It's for his own good if he stays in hospital until he is completely recovered.'

'I'll mention that to Hauzer,' Dvorník said. 'When is he visiting?'

'Tomorrow afternoon,' said Peiperová. 'He's taking Captain Slonský's journalist friend, Mr Valentin.'

Hauzer was Dvorník's assistant who was very much the forgotten man of the department. This was largely because he spent a lot of time following people, at which he was uncommonly good, in large measure because he was so unremarkable himself. Even Dvorník had been known to switch the lights off on leaving his office having overlooked the fact that Hauzer was still there.

'Who's going to tell Valentin?' asked Navrátil.

'The trouble is,' said Peiperová, 'that we don't know which bar he's most likely to be found in. I could try ringing his newspaper to see if they can pass on a message to ring us.'

'It's probably not worthwhile going to a lot of effort,' said Mucha. 'Even if Valentin's arm could be twisted, he lives in a tiny flat, I believe. There wouldn't be room for a Slonský.'

The more he investigated, the less Dr Novák liked what he was finding. Biochemical analysis of the victim's blood led him to believe that her pain levels had been high for a prolonged period. He had found no trace of the missing uterus, fallopian tubes or ovaries, nor had his team discovered any tool in the flat that might have been used to remove them. The blood-covered knives in the kitchen were not the right size to have inflicted all of the cuts he saw, though it was possible that they had each been tried in turn. However, the absence of blood directly under or on the lower surfaces of the knives suggested that blood had been poured over them. But the biggest puzzle was how someone who must have been covered in blood had apparently walked out into the street without attracting notice.

He had concluded that the blood in the hallway was the result of deliberate spreading of the victim's blood by the killer. There were no footprints in it, suggesting that he — Novák automatically assigned the male pronoun to him simply because the preponderance of such murderers were male — had walked backwards, strewing the blood behind him.

A second question was why the neighbour had heard what she called "a commotion" but not, apparently, any screaming. With so little of the victim's vagina still in situ it was hard to be certain whether sexual activity had taken place; he was inclined to think it had, but he had found no trace of semen on her. Perhaps she had been penetrated with some inanimate object.

Of one thing Dr Novák was utterly certain. He had never seen this man's handiwork before, and he did not want to ever see it again.

As part of the campaign to keep Slonský in his hospital bed, Navrátil had asked everyone not to mention the murder at Černý Most, reasoning that Slonský would try to use it as evidence that his presence was urgently required in the outside world. Since Slonský rarely bothered with newspapers or the television it was quite likely, thought Navrátil, that his boss would remain in ignorance until one of them told him, which would not be anytime soon.

This stratagem came to grief courtesy of the man in the next bed.

'You're a policeman, aren't you?' he asked Slonský.

'Captain in the criminal police.'

'That's a bad business out at Černý Most, isn't it?'

'What business?'

'Woman killed in her flat there. Whore or escort or good-time girl, whatever you want to call her. Here!' He handed his newspaper to Slonský who read the article carefully.

'It doesn't tell us much, does it?' Slonský said at last.

'What's there to tell? That sort of woman must take chances with her safety all the time. It's not surprising that it ends badly so often. It beats me why any woman would carry on with it.'

'Poverty usually,' snapped Slonský. 'Or a man telling her that's what she's there for and threatening to carve her up if she doesn't.'

'Still,' persisted his neighbour, 'it must be difficult to prove which particular client did it. I mean, they don't keep receipt books, do they?'

'No,' conceded Slonský, 'but the criminal police tries just as hard on every killing. These women are still citizens entitled to our best efforts. The old idea that they bring it on themselves by the life they lead is just victim-blaming to excuse not making the effort. If I wasn't banged up in here with this knee I'd be going door to door in Černý Most now, just like I would for any other murder.'

'You're missing out on all the fun, then.'

'If you think a murder enquiry is fun, you're got as perverse an idea of fun as this killer. Is there a telephone here patients can use?'

'I don't know. You could try asking Sister.'

'I doubt she'll tell me.'

'Are you surprised? I admire the woman for making you stay when every fibre of her being must be wishing you weren't here. You're not the easiest patient, are you?'

CHAPTER 4

On the basis that the majority of those at home during daytime would be women, the job of going door to door had been assigned to Peiperová and Jerneková. Krob was trawling through unsolved murders in the Czech Republic looking for any cases with similar features, while Navrátil was trying to put together some sort of dossier on the victim.

Access to State databases gave him some basic information. Her name was Kateryna Teslenko, and she was twenty-eight years old. She had been resident in the Czech Republic for around four years.

Navrátil checked for past residents at that address and his suspicions were aroused when he discovered that for the first seven months or so she had shared the flat with one Viktor Veremchuk, who was described as a carpenter. Ordinarily, Veremchuk would have had difficulty in obtaining a work permit, but he had been issued with a green card on compassionate grounds. This green card allowed him to work for up to three years but only in the job listed on the card. In Veremchuk's case, the reason given for awarding him a card was that he hailed from a town close to Chernobyl and had not been able to find any long-term work in Ukraine. He had argued that he wanted to make a new start because Ukraine now held too many bad memories for him.

Kateryna Teslenko was described as a singer and dancer on her form. It was unclear whether their relationship had ever been formalised. The clerk who granted permission to work had noted that this needed elucidating before the grant was made but had then done nothing about it and the permits had been issued anyway. Nothing about this was in any way unusual. Navrátil had previously seen examples of dead people being issued with new driving licences and even one instance of a man who had been mistakenly named on a death certificate, a fact which did not come to light until he attempted to borrow money at a bank which declined to make any advance to a person who was legally deceased and therefore could not be made to pay it back.

Navrátil could not help but notice that this "temporary" three-year card had been renewed twice, which led him to wonder what the point of the system was. Veremchuk seemed to have been resident in Prague for around eight years in total, but had not come to the attention of the authorities in any way. The small difficulty with verifying this was that he did not appear to be registered at any address, and nobody seemed to think that it was their job to rectify this omission. He had not been employed by anyone for around five years, and he had not paid a crown in tax for most of the time he had been in the country. He had not attended a hospital and did not have a driving licence valid in the Czech Republic, though he would have been required to obtain one within three months of his residence permit being granted.

'It's a bit of a mess, isn't it?' said Colonel Rajka when he was presented with Navrátil's findings.

'That's an understatement, sir.'

'So we don't know where he is, we don't know what he does, he may not be in the country anyway and we don't know what his relationship with Ms Teslenko was.'

'That's a fair summary, sir. Though surely he would have trouble leaving the country without showing his passport, and the border guards should be checking when someone entered when they try to leave.'

Rajka knew that Navrátil was a competent and tenacious officer, but he was also rather naïve at times. Well, about most things, if the truth be told. 'Navrátil, the border guards are the officers we don't want trying to do any policing in the Czech Republic. That's why most of them finish up on the borders. It wouldn't surprise me if some of them don't even know how to turn the computers on. Your best bet is to ask them for their lists of unreconciled travel documents.'

'I'm sorry, sir, I don't know what those are.'

Rajka gestured for Navrátil to take a seat. 'For airlines, we know who is travelling and passport details are submitted in advance. That means they can be checked before they leave and if there are any anomalies they can be ironed out. It's not the same for land travel, where people can just turn up at the border with no notice.'

'I can see that, sir.'

'So the procedure is slightly different. The passports are recorded and subsequently matched to either their ID card, if they're Czech, or to the document used when someone entered the country, if they're foreigners. This leaves two possible types of discrepancy. There can be those who have come but not gone, in which event they should still be resident here, or they can have gone without apparently having come here, which are the ones the border police are most likely to find. They produce lists of those cases.'

'Are they extensive, sir?'

'Too extensive for my liking, Navrátil. You won't have any hope of checking them all out. But if I were a Ukrainian trying to get back to Ukraine I'd drive through Slovakia because there's a land boundary there and it means only having to cross two borders. And fortunately the Slovak Border Police operate the same system — hardly surprising since we both inherited it after the Velvet Divorce. So it seems to me that we start with those who left the Czech Republic to go to Slovakia, and then left Slovakia to go to Ukraine. That should narrow things down a bit.'

'We have a photograph of Veremchuk on his original application to stay, so we could try matching that to anyone on those lists who didn't leave on the same document as the one they used on arrival.'

'Exactly. It'll be a long job, I'm afraid, and it may prove Veremchuk is still here somewhere. Of course, we joined the open borders scheme a few months ago so we may not have anything useful since then except video footage. You could try asking the border police directorate to do it. It'll give them something to do while they're sitting in those little huts.'

Slonský strode the length of the ward confidently, opened the door to the toilet cubicle, and sat on the seat. 'Jesus Maria, that hurts,' he muttered, rubbing his knee with gusto.

His latest wheeze had been to try to pretend that there was nothing wrong with his knee and that he was making a remarkable recovery. To that end he had adopted his most stoic face when a young doctor grabbed his ankle and rotated his leg, resolutely claiming everything was fine while his knee ligaments were pleading with him to give the doctor a retaliatory kick in the chops.

He had declined his evening painkillers on the grounds that he no longer needed them, but not before he had sneaked an extra couple at lunchtime while the nurse's attention was diverted; he had allowed the physiotherapist to put his limb through a cycling motion and insisted on an extended session although he was close to tears by the end; and now he had discarded his crutch when visiting the toilet, marching boldly down the ward like an army recruit and making enough noise with his slippers to ensure that the medical staff noticed him doing it.

The outer toilet door was opened gently and a timid voice could be heard.

'Mr Slonský, are you in there?'

'I might be,' he replied. 'Who wants to know?'

'You've got a visitor,' the nurse replied. 'A Mr Valentin.'

'Small, scruffy fellow, little beard, thin on top, looks like he needs a good feed?'

'That's the one.'

'I'll be right out.'

Slonský levered himself to his feet and gingerly put some weight on his repaired leg. It caused him to use a word he always associated with a cuff round the ear from his beloved grandmother when he was about ten, but he flexed the knee gently and steeled himself for a jaunty perambulation back to his bed.

Valentin was sitting on a wooden chair at the side of the bed, dipping his hand into a paper bag and rummaging through the contents.

'What have you got there?' asked Slonský.

'Some grapes.'

'Why grapes?'

Valentin shrugged. 'It's what you take people in hospital, isn't it?'

'They're for me?'

'Of course.'

'So why are you eating them?'

'I'm just checking they're not poisoned. Plus, you were a long time coming.'

'I was otherwise engaged when you came. There are some things you can't hurry, you know.'

'Anyway, I hope you like grapes.'

'It's a long time since I had any. If I don't I can always tread on them and drink the juice.'

Valentin looked furtively over his shoulder and swiftly produced a bottle from his inside pocket. 'Your special liniment,' he explained.

'Liniment? Why do I want liniment?'

'Sniff it,' Valentin ordered.

Slonský held the bottle so that he could see the label.

'I washed it out carefully,' Valentin insisted.

'Just as well. I'm not sure I fancy "Golden Horse Rub",' Slonský answered, before removing the cap and sniffing cautiously. 'Ah, that sort of liniment! That smells like good quality liniment.'

'It's fifty per cent, ten-year-in-the-cask liniment.'

'I'll enjoy rubbing that into my throat later. Thank you.'

'I don't think you've ever said thank you to me before,' Valentin said. 'It's quite touching.'

'Put it down to my being in excruciating pain.'

'Knee giving you gyp?'

'That too. But it's mainly psychic pain. I've got to get out of here.'

One of the senior nurses walked past and inspected him closely without breaking stride. Slonský smiled weakly. 'She terrifies me. Like Stalin with boobs.'

'Her moustache isn't as impressive as his.'

'True, but give her a couple of years and you never know. How come you're here on your own? Did Peiperová's system fail?'

'Of course not. I'll tell her you suggested such a thing and I wouldn't want to be in your shoes.'

'Hell, no. I can't cope with her and Sister Stalin bossing me around.'

'No, Hauzer brought me. He's trying to find somewhere to park the car.'

'Good luck with that. Visiting time ends in ninety minutes.'

'So, aside from being in agony, how are you?'

'Bored. What is the point of a jigsaw? Why take a perfectly good picture and chop it up so you can put it back together again? I don't play chess, that man in the corner with the bad arm cheats at cards — I'm sure he tucks a Queen or two in his sling when he thinks we aren't looking — and my brain is grinding to a halt for lack of suitable high-quality lubrication.'

'Maybe I can get you signed out for an hour.'

'Now you're talking. I was going to ask you if you could leave a couple of bottles outside on the windowsill during the night.'

Valentin looked out of the window. 'It'll be tricky. We're two floors up.'

'Are we? Damn. I can't remember when I last went this long without a beer.'

'How long has it been?'

Slonský glanced at the wall clock. 'Fourteen days, nineteen hours and eight minutes. Not that I'm counting.'

'Still, it'll give you a nice rest,' Valentin said cheerily.

'I don't need a rest,' Slonský snarled in reply. 'I don't want them to find out they can manage without me. It might give them ideas. If this is what retirement is going to be like I don't want any part of it. If they throw me out of the police I'm going to put my service pistol in my mouth and let someone else worry about cleaning it all up.'

'You don't mean that?' Valentin asked anxiously.

'No, I don't suppose I do. What would be the point of going through everything we've been through in life and then jacking it all in?'

The ward door opened and Hauzer looked around, giving a happy smile of recognition when he saw Slonský. Invited to find himself a chair, he borrowed one from the nurses' table and placed it alongside Valentin's, pausing before he sat to pat down his pockets before producing an envelope from his jacket.

'Colonel Rajka asked me to give you this, sir.'

Slonský read the note attentively. As a trained detective, Hauzer could see from Slonský's colour that he did not like what he was reading. For that matter, so could Valentin, who edged his chair back a few centimetres in case there was an explosion.

'Bastards! Of all the mean, low … bastards!'

'Has someone upset you?' Valentin asked.

'It's those bastards in Human Resources,' Slonský seethed. 'Bastards!'

'I think we've got that bit now.'

'They've written to Rajka pointing out that once an officer reaches minimum retirement age there are certain requirements that have to be met before he can be kept on. His contract comes up for renewal each year.'

'You knew that.'

'Yes, but they've "reminded" Rajka that if I'm on sick leave at the end of my additional year it's normal practice not to extend the contract any longer. That way they're not obliged to keep paying me.'

'When's your year up?' asked Hauzer.

'My birthday, the eleventh of November.'

'That's less than nine weeks away,' Valentin calculated.

'I've got to get out of here and get back to work.'

'You can barely walk, sir,' Hauzer objected.

'I can think, lad. I can answer the phones. I can make coffee. No, scrub that, I'm no good at making coffee. But I can find something to do. Even if I can't I've got to be in that building on the eleventh of November looking busy. Rajka can fend them off if I'm there, but he needs me at my desk by then. Well, don't just sit there — how am I going to get out of this place?'

CHAPTER 5

The young woman was physically unharmed but very shaken.

She had been running through Letná Park when she was grabbed by a man and dragged towards some bushes. Since it was late afternoon and there had been some light rain the park was relatively quiet, but by good fortune another man had already been in the bushes and had frightened the attacker away.

The first policeman to attend was very inexperienced so he had called for a detective to help, and Peiperová had responded. Naturally, Jerneková, who was still in training, had tagged along to see how these things are done, and now she was sitting with the victim on a bench while Peiperová sent a description of the attacker for any nearby officers to keep a lookout.

'I had my earphones on so I didn't hear him approach,' explained the young woman.

'There's a lesson there,' Jerneková replied.

'I'd always thought I'm young, I'm fit, I could fight a man off, but he lifted me right off the ground and pinned my arms.'

'Yeah, a lot of women think they can fight a man off or knee him in the dangly bits, but we're shorter. If you're going to get a good kick in it throws you off balance and he can just scoop you up. It's like my mum used to say, you'll only get one kick in, so make it count. Anything half-hearted will only annoy him.'

Peiperová returned with the rescuer, a man of about fifty with a small but very vocal terrier in tow. The similarity with her own companion was obvious.

'Is she all right?' said the man.

It was unclear how he could have frightened off a determined attacker, given that he had the appearance of an unmarried librarian who lived with his older sister; not surprisingly, that was exactly what he was.

'This is probably a stupid question,' Jerneková began, 'but what were you doing in the bushes in the first place?'

'Oh, this is so embarrassing! Am I in trouble?'

'This lady says you were standing there with your fly undone.'

'No! Yes, I suppose so. But it's not what you think.'

'What do I think, then?' Jerneková demanded.

'I hesitate to say in front of ladies.'

'I've never been called a lady before, so let's hear it.'

The man coloured and turned his eyes away to one side. 'It's a long way home and I have a bit of a problem with my waterworks,' he explained, dropping his voice to a whisper on the last word.

'We should be grateful you bothered to go behind a tree, then,' said Jerneková.

'I didn't mean any harm. If I go to prison I'll lose my job!'

Peiperová decided to intervene. 'There's no danger of that. In the circumstances we can overlook the public nuisance. We're grateful to you for stopping the attacker.'

'It wasn't really me,' he said, 'but Jarmila.'

'Jarmila?'

They looked at the young woman who was as puzzled as they were. The man pointed downwards. 'Jarmila is my dog. She's not very fierce, but she yaps a lot. And she didn't like him. She's very protective of my sister,' the man explained.

'I see,' said Peiperová, though she didn't.

'I don't,' Jerneková added.

'Well, I suppose she feels protective of women in general,' the man elucidated.

Jerneková looked at the little terrier quizzically, as if assessing what earthly use the protection of a dog like that would be.

'Nevertheless,' Peiperová continued, 'the dog did a good job.'

'Bitch,' said Jerneková. Realising that Peiperová appeared to be about to blow a fuse she quickly expanded her comment. 'She's not a dog. She's a bitch.'

'Oh. I thought you meant … never mind. Can you describe the attacker, sir?'

'Not really. He was a good ten centimetres taller than me, so a bit over one metre eighty. He was wearing one of those things boxers wear, you know? With a hood, navy blue, I recall. I couldn't really see his face. Clean-shaven, I think.'

'What about you, madam?' Peiperová turned to the young woman.

'I didn't see his face. He had big hands, covered in sandy-coloured hair. The index finger of his right hand had a black patch on the nail. I can't tell you much else.'

'There was one thing,' the dog walker offered. 'I think he was a foreigner.'

'Why do you think that?' Peiperová asked.

'When Jarmila snapped at him he said something, but it wasn't Czech. A bit like Czech but not Czech, if you know what I mean.'

'Slovak?'

'No, I'd have understood that. Slav, but not Czech, I'd have said.'

When Valentin arrived back at the hospital in response to Slonský's message he was not in the best of moods. Being woken as early as five past ten did not help, but he had responded to the call for help for friendship's sake, and now found himself intercepted on the way to Slonský's bed by a senior doctor who asked him to step into a small room and take a seat.

'I understand that you are willing to look after Captain Slonský,' the doctor began.

'Yes, if it means he can get home earlier.'

'I must admit that we hadn't entirely understood the nature of your relationship with Mr Slonský,' the doctor growled.

'Relationship?'

'Yes. Of course, we are entirely non-judgemental about these things nowadays. I just want to be sure that you realise that your practices carry health risks.'

Valentin felt sweat collecting under his collar. 'What exactly did Slonský tell you?'

'There's no need for embarrassment. We're men of the world.'

'Yes, I think, maybe…'

'You don't have to explain. I suppose it's natural to conceal those kinds of preference. You must experience a lot of prejudice.'

'I think I need to say something,' Valentin began, but then bit his tongue as he realised that he was Slonský's best hope of getting out, and if that meant that the hospital staff had to be misled into thinking they were a gay couple, he ought to go along with the deception.

'Yes?' the doctor raised an eyebrow.

'We don't actually have any ... er ... practices,' Valentin mumbled, feeling quite queasy at the thought of them, at least with Slonský. 'It's more a matter of companionship.'

'Of course. These things are important in your twilight years.'

Valentin fleetingly wondered if slapping a specialist would make Slonský's eviction more or less likely. 'We don't do that kind of thing,' he muttered instead.

'None of my business,' the doctor said briskly. 'My sole concern was that you should be under no illusions about the implications for your health.' He stood and held the door open for Valentin. 'Haemorrhoids are no laughing matter,' said the doctor, wincing slightly.

Slonský was unrepentant. 'A real friend wouldn't be carping about helping a mate out like this,' he said.

'You could have warned me,' Valentin grumbled. 'It was highly embarrassing.'

'What is there to be embarrassed about? You're not anti-gay, are you?'

'Of course not. Live and let live is my motto. I just don't feel comfortable with lying to a doctor.'

'I would have told you, but the doctor got to you first.'

'It wasn't just that. It was the mental stress of trying to guess what kind of piffle you could possibly have told him that made him think that we are ... together.'

'All I said was that you would be taking care of me. On a 24/7 basis. He must have put the rest together himself.'

'You didn't suggest that we were romantically linked?'

Slonský looked a little awkward. 'Not in so many words.'

'Well, what did you say in so many words?'

'I forget. Something about being closer to you than anyone else. Which is true, by the way.'

'It may be true, but it's downright misleading.'

'Only if you want to be misled. Did he insist on all the intimate details?'

Valentin coloured. 'No, thank God. I don't think I could have made up anything convincing.'

'But did it work? Can I go home with you?'

'Yes and no.'

'How do you mean, "yes and no"? It's either yes or it's no.'

'In theory you can, but I don't have any way of taking you, do I? I don't drive.'

'I'll pay for a taxi.'

Valentin had heard this one before. 'Have you actually got any money on you?'

'Ah. Not as such.'

'I thought not. So what you really mean is that you'll call a cab which I will pay for.'

'I'll pay you back.'

'That'll be a first.'

'I beg your pardon!' Slonský yelped. 'When have I ever not paid you back?'

Too late, he noticed the doctor walking towards him.

'Could you conduct this lovers' tiff outside?' the doctor asked. 'People are trying to sleep here.'

Krob put the telephone back in its cradle. 'That was Mr Valentin. It seems Captain Slonský is being allowed to go home.'

'To whose home?' chorused Navrátil and Peiperová.

'His own, presumably,' Krob guessed. 'It can't be Mr Valentin's because he only has one room.'

'I've never been to the Captain's flat,' said Jerneková. 'What's it like?'

'I don't know,' Navrátil replied. 'None of us have ever been either.'

'Should we drop in on him from time to time to see how he is?' asked Krob.

'I think we should probably wait to be invited,' Peiperová said. 'We've all got his mobile phone number, so we can call him to keep in touch.'

Her telephone rang. As she answered it she pulled a face. There appeared to be no opportunity to talk as she listened and made notes, then hung up with a curt "goodbye". 'How does he do that?' she enquired.

'Do what?' asked Navrátil.

'Call when we're thinking about him.'

'Don't ask me,' said Navrátil. 'I'm still trying to work out how you manage to answer questions I haven't got round to asking.'

'It's called female intuition. I can read you like a book.'

'I can't,' Jerneková interjected with a smile, 'but I'll learn.'

'Anyway, what did the Captain want?' Navrátil asked.

'He just wanted to let us know that he's being discharged but he's going to his own flat and he'll see us all tomorrow.'

'He's coming into work?' Krob whispered.

'So it seems,' Peiperová replied.

'Given the state of his knee, he's either very brave or very stupid,' Krob continued.

'Anyone want to place a bet?' asked Jerneková.

CHAPTER 6

Peiperová was perplexed. 'Is this really all we have?' she asked.

'I'm afraid so,' Sergeant Mucha replied.

'But surely there are many more sex attacks in the Czech Republic than these?'

'Undoubtedly. I'm sure there are many that don't get reported. But of those that are, these are the unsolved ones.'

'Why so few? Are Czech men less likely to commit sex offences than other nationalities?'

Mucha considered the proposition and brought his lengthy experience to bear on the matter. 'I don't think so,' he said. 'It's just that they're more inept, so more of them get caught.'

'We think this one may have been a foreigner. Does that narrow things down at all?'

Mucha tapped a few keys and waited. 'Sadly not. Foreigners punch above their weight in the sex offences league. Some of them come here for that very reason.'

'Then we'd better catch a few and put a stop to that,' said Peiperová with a very determined look on her face.

Slonský sat on the end of his bed and rolled up his trouser leg to look at his knee. For all his bravado, the climb up the stairs to his flat had been excruciatingly painful and he just wanted to check that all the bits that should be inside his knee were still there, because his stitches were giving him the idea that one or two pieces of knee might have escaped.

Valentin turned his head away. He was squeamish about stitches, scars, blood (especially his own) and bodily fluids generally, added to which he was acutely aware that he had not eaten that morning. 'Anything I can get you before I go to work?' he asked.

'You're going to work?' said Slonský. 'When did this lifestyle change come about?'

'I have to earn my keep,' Valentin explained. 'I don't get sick pay like some others I could name.'

'I'm getting sick pay because I'm sick,' said Slonský. 'I'm not malingering. I didn't ask to be wounded in the service of my country, you know.'

'This isn't the Battle of the Dukla Pass. You fell over on some wet cobbles.'

'While apprehending a dangerous criminal, which is what I am paid to do.'

'He's a burglar, not a murderer.'

'Maybe he's just a failed murderer, did you ever think of that?'

'You mean he would have killed you if he could, but he messed it up?'

'The facts could bear that construction,' Slonský doggedly claimed.

Valentin threw his cap on the pile of newspapers and flopped into the only chair. 'You're going to have to make your mind up,' he said. 'Either you're grievously injured and knocking on death's door, or you're fit for work and itching to earn that new contract. You can't be both.'

Slonský turned this dilemma over in his mind for a few moments. 'When I'm at work, I'm fit for work,' he decided, 'but in the privacy of my own home I'm allowed to say that my knee hurts like hell. It shows the trust I have in you that I don't attempt to dissemble in front of you. I let you see things as they really are.'

'So your knee really hurts?'

'Like nobody's business. It feels as if someone has jammed a bayonet in one side and out of the other.'

'Maybe that's nature's way of telling you it's time to pack it in and settle down to a quiet retirement.'

Slonský glowered at Valentin. 'I thought you were a friend,' he hissed.

'I am. If I wasn't I'd have told that doctor that I didn't know what you were talking about when you claimed we were a couple.'

'We bicker like one.'

'I'm not bickering. I'm trying to get you to see sense. Though I don't know why I'm bothering, because I haven't managed it in nearly sixty years so why should I think I might be able to do it now?'

'You've got a sharp tongue, you have.'

'Hark who's talking. Now, is there anything I can do for you before I leave?'

'Yes, actually there is. If I'm going back to work tomorrow I need a vital piece of equipment.'

'What's that?'

'A new belt. I can't detect crime walking round holding my trousers up. I've faded away to nothing in that hospital.'

'You still look pretty substantial to me.'

'They hardly feed you, and when I complained they said that I didn't need my usual calorie intake because I was being inactive.'

'Fancy that — anyone daring to call you inactive.'

'I know! The cheek of it. Besides, whatever my body is doing, my brain is racing. It can't cope with that low-octane fuel they were giving it.' Slonský lowered his voice as if about to impart a scandalous secret. 'Do you know they tried to give me that muesli stuff once?'

Valentin knew that a loud tut was expected of him and duly obliged.

'If I had a new belt,' Slonský concluded, 'I could stagger down the stairs and across the street to the bar and get myself some lunch, not to mention beginning the long process of brain rehabilitation with a few glasses of top quality brain fuel.'

'I'll find you a belt,' Valentin sighed. 'What size?'

'How the hell do I know? Five centimetres less than this one, I suppose.'

Slonský slipped his belt out of his trousers and offered it to Valentin, who accepted it gingerly like a man handed a dead snake.

'You'll be here when I get back?' Valentin asked.

'Of course, I can hardly go out with no means of holding my trousers up, can I?'

'You could use a bit of string.'

'I could, if I had any string, which I doubt. We take belts off people when we arrest them, you know, in case they try to top themselves.'

'Why would anyone want to do that? Imagine being found dangling from the ceiling with your pants round your ankles. It's not very dignified.'

'I think the general view is that people who are miserable enough to kill themselves are not too worried about who sees their underwear,' Slonský added.

'You surprise me. If I decide to end it all I'm going decently dressed.'

'If you don't get a shift on and get me that belt they'll be finding you at the foot of the stairs in your overcoat.'

'I can take a hint.'

Navrátil had taken a leaf out of Major Klinger's book.

Klinger, head of the Fraud Squad, of which he composed precisely fifty per cent, was perhaps best known as the most compulsive cleaner in the police service. According to Slonský, Klinger was single-handedly keeping the Czech disinfectant industry going with his mania for polishing door knobs and work surfaces. Not only that, Klinger was one of the country's biggest consumers of sticky notes and highlighter pens.

His system for marking up case notes using a range of colours had never been completely elucidated despite the efforts of some of the finest minds in the Czech Republic. Even Sergeant Mucha, a known connoisseur of bureaucracy and a man whose ability to read the handwritten notes of long-departed officers was legendary, had confessed himself bewildered by what exactly was denoted by the lavender pen marks.

Navrátil was developing his own system as he waded through the metres of printout supplied to him by the Border Police who regretted that they were unable to spare officers to make the comparisons themselves. On the theory that it was unlikely that Veremchuk had managed to leave the country disguised as a woman, he began by highlighting all the women's names in blue. The next step was to use his orange highlighter to distinguish anyone whose ethnicity suggested that a Ukrainian man would not successfully pass for them. There were a small number about whom something was definitely known that ruled them out — for example, that they were in a Czech prison when Veremchuk entered the country, or they were missing a body part. At the end of this Navrátil was still left with far more names than he would have thought possible. It seemed that if Veremchuk was no longer in the Czech Republic — and that remained to be tested — there were at least one hundred and sixty-eight other people whom he might have pretended to be.

Police procedure can only take you so far, Navrátil decided, and he reached for the telephone. It was a shame that Major Lukas had left the department, because he was a fluent Russian speaker. At a pinch, Captain Slonský would have sufficed, who at least had learned Russian at school, even if his vestigial vocabulary now ran only to those words that he would not have learned at school. As for Navrátil, he spoke English, but not Russian, and certainly not Ukrainian.

Fortunately for him the telephone was answered in Kyiv by Captain Solovyov, who spoke Russian but patriotically refused to do so, and who suggested that they speak English to each other.

Navrátil explained that they had found the body of a Ukrainian citizen and were now attempting to trace her boyfriend, a man named Viktor Veremchuk, who appeared to have irregular papers. He had arrived in the Czech Republic eight years before, but he might have left under some other name.

Solovyov asked for the date when Veremchuk had first arrived, and then announced that he was going to check the exit details for that day. Navrátil held on, and it was only a couple of minutes later that Solovyov returned to the phone.

'Found him,' he announced. 'Veremchuk, Viktor Efimovich. The interesting thing is that we don't appear to have a citizen of that name, so maybe he entered your country under an assumed name and left under his real one. Do you have a photograph of him?'

'Yes, we do,' Navrátil said. 'I'll scan it and email it to you.'

'Thanks,' said Solovyov. 'I'll see if we can match him to any known bad boys here and I'll get back to you.'

Navrátil made the copy and sent it to the address that he had been given. Anticipating that it might be days before he heard anything he settled down to read the scenes of crime report about the apartment block where Kateryna Teslenko had been found, but was soon interrupted by the ringing of his telephone. It was Solovyov.

'That was quick,' Navrátil said.

'I don't need to look through the files for that one,' Solovyov explained. 'That's a man called Oleg Yeremenko, and if you've got him you're welcome to keep him.'

'He's a known criminal, then?'

'Technically, no, because he's never been convicted, but he's an enforcer who works for one of the ethnic Russian gangs here. He's seriously bad news. We'd been wondering where he'd got to, but we thought he was probably holding up an elevated highway somewhere.'

'Come again?'

'Buried in the concrete. A significant number of our gang members just disappear and we don't find them again until someone digs up some foundations or repairs a road.'

'Is there any particular reason why he would come here eight years ago?'

'I can't say why he chose Prague, but I think he was probably keen to leave the Ukraine after the opium war.'

'Opium war?'

'Ukraine had a reputation as a crossing point for the drugs trade. Raw opium coming in from Turkey, Azerbaijan or Afghanistan went westwards, while processed heroin went back the other way, and the exchanges happened here. We were seizing four or five hundred kilograms of the stuff every year, but that was probably the tip of a very big iceberg. And we wouldn't have seized that much if it hadn't been for the enthusiastic support of two of the biggest gangs. One was ethnic Ukrainian, and the other was ethnic Russian, and they fed us information about the other gang's activities. But alongside that they attempted to disrupt each other's business with kidnappings, thefts and shootouts in the streets. Yeremenko disappeared just after a Turkish courier was shot at point-blank range in a police station, which was more than a little embarrassing for my colleagues.'

'The courier had been arrested, presumably?'

'Yes, he was driving a battered old minibus that had more heroin in it than sound steel. The seat cushions were stuffed with bags of white powder.'

'But if he'd been arrested why would Yeremenko shoot him? Surely the other gang was already damaged by the seizure?'

'It wasn't the other gang. The Turk was driving for the Russians. Yeremenko was making sure he couldn't share any information that we might find useful.'

'How did he get access to someone in custody?'

Solovyov laughed. 'Sheer nerve. He pretended to be drunk and was brought in to sober up. Before he'd been searched he overpowered a guard, stole his keys and got into the corridor where the holding cells were. He shot the Turk through the bars, put the guard's jacket on and slipped out when everyone came running in at the sound of gunfire.'

It rang all too true to Navrátil. It was all too likely that the police running in left the door unlocked behind them. 'But why would that upset the Ukrainians?' he asked.

'Because Yeremenko used a gun we could link to one of their men. It seems that he had deliberately tried to frame the Ukrainians for the murder of the Turk, and, understandably enough, I suppose, they didn't like it. Fortunately we had cameras in the corridor that proved who the killer actually was.'

'But nobody intervened?'

'Nobody was watching the screen just at that moment. They were too busy trying to process the gang members we'd arrested.'

'Do you know of any link between him and Kateryna Teslenko?'

'That's the woman, presumably?'

'His girlfriend, perhaps.'

'I can't say I think much of her taste.'

'Some women like older men.'

'If she was twenty-eight, then there's twenty-three years between them.'

Navrátil double-checked his file. 'Veremchuk was forty-two, it says here.'

'He may have been, but Yeremenko is fifty-one. It looks like in addition to all the murders and kidnappings he may have lied about his age.'

Typical, thought Navrátil. *You can't trust criminals.* 'Do you know anything about the woman?' he asked.

'What was her name again?' asked Solovyov.

'Teslenko. Kateryna Teslenko.'

'Give me a moment and I'll run it through our computer.'

Navrátil could hear Solovyov whistling cheerfully as he waited for the results. The whistling suddenly stopped.

'Well, I'll be…' murmured Solovyov.

'Something interesting?' Navrátil asked, as much to remind Solovyov that he was still there as that he expected it to be of interest to him.

'Young Ms Teslenko doesn't have a criminal record,' Solovyov explained, 'but according to our database she is the daughter of Grigory Darmant.'

'Who is?'

'Grigory Darmant? He's an enigma. He's probably responsible for a large percentage of our crime though, of course, he doesn't have a criminal record because he is also a respectable entrepreneur and a big supporter of our ruling party.'

'Why did she use a different name?'

'Her mother isn't married to Darmant now, probably because they're divorced.'

'And is there any link between Darmant and Yeremenko?'

'Almost certainly. They're both ethnic Russians, and generally speaking villains stay within their ethnic groups here. It's purely practical — if you're a Ukrainian going to work for the Russians they won't trust you and your own will disown you.'

'Do you think Darmant will be upset when he hears that Kateryna has died?'

Solovyov considered for a moment or two. 'I don't know about upset. But he won't forget an insult. Whoever did it, it would be good for them if you caught them before he does. It could save them a deal of pain.'

CHAPTER 7

Equipped with his new belt, Slonský had hopped down the stairs and sat on the windowsill for a moment before attempting to cross the road. There was no point in denying it; his leg hurt like hell. Unless he could come up with some cunning subterfuge, it would be obvious to everyone that he was not fit for duty.

He pushed himself to his feet and made his way to the side of the road. A pedestrian who waits for the Prague traffic to stop is in for a long wait, even if they use the official crossings, it being the long-held belief of many Czech drivers that when it comes to traffic lights amber is a paler shade of green.

Taking his life in his hands, Slonský stepped off the kerb and made it all the way across the road with only two horns blaring at him. He was particularly stung by one of the drivers who called him "a brainless cripple". Slonský may not have been inclined to political correctness, but he was beginning to understand what people with a disability had to put up with, and he didn't like it. He was almost moved to sympathy, but he could see a welcoming door opening in front of him, through which issued the enticing sound of people having a good time.

He limped to a stool and dropped his considerable weight gratefully onto it. A young woman in black appeared in front of him; since she was wearing an apron and a pouch he deduced her to be a member of staff.

'Are you all right there?' she asked solicitously. 'You wouldn't like a chair with a back?'

'They're all the way over there,' Slonský moaned, at which the young woman turned, strode across the room and returned with a sturdy chair that she placed by a nearby table, moving the stools away to make space. The chair did not match any of the other chairs, but no true Praguer drinks in a bar with matching chairs. Eclecticism is the order of the day.

'Thank you,' he said.

'Think nothing of it,' she beamed. 'We must look after our senior citizens, mustn't we?'

Slonský bit his tongue. There was nothing to be gained by a response. Instead, he made a mental note to bring Jerneková in here for a drink some time and wind her up about something. That would teach them.

He ordered a large beer and some fried cheese and rubbed his knee. He rarely ate fried cheese, because, frankly, he had to make some concession to keeping in trim and the calories in fried cheese had more zeroes than a Zimbabwean bank note. Not only that, it gave him vicious wind for some reason. He had a robust constitution and could eat or drink almost anything without ill effect, but he had noticed that by his fifth or sixth piece of fried cheese his insides would be bubbling like a volcano.

The beer arrived and stood patiently in front of him, awaiting its fate. It looked cool, inviting, crystal clear, promising; he closed his eyes and poured the liquid gold over his tongue. Little sparkles tingled across its surface as if his taste buds were greeting a long distant friend. The cold liquid gurgled down his throat and splashed into his stomach and then, wonder of wonders, he could feel his brain cells spontaneously return to life.

By the end of the second glass his mental processes were purring like a Formula 1 engine. He did not care to make the experiment, but he was confident that he could polish off a sudoku puzzle in a few minutes. He totalled his bill mentally in a matter of seconds.

Normal service had been resumed. The Slonský brain was back in business.

Peiperová was studying the printout with a determined look while nibbling the top of her pencil in perplexity. 'There are just too many possibilities,' she concluded after a while.

'Well, we can't give up,' Jerneková argued. 'This is exactly the kind of thing the police are there to put a stop to.'

'There are other police to do that, Lucie. Our job is to catch the particular man who tried to molest that woman in the park.'

Jerneková leaned back in her chair to have a good stretch. 'I don't mind standing around the park trying to lure him,' she said, 'but I draw the line at jogging. And I'd want to take my gun.'

'I don't think he'll try to grab you if you've got a gun.'

'I could conceal it somewhere.'

'Guns aren't easy to conceal, especially if you're in tight clothing.'

'I could shove it down my pants,' Jerneková suggested, 'though knowing my luck I'd shoot my own clit off.'

Navrátil, who had been standing in the doorway unnoticed waiting for a break in the conversation, decided to go for a coffee first to give himself time to purge the image from his brain.

Peiperová observed the movement and chased after him. 'Did you want something?'

'Just to bang heads together. I'm getting nowhere and I thought you might have some ideas.'

Peiperová ran back to her desk and grabbed the file she had been using. 'I'll do you a swap. You read this and I'll think about your case for a while.'

'It's a deal. Shall we grab a coffee?'

'Not for me, thanks,' Jerneková called from her desk.

The taxi pulled up outside the police headquarters and Slonský alighted. It was amazing how much better his knee felt after a litre of the Czech national product, so much so that he attempted to ascend the steps like Gene Kelly before grimacing and emitting some coarse language.

He hobbled to the door and entered the familiar foyer once more. At the desk Sergeant Mucha looked up and smiled. 'Welcome back,' he said. 'Are you working or just here to hand your sick leave papers in?'

'Don't even joke about it,' snarled Slonský. 'Is there a chair somewhere?'

'We don't have them in here,' Mucha told him. 'The drunks only throw them. There's a bench against the wall there.'

'How can I hold a private conversation with you from all the way over there?' Slonský asked, neatly glossing over the fact that most of their conversations were conducted at a volume that could be heard from the street.

Mucha had an idea. 'Hang on,' he said, and disappeared into the little storage area behind the desk. 'Aha!' He reappeared with a lightweight wheelchair and unfolded it by the desk. 'There you go. We have to have one of these for the convenience of service users who find the walk to the cells too difficult.'

'Does it help?' asked Slonský.

'Not really. They complain like hell when I push them down the steps. It might be an idea if we got a lift put in one day.'

'I should keep that to yourself. We don't want the word to get around that we've gone soft on criminals.'

'So,' asked Mucha, 'to what do we owe this personal appearance? How long is it since you got out of hospital?'

'Nearly four hours,' Slonský replied. 'I'm bored.'

'Well, I'm sure your colleagues will be pleased to see you. Navrátil is dealing with a particularly nasty murder and Peiperová is trying to track down a sex attacker who tried to abduct a young woman in the Letná in broad daylight.'

Slonský looked wistfully at the staircase. 'I'm unlikely to make it up there before the end of the day,' he sighed.

'I'll ring and get them to come down,' said Mucha.

Since Navrátil and Peiperová were still in the canteen and Krob was having his physiotherapy, Jerneková took the call and detoured to collect the lieutenants on the way. As they reached the bottom stair and turned into the foyer Peiperová's hand shot to her mouth.

'Sir! I didn't realise it was as bad as this.'

'It is what it is, lass. I'll just have to make the best of it. But I'm determined not to let this impede the ceaseless search for justice.'

'How long are you going to have to use one of these, sir?' asked Navrátil.

'Who knows? But I've got to be out of it by the eleventh of November or I'm out on my ear.'

'Why?' asked Jerneková. 'Are they seriously going to chuck out one of their best detectives just because he's in a wheelchair? It'd be a public relations disaster. If I were you I'd stay in it.'

'Lucie,' hissed Peiperová. 'Think what you're saying.'

'What?'

'You can't talk like that to someone who's confined to a wheelchair.'

'I know,' said Jerneková, 'but he's swinging the lead, isn't he? Look at the wet footprints on the floor. He walked in here and then got in the chair.'

Five pairs of eyes followed the glistening trail to the door.

'Well spotted, Jerneková,' said Slonský. 'I wondered who would be the first to notice that.'

CHAPTER 8

The woman was well kept, thought Slonský when she gave her date of birth. He felt like saying "Are you sure?" but that seemed impolite, even by his standards.

'Forty-three years old,' he said as he tapped the numbers into the report form, followed by the details on the business card that she had given him.

'Now,' said Slonský, 'what's the nature of your complaint?'

Petra Linhartová looked around, seeming rather uncomfortable with the whole process. 'This is embarrassing,' she said. 'You don't have a woman officer I can speak to?'

'Unfortunately, they're both out at the moment on urgent business.'

Slonský did not disclose the nature of that errand although he knew perfectly well that they had sneaked out to buy a birthday present for Officer Krob.

Petra Linhartová sighed. 'You'll take my complaint seriously?'

'Of course. I take every complaint by a citizen seriously. And you may rest assured that whatever you're going to describe, we've heard it all before.'

'I doubt you've heard this one,' she said.

'Try me,' Slonský replied.

Petra Linhartová flicked a lock of her blonde hair back from her eyebrow, fixed her gaze on the clock above Slonský's head, and began her account. 'You'll see that I hold a very responsible job. I work long hours and I live alone. So for some time I've used a laundry service. It's not that I think doing my own laundry is beneath me,' she hurried to assure him, 'but I can earn more than enough in a couple of hours to pay for the service.'

'I'm not judging you,' Slonský answered. 'It may comfort you to know that I also live alone and do the same thing.' *If I remember*, he added mentally, *which is not always guaranteed.* And if you count pushing a refuse bag full of clothes through the door of the flat two floors below so the old woman who lived there could wash and iron it for him in exchange for a bit of pin money as "using a laundry service".

'Well, I changed provider a few months ago and generally I've been very happy with them, but the last three or four deliveries have been short.'

'Short? In what way have they been short?'

'I'm missing some panties.'

Slonský's pencil refused to descend to his pad but stayed resolutely poised in mid-air awaiting further details. 'Panties?'

'Yes,' Ms Linhartová replied. 'They're not bringing back all the panties I give them.'

Now it was Slonský's turn to wish that Peiperová and Jerneková had been there. 'And you know this — how?' he asked.

'At first I thought it was just a mistake and they would turn up next week or they'd been put in the wrong delivery and somebody would return them.'

'Or perhaps you were mistaken about whether they had gone?'

'That might have been possible, except that the matching bra came back. Anyway, now I have absolute proof.' She opened her bag and produced two sheets of A4 paper. 'This one is the bundle of items I sent last week. And this is the same bundle when it was returned. You see? Two pairs of panties are missing; those pale blue ones, and the white ones with the red polka dots.'

There was no disputing the photographic evidence. Two pieces of underwear were in one picture but not in the other.

'And how many pairs do you think have gone missing in this way?' Slonský asked.

'Five or six.'

'Approximate value?'

'Value?'

'I know it seems strange,' Slonský explained, 'but I have to put down the worth of the stolen items.'

'You mean what they're worth now, or what I paid for them?'

'Let's go with replacement value. I can't imagine there's much of a market for used knickers.'

'You'd be surprised,' said Petra Linhartová, who thought for a moment and then suggested a number. It sounded improbable to Slonský whose experience of underwear purchases involved a multipack of identical items once in a blue moon. It seemed that Petra Linhartová was used to paying as much for a tiny scrap of cloth as he paid for three or four pairs of underpants.

When Petra Linhartová had gone, mollified to some extent by Slonský's assurance that the criminal police service would do everything in its power to retrieve and safeguard the women's underwear of Prague, Slonský flopped back in his chair and considered which of his team should be handed this enquiry.

Navrátil? No. The poor lad would probably find it difficult to say the word "panties" aloud, though since his recent marriage it was not impossible that he had finally seen some. Besides, he had a particularly nasty beheading to sort out.

Peiperová? It should not really need a lieutenant to deal with this.

Jerneková? As a woman, she could be expected to have more empathy with the victim, but then Jerneková and empathy in the same sentence struck Slonský as an unlikely pairing. She would probably tell the complainant that anyone who sends her underwear out to be laundered deserved to have things stolen.

Krob it was then. At least it was something he could do while his shoulder was out of action.

Slonský allowed himself to reflect briefly that whenever he undertook that sort of exercise, the answer always seemed to be Krob. Perhaps this spoke of some subconscious admiration for Krob's even temper and patience, he thought; no, that couldn't be it, because he was very comfortable in his own skin. Slonský liked to tell himself that he was too old to change; in fact, he had changed a lot over the past few years, but chose not to admit to it, as if flexibility were a weakness.

Occasionally, he would replay the awkward conversation to which Captain Lukas had summoned him in the first days of 2006 at which Slonský had been informed that his days of working alone were over. This was such a shock, as if all those years of making himself as objectionable as he could to his partners so that they would leave him in peace had been for nothing. The only one who had stuck working with Slonský for any length of time was Lukas himself, back in the days when he was a junior lieutenant and Slonský was a mere patrolman; a patrolman who didn't often drive, because Lukas preferred to do that himself, no matter how many times Slonský apologised for the incident with the archway (it wasn't as if he was the only policeman who had ever written off a vehicle, after all).

Lukas had explained that he was required to arrange for a young graduate from the police academy to be mentored, and that Slonský was the obvious — indeed, the only — choice. Slonský demurred, but was then reminded that he was coming up to the age of 59, after which his contract could only be renewed with the agreement of his line manager, and that Lukas' consent could well depend on whether he needed to keep an officer because he was a good mentor for a young recruit.

'I don't really have a choice, do I?' Slonský had said.

'Of course not,' Lukas replied. 'It's the Czech police way. But it was important that you realised that for yourself.'

In the event, Jan Navrátil had been a breath of fresh air. Slonský had shed the years like someone getting a young puppy. Navrátil was eager to learn, intelligent, diligent and gifted; he was also so strait-laced that Slonský occasionally pondered how the young man thought he had come to be, since the idea of his parents having had sex would not have occurred to him.

Slonský had watched Navrátil growing closer to Kristýna Peiperová over the next two years with a fascination that this was what young love was like; except that it was the wrong way round. Slonský could picture Navrátil singing about raindrops on roses and whiskers on kittens, whereas Peiperová, though very feminine, was ruthlessly practical. Of course, what had sealed his relationship with Navrátil was the regular arrival in the office of samples of Navrátil's mother's baking. She made a mean cinnamon bun and her cheese straws were beyond compare. Slonský was pleased to hear that Mrs Navrátilová had been giving instruction to Peiperová in this regard. He could see the value of mentoring where excellent cheese straws were the result.

Colonel Rajka leaned on the door frame and spotted Slonský at his desk.

'Captain Slonský!' he said. 'Could I have a word?'

Slonský began to lever himself out of his chair.

'Stay where you are. I'm sure Lieutenant Navrátil won't mind making himself scarce for five minutes while we have a little chat.'

'No, of course not,' agreed Navrátil, though it was actually quite inconvenient at that precise moment, given where he had got to in checking his printout. 'I'll get a coffee.'

'Good idea,' said Slonský. 'Best get me one too. It'll save you a trip later.'

Rajka sat across the desk and opened a green folder. 'I thought you might be able to help me with something that is puzzling me.'

'I'll certainly try, sir, though the chances that I'll be able to answer something that you can't…'

'Cut the flattery, Slonský. I'm immune.'

'Of course, sir.'

'I've received your medical report from occupational health. It was passed to Human Resources as usual and someone there has noticed a discrepancy. You'll see that on your police record your date of birth is given as 1949 and yet your hospital discharge summary says 1947.'

Slonský felt an unusual sensation of embarrassment. He dreaded retirement which was looming ever closer, so when, a short while before, he had been left unattended in the Human Resources department with his record on a computer in front of him and someone already logged in, it had been the work of a few moments to amend his date of birth in a favourable direction.

'You see,' Rajka continued, 'I would have assumed that our record was correct, but it looks very much as if you joined the police force when you should have been doing your national service; and you were doing your square-bashing when you were still at school.'

'I'm sure there's a perfectly good explanation for this error, sir,' Slonský muttered.

'I'm pleased to hear it. Just be a good fellow and trot along to HR to give it, and then we'll say no more about it. After all, falsifying police records is a very serious offence, isn't it?'

'It certainly is,' agreed Slonský. 'I'm going to get to the bottom of this, sir. Leave it to me.'

'Do you need me to fetch that wheelchair from downstairs?' Rajka asked.

'No, sir, I'm perfectly fit to walk to HR.'

A few minutes later, Slonský was leaning heavily on the wall at the top of the stairs to compose himself before pushing open the door to the department that he still called Personnel. The young woman at the desk received the green folder and went off in search of someone who knew something about the case.

Slonský grimaced, but there was no choice. There he was with an unguarded, logged in terminal. He typed in his name, changed the date of birth back, clicked on the F10 button as instructed, and then retreated a couple of metres so that he was far from the keyboard when she returned.

'Lieutenant Hladík will see you in the interview room, Captain. I'll buzz you through.'

"Buzzing you through" turned out to mean that she pressed a button under the counter which allowed Slonský to push on a small low door at the end of the counter; except that he did not know this, and failed to do so.

'When I press the button, sir, you just push on the gate,' the young desk officer explained.

They tried again. Slonský pushed on the gate, but that was all he did, with the result that the gate sprang back after a moment and slapped him on his bad knee, causing him to howl with pain and collapse on the floor.

The young woman was torn between rendering assistance and fetching help, but seeing Hladík approaching, she drew his attention to his interviewee's predicament. Hladík knelt beside him.

'Slonský, Captain Josef?'

'So am I. That's a coincidence,' said Slonský feebly.

'He didn't bang his head?' Hladík asked the clerk.

'I don't think so, sir. Maybe when he hit the floor?'

'You'd best notify Colonel Rajka. And send for a doctor.'

Rajka arrived surprisingly quickly, almost as if he had been expecting to be summoned, though his face when he saw his best officer lying on the floor was a picture of bafflement. 'What happened here?' he demanded.

'I'm afraid Captain Slonský's knee got trapped in our new security gate,' the clerk explained.

'And how can that happen? Surely the gate should not close on someone's leg?'

'I'm not sure,' she said. 'It's never happened before. Usually I just push the button and people walk in. Captain Slonský seemed to take a long time.'

'Well, of course he did,' Rajka thundered. 'He's been off work for a while with a service-related leg injury.'

Hladík stood up, straightened his tie and saluted smartly. 'I'll arrange for an engineer to look at the gate straight away, sir.'

'Good. Well, while I'm here, let's get to the bottom of this issue, shall we?'

Slonský groaned loudly.

'A doctor is on his way, sir,' Hladík announced. 'You just lie there.'

'I can't do anything else,' moaned Slonský. 'Oh, the pain!'

The young woman knelt beside him and held his hand, which seemed to improve his condition somewhat.

'Now, the problem is, sir,' Hladík explained, 'that this discharge letter says 1947, whereas if you look at Captain Slonský's service record it says … oh.'

'That looks like 1947 to me,' said Rajka.

'Yes. Yes, it does, doesn't it? I can't think why…' A confused Hladík grabbed the copy he had printed out, but despite staring at it very hard for some seconds it continued to say 1949. 'I'm very sorry, Colonel…'

Rajka was generally a very even-tempered man, for which his colleagues were very grateful, because an enraged Olympic wrestler would be difficult to handle; but he was clearly a rather unhappy superior officer as he addressed the young lieutenant. 'You have wasted my time, and that of Captain Slonský, on a wild goose chase about a discrepancy that doesn't actually exist, and, into the bargain, set back his recovery from an injury received in the line of duty.'

'I can't apologise enough, sir…'

'That's right, you can't. Now, just a few days ago your department wrote to me saying that if Captain Slonský was not back on duty by 11th November next his contract would not be extended. If he is not on duty then as a result of an injury sustained through your department's negligence I have no doubt that this requirement will be waived,' Rajka hissed.

Well, this is turning out very well, thought Slonský, not forgetting to moan every few seconds.

'I'll see to it right now, sir,' Hladík replied.

'Good. If you do, I will use my influence with Captain Slonský to see that the matter ends here.'

Ten minutes later Rajka was in possession of a letter assuring him that Captain Slonský's contract was being extended for another year, while Slonský was being helped into a wheelchair by a doctor and a paramedic who, after a thorough examination, concluded that no lasting damage had been done, though no doubt it had been a nasty shock for an older man. They carefully wheeled him back to his desk where he gingerly clambered out and resumed his seat, thanking them profusely for their help.

When they had gone, Navrátil could not contain his curiosity any longer. 'What happened to you?' he asked.

'Never mind that,' said Slonský. 'This coffee has gone cold.'

CHAPTER 9

'Sex attackers attack. It's what they do,' opined Jerneková. 'Sooner or later he'll whip it out again and we'll nab him.'

'Maybe,' agreed Peiperová, 'but not necessarily in the same place. We can't station officers in every park in Prague just in case.'

Jerneková speared another gherkin with her penknife.

'Can't you use a knife and fork like everyone else?' Peiperová enquired.

Jerneková looked puzzled. 'I don't bring a knife and fork to work. But I always have my trusty penknife. It may come in handy if this fellow gets his todger out around me.' She inspected the gherkin with a little momentary distaste. 'Just as well these aren't pink,' she concluded before clamping it between her teeth and biting.

'Are you taking this seriously?' asked her boss.

'I never take sex crimes anything other than very seriously. We're going to nab him. It's just a question of how.'

'Well, any ideas you have will be appreciated.'

Jerneková chewed and considered. 'Here's a thought. Suppose we can narrow down what type of attacker he is?'

'Come again?'

Jerneková leaned forward and stared at her desk blotter to collect her thoughts. 'Most criminals commit the same crime in the same way, right? Cat burglars don't suddenly become forgers, and so on.'

'Yes,' conceded Peiperová reluctantly.

'He attacked a grown woman, so let's throw out all the past cases where the victim was a child.'

'That seems reasonable.'

'This description we've got. It's pretty general, I grant. But it's clear that the assailant is quite fit. Suppose he's also a jogger? He goes where joggers are to be found. He likes fit women.'

'So he chose the site because he'd been there before?'

'Of course. He needs to know where he'll run if it all goes tits up, if you'll pardon the expression. He believes he can outsprint the women he attacks.'

'Over a short distance he probably can. She'll have to stop and turn before she can pursue him, and most women won't. I imagine they want to get out of there as fast as possible.'

'So where do joggers congregate?'

'Lucie, the streets are full of them.'

This was something of an exaggeration. For many men in Prague, physical exercise was just a notional possibility, not something in which they indulged; something that was a good idea for other people.

'Yes, but this kind of attacker doesn't hang around streets. He needs a bush or something like that to drag her to.'

'So we're looking for a park with a bush in it. That'll narrow things down,' Peiperová muttered.

'There's more,' Jerneková continued, apparently immune to sarcasm. 'There were a few joggers around. Why did he pick this woman?'

'She had earphones in so she couldn't hear him.'

'And he could see that as she ran along?'

Peiperová had to admit that her trainee had a point. The runner had some sort of little electronic box, but it was attached to the waistband of her shorts at the back; and while there were leads connecting the earphones with the box, they were black and she was wearing a black running vest. They wouldn't have been easily seen.

'Maybe he likes a particular type of woman — blonde, brunette and so forth,' Jerneková suggested.

'Well, this one was tall and blonde.'

'Phew!' Jerneková announced. 'I'm safe twice over then.'

'Maybe he'd been watching her for a while, so that's why he knew she had earphones.'

'Or he's seen her there before.'

'Would you say she was pretty?'

Jerneková pondered the question for a while. 'Not especially. But then I'm not a bloke. And I'm not gay either, before you ask.'

'I wasn't going to,' Peiperová protested.

'No, well, people do. They think if you're not married or dating you must be. Can't they understand that you can find men and women equally unappealing?'

'It's your business. You don't owe anyone an explanation.'

'I mean, it's not as if I haven't had offers,' Jerneková continued, warming to her theme. 'Plenty of them. All creeps, of course. And my mother used to say I was too choosy! Well, I was choosier than her because I wouldn't have chosen Dad. And if I had, I'd have taken a kitchen knife to him if he knocked me about.'

'Did your mother suffer from domestic violence?'

'No. She got hit about. You have to be middle class to have "domestic violence". It's like skin rashes. Better-off families have dermatitis or eczema, but we just got scabs.'

'That's awful, Lucie. Why did your mother put up with it?'

Jerneková shrugged. 'What else could she do? How would she have got a new flat? How could she keep us on her wages?

The best she could do was to keep Dad topped up with vodka and hope he slept more than he slapped.'

Peiperová was not entirely sure how the conversation had come to this point but wanted to draw a line under it now. 'I'm sorry that happened to you,' she said.

Jerneková sniffed. 'It didn't affect me. Mum kept him away from me, most of the time.'

'Only most of the time?'

'I got a couple of leatherings. And the other stuff.'

'Other stuff?'

'Can we not talk about it? It's done now.'

'Of course. If you ever decide you do want to talk…'

'I know. And rest assured you'd be the first one I'd turn to. Anyway, why did you ask about her looks?'

'Because there must have been a hundred women in that park when he attacked, and yet he chose one who could probably outrun most of us and who doesn't strike me as a great looker. So why did he choose her?'

'The challenge? Or maybe he just likes sweaty women in Lycra?'

'Or maybe it isn't a sex attack at all? We're just assuming that it was because he's a man and she's a woman.'

'It wasn't just us,' Jerneková pointed out. 'The first policeman on the scene said it was when he phoned it in. That's why they sent us.'

'Yes, but suppose he was wrong? I mean, a sex attack in a crowded park is taking a big chance. If he was just trying to mug her, that would be understandable.'

'Why would you mug someone with no bag in running kit? She obviously wasn't carrying anything valuable.'

'She'd have the keys to her apartment. She had her music player on her waistband. She'd probably have a phone somewhere, because most women have a phone these days.'

'But she didn't have a backpack or one of those things you hang at your waist. If she had a key it must have been in her wristband or the pocket of her shorts. There were plenty of other women with a lot more worth stealing in that park.'

'So if not sex, and not theft, what are we left with?'

'Something about her. She wasn't picked randomly in the park. She said she goes there three or four times a week. She was targeted.'

'Let's dig a bit more into Ms Zechovská, then. See if we can't find some reason why someone would try to attack her.'

Slonský flicked his eyes up and down Navrátil's list before plumping decisively for one about a third of the way down.

'Why arrest him, sir?'

'I don't like his name. It sounds aggressive.'

'We can't arrest someone just because we don't like his name.'

'It's as good an idea as any you've given me in the last half hour. Anyway, we did in the first half of my career. Ah, Navrátil, what you missed by being born too late! Those days when you could just add a name to a list and get your neighbour arrested because he'd annoyed you.'

'You've repeatedly told me how you hated those days.'

'I did. But it was a great time to be a policeman. You had a list of crimes, and a list of criminals, and you just picked one off each and paired them up. Crime solved. And if, by some happy chance, we actually caught someone in the act, that was even better. Collar someone doing a bit of shoplifting, and you can pin all the unsolved shopliftings within five kilometres on them.'

'Didn't their lawyers object?'

'Of course not. We were the police, after all. The lawyers knew we wouldn't have arrested someone unless they'd done something. Do you remember when the Romanians got rid of Ceauşescu in '89?'

'No, sir. I'm too young.'

'Well, he had a defence lawyer at his trial, but once the prosecution had summed up the defence lawyer gets to his feet and starts telling the court Ceauşescu and his wife are guilty as hell and deserve the stiffest punishment going, only not death, please, because they're loopy. That might not quite be verbatim.'

'I should hope not.'

'Anyway, that's what a lot of trials were like when I was your age. Sometimes the defence lawyer did a better job of putting the case against his clients than the prosecutor did. I remember one when the prosecutor was floundering and the defence counsel had to remind the court that the stolen property had been found in the defendant's flat.'

'And had it?'

'Yes,' said Slonský. 'Hardly a surprise, considering we put it there.'

'Didn't you have any pangs of conscience about that sort of thing?'

'Of course I did. But I also wanted to eat now and again, and people who stepped out of line got sacked and couldn't get another job. And I didn't have family or friends to feed me. Conscience is a luxury, lad. Poor people can't always afford one.'

'I'm glad I didn't live then.'

Slonský considered for a moment. 'It had its pluses, I suppose. Sausage was cheap. You never knew what was in it but it was affordable. And I could afford to go to the movies.'

'I didn't know you liked going to the cinema.'

'I don't. I never went. But I could afford to go if I wanted. That's the real test of democracy, lad. It's not what you can do; it's what you don't have to do if you don't want to. Like stitching suspects up, which just proves my point. Let's get some coffee if we're going to continue this discussion.'

After his latest session of physiotherapy Krob had managed to raise his right arm above his head, which would have been no big deal a year ago, but was something of an achievement now. He had been given a rubber ball to squeeze to build up his grip strength after so long with an arm in a sling, and was looking forward to picking up his son with both arms for the first time in quite a while.

Between celebratory slurps of coffee Navrátil was bringing Krob up to speed on the investigation. For someone who was taking no notes, Krob seemed to grasp the fundamentals quite quickly.

'Where did you park?' Krob demanded.

'Excuse me?' said Navrátil.

'Where did you park?'

'At the mall.'

'That's too far for a bloodstained man to risk. Either he lives close enough to walk, but even then it's a risk if he's covered in blood, which he surely must have been, or he parked nearby.'

'Or somebody drove him and waited,' Slonský helpfully added.

'He may have worn a coat to protect him from the blood,' Navrátil explained.

'Of course,' agreed Krob, 'but he didn't leave it there, so he'd be carrying a bloodstained coat, and even in Černý Most that's going to get noticed.'

Actually, thought Slonský, if there's one area of Prague where being spattered with blood might not seem out of the ordinary it was Černý Most, some of which was only built around the time the Berlin Wall came down and did not seem to have established a community feeling of its own. It was true that in much of Prague the locals might take the view that if a man wants to go round in a bloody jacket that is his business, but in Černý Most it was more likely to cause passers-by to cross the street and resolve to say nothing about it.

Navrátil chewed his lip in thought. 'So where could he have parked where nobody noticed him?'

'They may have noticed him all right,' Slonský threw in, 'but that doesn't mean they're going to tell us about it unless we specifically ask — and maybe not even then.'

Jerneková flipped her notebook open and began to read. 'Zechovská, Paulina. Born 13th December 1982. Registered address is in Radlice, not the Bubeneč address she gave us, but that's easily explained, because the Radlice address belongs to her parents, so she doesn't seem to have told anyone when she moved out.'

'Nice area,' commented Peiperová

'Dad got rich on trucking. Well, he calls it logistics management, but basically he owns a lot of lorries.'

'And the Bubeneč address?'

'I can't find anyone registered as living there, but that's not surprising, because it doesn't exist.'

'You're kidding me.'

'No, I'm not. If I was kidding you I'd have a daft grin on my face now.'

'So how does this woman expect us to bring anyone to trial for assaulting her if she gives us a false address?'

'She doesn't. She doesn't want us to find her, therefore she has something to hide.'

'That's a big leap. She might just have been scared.'

'Oh, come on! Even when I've been frightened out of my wits I've never forgotten where I lived. She must know the area, because she gave a genuine street but a bogus house number. They don't go up that high.'

Peiperová turned this information over in her mind. 'Joggers surely prefer a nearby park. Bubeneč isn't too far away to be realistic. Maybe she does live there, just not at the address she gave us.'

'Okay, so she may know there's a street called Pelléova. Do you know that part of town?'

'No,' said Peiperová, 'but let's drive round a bit and familiarise ourselves with it. Who knows, we may see someone we know?'

'One thing's for sure. We won't find her in the park. If she wants to avoid us, she'll stay well clear of there.'

Bubeneč is a curious district, a mixture of office blocks and quiet residential streets, some of them with houses on only one side. At one time it was a separate little town, regarded as a desirable place to live by those to whom city life was uncongenial. Slonský had never understood this, because he could not imagine anyone not wanting to live in Prague, but before the Second World War it had become popular with émigré Russians who did not want their whereabouts to become known to Stalin, a view reinforced when they heard what had happened to Trotsky in far-off Mexico City. In recent times another bunch of affluent Russians had come to live there. The Russian Embassy was here, and there was a cultural life in the district that attracted new arrivals to settle there, so that many Praguers called it Little Moscow.

Peiperová and Jerneková were not from Prague, and although Peiperová had been there for nearly three years she had not yet acquired the full level of suspicion of all things Russian that marks a Prague native.

They found Pelléova and drove up and down a couple of times. There were too many possibilities to guess which house Zechovská might actually live at, but since it was nearing the time when she had been jogging the other day they decided to head for Stromovka Park, where there was a large open patch of grass to run in, reasoning that if Zechovská had given a false address that probably meant she did not want the police looking too closely into her life, and that she had some idea who might have been behind an attack on her. Either she would get some protection, or she would take care not to jog near bushes or huts.

'I don't see any young women running alongside large men in black suits,' Jerneková commented.

'Neither do I,' agreed Peiperová. 'Still, since we're here and it's a warm day how about a coffee?'

They walked across to the refreshment kiosk and placed their orders. The young man who served them wore a tight black T-shirt and a gold loop in his left ear, his black hair swept back and maintained in position by an improbable amount of gel. His head looked as if a giant black slug had rested there for a nap.

Peiperová held out a banknote and accepted the small change he offered in return, dropping a little in the cup marked

TIPS which was surprisingly empty given how many people were cradling cups around them.

Jerneková accepted her drink from him. 'Thanks, Honza. Seen Paulina around lately?' she asked conversationally.

'Paulina?'

'My running pal. Bit taller than me, blonde ponytail.'

'Oh, that Paulina! No, now you mention it, not for a few days.' He busied himself emptying the coffee grounds from the machine.

'I'm a bit worried about her, to be honest,' Jerneková continued. 'You know she got bothered the other day?'

Honza looked concerned. 'Bothered? Here?'

'No, in Letná. I told her to stay closer to home if you're jogging alone, or wait for me to finish work, but you know what she's like.'

Honza chuckled. 'Probably thinks nobody would try it on with her given that goon of a boyfriend she's got.'

'I've never met him. She won't introduce me in case I try to entice him away from her.'

Honza could not disguise the look that suggested this was an unlikely outcome. 'I don't even know his name,' Jerneková prattled on. 'She just calls him Him or His Lordship.'

'I don't know it either,' said Honza, 'and if you ask me that's healthier for both of us.'

'Yes, I suppose so. Good coffee, by the way.'

'Thanks. See you again sometime.'

As they walked away Peiperová waited until they were out of earshot before interrogating her junior. 'Honza? Do you know him?'

'Never seen him before. But he's got an ID card hanging on a lanyard by his jacket. Anyway, we young people have such full social lives we can't remember who we've met and who we haven't, so he wasn't going to admit he didn't know me.'

'We young people? You're older than I am.'

'Yes, but you're married and therefore off the market. I, on the other hand, am unattached.'

'You never go out anywhere to meet men.'

'Not strictly true. I went to the wrestling a couple of weeks back.'

'On your own?'

'Yeah — I can't be bothered with all that small talk when men are getting body-slammed in front of me. And the last guy I went with took exception to me shouting to one of the wrestlers to bend the other guy's leg back until his foot went up his arse. Not ladylike, apparently. Who knew?'

CHAPTER 10

The telephone call came just in time to stop Navrátil joining the others for coffee.

'Solovyov here. I thought you might like to know that our officers at the airport tell us Grigory Darmant is about to board a plane to Prague.'

'Thanks for letting us know.'

Navrátil scribbled himself a note in case he forgot this important information while descending the stairs to the canteen, which he did with such rapidity that he arrived before Slonský reached the front of the queue.

'Ah! Good timing, lad. I seem to have left my wallet in my coat pocket.'

'You may want to put that pastry back, sir. Darmant is on his way here.'

'Darmant?'

'The victim's father.'

'Oh, that Darmant! Let's see who meets him, shall we?'

'That's what I thought. Krob and I will be there. Do you want to come too?'

'Best not.' He indicated his knee. 'I'd only slow you down. But before you go running off, there are two questions you need to answer.'

'Yes, sir?'

'First, what are you going to do if Yeremenko is there?'

'Invite him to answer some questions for us.'

'And if he refuses?'

'Bring him in. As partner of a murder victim he's automatically a suspect. You say yourself that most people are killed by people they know.'

'And I'm right. Take Dvorník and Hauzer though. If Yeremenko gets difficult you may need some extra hands.'

'And the second question?'

'Have you got fifty crowns you can lend me?'

Even if you had never seen a photograph of Darmant you would have recognised him as he entered the arrivals hall, thought Krob. A heavyset man in his mid-fifties in a well-tailored suit with a gold watch like an ankle tag and two large men walking just behind him. They strolled through the security gate without the least hesitation before Darmant paused in the doorway to scan the people waiting, many of them bored men holding up cards with names scribbled on them.

Yeremenko was not there; or, more accurately, he did not appear to be there. But, reasoned Krob, if none of these waiting cab-drivers is waiting for Mr Darmant, how is he going where he wants to go? Who else does he know in town? The obvious answer was to follow Darmant to see who met him, because he clearly expected someone to be there.

One of the bodyguards leaned over and murmured in Darmant's ear. He nodded, and started walking towards the exit doors, Krob strolling along a parallel path thirty metres away.

Navrátil was patrolling the pick-up zone. Seeing Krob he shook his head gently; no Yeremenko in the queueing cars. Darmant's telephone must have rung, because he held it to his ear, pointed to the right and his little party veered in that direction. Krob casually ducked behind an advertisement board as they walked past him.

One bodyguard dumped the trolley and the two men divided the baggage between them. Neither seemed to have the least difficulty in carrying forty kilos. Darmant assisted by taking his own cabin bag. To Navrátil's horror, they clambered aboard a courtesy bus.

'They're going to the car hire place,' he hissed into his microphone.

'So are we,' Dvorník replied, and Navrátil spotted an unmarked police car gliding into the traffic, Hauzer at the wheel. 'But which one?'

'Czechocar,' Navrátil replied. He looked around for Krob, but could not see him anywhere. 'Where are you, Krob?' he asked.

For a moment there was no reply; then he heard Krob apparently addressing a person near him. 'Excuse me — is this the bus to the Czechocar rental desk?'

Navrátil returned to his car. He would be later than the others getting to the rental area but there was no point in staying where he was.

Dvorník was not built for speed. Slonský had been heard to observe occasionally that he wished he knew the make of double bed that Dvorník and his wife shared, since it was obviously a well-built piece of furniture if it could survive the conjugal activity of two leviathans. Despite his girth, he could move quite quickly when he wanted, and he was first to the door, alighting from the car as Hauzer pulled up.

Hauzer went straight to the desk, flashing his police identity card to the astonished woman at the counter. 'Have you hired a large vehicle to a man called Veremchuk or Yeremenko in the last few minutes?' he demanded.

'He's just gone to collect it.'

Hauzer ran to the collection point, hoping that Yeremenko had not got a head start on them, but trusting that he would have to wait for Darmant. As he arrived a large silver car started up, its daytime running lights catching his attention. He walked over and spoke to the driver. 'Good afternoon, Mr Yeremenko. Prague Police. I'd like you to switch off the engine and give me the keys, please.'

'I have an appointment to meet someone.'

'We know. But I'm afraid our meeting takes precedence.'

Yeremenko made no move to turn off the engine, but the passenger door opened and he heard a click. Turning to that side he saw Dvorník crouching and an automatic pistol levelled in his direction.

'It would be a bad idea to decline our invitation,' Dvorník assured him.

The courtesy bus pulled up and the passengers tumbled out. Darmant and his men ignored the rental office and went directly to the car pickup area, arriving just in time to see Yeremenko climbing into the rear seat of a car at the behest of a man with a gun. One of Darmant's men made to intervene but was restrained by a firm grip on his arm.

'What do we do now, boss?' he asked.

Krob stepped forward. 'Prague Police, Mr Darmant. My colleague and I will be very happy to drive you wherever you want — after we've had a little chat at the station.'

Krob's offer, though well intentioned, proved impractical, because Navrátil's car could not take five men and four suitcases, but fortunately the airport police agreed to take the bodyguards and the luggage direct to the hotel where they were booked in. Again, one of the bodyguards seemed unhappy with this arrangement, but Darmant calmed him.

'I'm sure that no harm will come to me while I am in the company of the police,' he smiled grimly. 'I'll follow shortly. After all, I'm not being arrested, am I?'

'Not at all, Mr Darmant,' Navrátil assured him. 'We thought you might be able to give us some information that will help us to catch your daughter's killer.'

'I'll tell you everything I know,' Darmant said through a thin smile, 'but I doubt it will help you much. My daughter's life is … was here, and mine is elsewhere.'

Dvorník and Hauzer were not making much headway with Yeremenko, largely because they had known next to nothing about the case until summoned to help at the airport, but Dvorník had been around long enough to know that precious interview time must not be wasted and that the main aim must be to get the interviewee talking.

'Yes, Kateryna Teslenko was my girlfriend. We'd been together a few years,' Yeremenko said.

'And you were still on good terms?' asked Dvorník.

'Yes. We didn't live in each other's pockets, you understand. I go away, she works late at nights, but we were still happily together when we could be.'

'But you lived somewhere else?'

'She needed space to live her own life.'

'And entertain other men occasionally?'

'Not for money. She wasn't that kind of girl.'

'Did I say she was? I was asking if she would allow other men into her flat.'

'In daytime, certainly. She didn't sleep with them, and she didn't bring men home from work.'

'What was her work, exactly?'

'She was a dancer.'

'Exotic?'

'If she had to, but musical theatre was her preference. If you've been to a musical in the last four years you've probably seen her in the chorus.'

'And you looked after her?'

'Obviously not well enough.'

'Do you know any reason why someone would want to murder her?'

'No.'

'Did she have any enemies?'

'It looks like she did, but I didn't know of any.'

'But you have.'

'I've crossed a few people over the years.'

'Has it occurred to you that somebody may have killed Ms Teslenko to get at you?'

Yeremenko sighed deeply. 'Every day.'

'But you didn't come here to identify her, or to offer any help, and you tried to run when we came for you.'

Yeremenko leaned forward over the interview table. 'I wasn't in Prague when it happened; I don't read the papers; I didn't watch the news. What help could I give? And of course I ran away. I didn't know who you were.'

'So how did you find out what had happened to her?'

'A friend rang me.'

'Friend's name?'

Yeremenko hesitated, but only for a couple of beats. 'Chigulin, Yurii. I'll give you his number.' He pushed his phone across the table. Hauzer found the number, copied it down and pushed the phone back again.

'Thanks,' he said politely.

'Happy to help.'

'What did this friend tell you?' Dvorník enquired.

'He said a woman answering Kateryna's description had been found murdered. He had gone over to her flat, knowing I was away, and found the police swarming over it, so he came away to phone me.'

Dvorník waited a moment to increase the impact of his next comment. 'I'm afraid she had been very violently attacked. Did Chigulin tell you that?'

Yeremenko shook his head. 'How violently? Was she raped?'

'I can't tell you. We don't have definitive pathology reports on that yet. But she had been stabbed several times.'

'Not shot?'

'No. Were you expecting her to have been shot?'

'No, not particularly. I just hoped she hadn't suffered.'

Dvorník did not think any answer he could give would help, so he just sat back and folded his arms.

Slonský had been happy to let Dvorník and Hauzer do the initial questioning of Yeremenko for two reasons. First, he was reserving his fire for Darmant; and second, he had just been served a hot sausage and sauerkraut when Yeremenko arrived at the station, and he saw no point in letting it go cold. Suitably fortified, he was laboriously climbing the stairs to fetch the file when he saw Navrátil blithely skipping down them clutching the very folder he wanted.

'Ah, that's the one. Thanks for fetching it.'

'I thought I'd interview Darmant. It's my case.'

'And I'm the captain, so every case is my case. But I'll just sit in at the back. You won't know I'm there.'

That's highly unlikely, thought Navrátil, but decided that it was sufficient to have won confirmation that it was his case.

Darmant was sitting very placidly in the interview room with a cup of coffee and a sandwich, from which he had taken a couple of bites.

'I'm sorry to have kept you waiting,' Slonský said as the detectives entered.

'No problem,' Darmant replied. 'I'm sure you're very busy.'

'We certainly are,' Slonský agreed as he took his seat at the table, ignoring Navrátil who was politely offering him the chair at the back of the room.

'Then I'm sure you'll be as keen as I am to sort out any little difficulties with speed,' Darmant smiled. It was rather unnerving. The only person Navrátil knew who smiled like that was Major Klinger. It was a parody of a smile, as if its bearer had been told the mechanics of how to smile without any reference to human warmth; though, on reflection, maybe human warmth was not expected in the Fraud Squad.

'Let us begin by saying how sorry we are for your loss,' Navrátil said.

'We are,' agreed Slonský. 'Both of us.'

'Thank you. It has been a great shock.'

'Ms Teslenko wasn't married, but doesn't appear to have used your name,' Slonský continued. 'Why was that?'

Darmant shrugged his shoulders. 'My name isn't always an advantage. And I was away quite a lot when she was a child. She chose to use her mother's name.'

'Were you ever actually married?'

'Married and divorced.'

'Is her mother still alive?'

'I don't know. We're not in touch.'

'But you must pay her alimony?'

'No, she settled for a lump sum and our best house.'

'And were you in touch with Ms Teslenko?'

'Yes, as much as one ever is with an adult daughter. She rang if she wanted something, or on my birthday, that sort of thing.'

'She made her own life, then?'

'Yes. She has — had — a very independent streak,' Darmant conceded. 'She got that from her mother.'

Navrátil began to wonder if he was going to get a word in during this interrogation for which Slonský had promised to sit at the back. 'Perhaps you'd excuse us,' he blurted out. 'Captain Slonský, could I have a quick word outside?'

'Of course, Lieutenant, as soon as this interview is over. We mustn't keep Mr Darmant waiting.'

'Then perhaps I could ask a question,' Navrátil said, a little louder than he intended.

'Of course. Ask away. Don't mind me,' said Slonský.

'Thank you. Mr Darmant, is it possible that your daughter was murdered by someone who has a grudge against you?'

'Certainly,' Darmant answered. 'In fact, I think it's very likely. Kateryna wasn't the sort to make enemies.'

'You would say that you have enemies, then?'

'Yes.'

'Could you give us some names?'

'Bring me a telephone directory for Kyiv and I'll start ploughing through it. We may be a while. I was hoping you might be able to narrow it down for me a bit.'

'Has anyone ever threatened you personally?'

'Oh, yes. But I don't think any of them did it.'

'Why not?'

'Because two are in a top security prison and one is believed to be under a highway in Eastern Ukraine.'

'When you say "believed to be",' asked Slonský, 'is that just guesswork or do you know something about it?'

Darmant smiled again. 'I'm hardly likely to tell you if I did, am I? But in the interests of openness, I have no doubt that he is dead. I just don't know where his killers buried him.'

'They didn't tell you?' Slonský enquired.

'You may not believe this,' Darmant told him, 'but it wasn't actually my men who killed him. He upset someone else too.'

'Careless of him.'

'Very. And even more careless to go to a casino, drink too much, and forget where his car was going to pick him up. I understand that some passers-by offered him a lift in their car.'

'How kindly of them.'

'It was, especially because he inconsiderately bled all over the upholstery on the back seat.'

'Nosebleed?' asked Slonský.

'Among other places.'

'When we find out who killed Ms Teslenko, I hope the matter of retribution will be left to the Czech state.'

'I hope so too,' said Darmant. 'But if it turns out that the killer is out of your reach, he certainly won't be out of mine.'

CHAPTER 11

'That's good work,' announced Slonský, tossing the report vaguely in the direction of his in-tray. The papers landed on the desk but slithered onto the floor.

'Thank you, sir,' said Jerneková.

'However, where does it get us? For some reason this woman…'

'Paulina Zechovská,' Jerneková supplied.

'This woman Zechovská, for no doubt perfectly good reasons of her own, doesn't want us to know where she lives and she gives us a false telephone number so we can't contact her. Which implies that she doesn't really want us to investigate the assault on her. I wonder why not?'

'Perhaps she already knows who the assailant is?' Navrátil suggested.

'No, that won't wash,' Peiperová argued. 'She was genuinely frightened.'

'She could know who he is and still be frightened of him,' Navrátil persisted.

'If it's a domestic incident she's in the perfect place to sort it out. The police are there and he can't say she called them, because a passer-by did.'

'And she gave us that curious fact about his black fingernail,' Jerneková added. 'That sounded like genuine information to me. I don't think she could tell us any more about him even if she'd wanted to.'

'The other possibility that occurs to me,' Slonský announced with argument-settling finality, 'is that she has an alternative method of investigating. And possibly punishing the guilty man.'

'You mean she'll get her boyfriend to duff him up?' asked Jerneková. 'Good for her.'

'I'm not sure that victims taking the law into their own hands is something we want to encourage,' said Navrátil.

'Bad for business, I suppose,' Jerneková agreed.

'I'm more worried about vigilante lawlessness,' said Navrátil sternly.

'Yeah — that too,' agreed Jerneková.

Slonský shook his head wistfully. 'They're not proper vigilantes these days. It's not like when I started out. I remember back after the Russians visited in 1968 we had no end of attacks on so-called collaborators. There was an incident when some fellows were planning to throw a party official out of a fifth floor window and I was sent to stop them.'

'Just you?'

'Well, no, but I was first up the stairs. You can tell it was a long time ago. Anyway, they were trying to open the window wide enough to get a fat party official out. Fortunately it was up to the usual standard of building work and the runner was kinked so the sash wouldn't go right up, but they'd got his top half out of the window when I got there.'

'Did you tell them to stop?' Navrátil asked.

'I certainly did, in my best official voice, as instructed at training school.'

'What did they do?' asked Krob.

'They told me to go and … well, they were impolite. So I drew my gun. They just laughed. So I fired a warning shot at the ceiling. Bad move. There was another floor above and I nearly took out a district party secretary. Got him right in the thigh. Anyway, they stopped pushing the fat one out of the window long enough for me to give them a stern warning.'

'Which was?' enquired Navrátil.

'I told them I didn't give two hoots about them throwing the guy from the window, but if he landed on an innocent bystander I'd run them all in. Strangely enough this seemed to calm them all down a bit.'

'So they didn't throw him from the window then?' Navrátil said.

'No idea,' shrugged Slonský. 'I just told them to stop and left them to it. He hadn't been launched by the time I got back to the car or I'd have seen him on the asphalt.'

'What a horrible way to go!' Peiperová opined.

'Fine old Czech tradition. We've been defenestrating people for centuries. Read your history books.'

Dvorník appeared in the doorway. 'Hauzer says they haven't moved from their hotel. But Daniel Kristoň just showed up.'

Slonský's eyebrow did some stretching. 'Daniel Kristoň? I didn't know there was a link there,' he said.

'Who's this Kristoň guy?' Jerneková demanded.

'He's a security consultant. Also a private detective. Probably rents out car park spaces too.'

'You think Darmant is hiring him to find out what happened to his daughter?' Navrátil asked.

'Well, since I'm not in the room I don't know. But my best guess is that Darmant is just getting a bit of background from someone familiar with what goes on behind the scenes in Prague. And he wouldn't have to hire Kristoň. Kristoň knows that if he uncovers anything of interest to Darmant there'll be a nice fee attached.'

'Is he shady?' Jerneková persisted.

'Of course,' Slonský replied. 'Everybody in Prague is shady. It's just a matter of how shady they are. I mean, you've only got to look around the canteen here to see how low some people can get, and we're the good guys.'

'Some people somehow manage to lead moral and upright lives,' Navrátil protested.

Slonský smiled thinly. 'So far,' he agreed.

'I was meaning you,' Navrátil explained.

'Oh! Thank you for that vote of support.' Slonský picked up his hat. 'Just slipping out for a few minutes. Whatever you're doing, carry on doing it. Dvorník, can I borrow you for a little while?'

Dvorník could hardly refuse, but in fact Slonský merely wanted a lift into town. Once there, he alighted, bought himself a coffee and a newspaper, and sat down to read it.

'What are you doing here?' hissed Hauzer.

'What are you doing here, sir, you mean. Budge up — this seat is a bit small for two.'

'When I sat here there was only one,' Hauzer murmured. 'Sir, you'll give the game away.'

'You think so? Well, now, Hauzer, what's the manpower position of the Czech Police service?'

'Pretty terrible. We're undermanned.'

'Exactly. And since we're so short of officers, what are the chances that two could be spared for an ordinary surveillance job in the lobby of a Prague hotel?'

'I see where this is going, but…'

'And since I'm known to be a policeman by virtually every naughty criminal in Prague, that suggests that you can't be, doesn't it? Anyway, you've found what I wanted to know, so by all means slip off back to the office and make Dvorník's day for him.'

'If you're sure,' Hauzer began doubtfully.

'I am. I'll get the Metro back.' Slonský unfolded his paper and began to read. After a while a member of staff oozed alongside his shoulder and asked if there was anything he could do. 'Certainly,' said Slonský, and told him.

Mightily offended, the young man took himself off, leaving Slonský to peruse the business pages in peace.

The doors of the elevator opened and a tall, pasty-looking man with receding hair stepped out. Slonský glanced upwards just to check who it was. 'Good morning, Daniel,' he said cheerily.

'Oh, Christ, it's you.'

'A greeting lacking in its customary warmth, Daniel. Aren't you pleased to see me?'

'Always. You know me, Lieutenant.'

'It's Captain now.'

'Captain? Congratulations!' Kristoň seemed sincere on that point at least.

'Thank you. Of course, we do not seek promotion for its own sake, but for the opportunities it presents to serve the people of the Czech Republic more efficiently.'

'Is that why you're here?'

'In a way. Instead of towering over me, why don't you give me a hand up and we could have a friendly coffee at that table over there?'

Kristoň lowered his voice. 'I'm not sure it's a good idea for us to be seen together.'

Slonský did not lower his. 'You mean people might jump to the conclusion that you're an informer?' he asked.

'I don't inform!'

'Of course you don't. You do your public duty, that's all. And I'm glad you don't expect a fee because I doubt that we could pay your hourly rate.'

'You couldn't,' Kristoň agreed.

'But I can buy you a coffee. If not here, then perhaps at the bar on the corner.'

Kristoň sighed and checked his watch. 'I can spare you half an hour.'

'It'll take us that long to hobble there,' Slonský complained, hoisting himself upright and limping towards the door.

'What did you do?' Kristoň asked.

'Injured in the course of duty.'

'Really?'

'Really. Pepa Mach.'

'That little runt? Is he still clambering up buildings?'

'Not at the moment. He's sitting in Pankrác awaiting trial.'

Kristoň held the door open so Slonský could pass through.

'Come on, lean on my arm,' Kristoň said.

'Thank you. Knee giving me a bit of trouble today. But then, I'm lucky still to have the leg, I suppose.'

'That bad?'

'I don't want to talk about it, Daniel. The nightmares have stopped at last and I don't want to trigger them again.'

'Of course,' muttered the embarrassed Kristoň.

Slonský flopped into the first available chair and placed their order. 'Pastry, Daniel?'

'Watching my weight,' Kristoň replied.

'Very wise. Bring two anyway, miss; I'm sure I can manage a second one if my friend can't.'

'You'll realise that I can't discuss my client's affairs,' Kristoň announced.

'He's a client, is he? You were in quick there, Daniel, I've got to hand it to you.'

'Mr Darmant has been a client for a while.'

'Has he? Good payer, is he?'

'I've no complaints.'

'I think it's terrible when professional men are kept waiting for their fees. If you've done a job for someone you should get your money the moment you're released from prison, don't you think?'

'Why should anyone be going to prison?'

'Well, whoever killed Darmant's daughter will be, won't he?'

'I sincerely hope so. Bad business.'

'You're right there. We don't want that sort of person wandering around Prague, do we? To which end, if any information should come your client's way that would assist the Czech Police in their enquiries, no doubt it will be forwarded at once and not used to pursue some independent personal enquiry.'

Kristoň looked shocked. 'It goes without saying, Captain.'

'Good. Say it anyway. Just to please me.'

'If I hear anything I'll let you know.'

'I'm sure you will, Daniel. After all, you know which side your bread is buttered on. That's what makes you a delight to deal with. However, I was more concerned about your client. I would hate to have to run in the grieving father if anything unofficial happened to his daughter's killer.'

Kristoň gazed into his cup morosely. 'He's not happy.'

'And who can blame him? And he hasn't seen the crime scene photos like I have. Believe me, they're not nice. Try to persuade him not to ask for them, there's a good fellow.'

Kristoň nodded. 'Message understood.'

Slonský fished in his wallet for a small slip of paper. 'That's my desk number. If I'm not there Lieutenant Navrátil will pick it up. You can trust him. He's a good lad. Nobody needs to know you've called.'

'Aren't all calls to the police recorded?'

'Are they?' Slonský was genuinely surprised to hear this, but then he recalled the technicians connecting gadgets to his phone in the past to intercept or trace calls to him, so it seemed it must be true. 'You'd best have my mobile phone number then.'

'Which is.'

'Damned if I know.'

Slonský drew the phone from his pocket and handed it over. Kristoň clicked on a couple of buttons and wrote the number on Slonský's tatty note.

'Some day you must show me how you do that,' said Slonský. 'I can't keep asking Peiperová.'

'Who?' asked Kristoň.

'Another lieutenant. Doesn't matter. Genius with technology. She can even get the kettle to produce good coffee. Anyway, thanks for this little chat. We must do it more often.' Slonský waved his arm and a taxi on the other side of the road executed a daring and probably illegal manoeuvre to pull alongside the café. 'Remember, Daniel, we're both rowing the same way on this one. Darmant might think he's untouchable, but so long as you're in Prague, you're not,' he said as he climbed into the cab.

CHAPTER 12

Sergeant Mucha had dealt with many strange requests at the station's front desk over the years, but this was one of the strangest. 'Are you sure?' he said.

'I can't get a new one on expenses,' Jerneková explained. 'I just thought there's bound to be one in lost property somewhere.'

Mucha shrugged and clicked the mouse on the screen, scrolling down slowly. 'Well, I'll be…' he exclaimed. 'They've got one at Břevnov.'

'Prague 6? That'll do. Can I book it out?'

'You can't just book lost property,' Mucha explained. 'By definition, it doesn't belong to us.'

'How long have they had it?' Jerneková demanded.

Mucha ran his finger across the screen. 'Fourteen months.'

'Well, there you are. The chances that someone will suddenly turn up to claim it this afternoon aren't great, are they? And if they do the desk at the Břevnov station can take an address and I'll deliver it to the door personally.'

Reluctantly, Mucha lifted the receiver and made the call. 'They'll bring it to the front desk,' he said. 'You'll need your ID.'

'Of course. They can't go round giving lost property to just anybody, can they?' Jerneková zipped up her jacket and made for the door, whistling happily. 'Oh — if Lieutenant Peiperová comes looking for me, I'll meet her there,' she announced.

Autumn was definitely on its way, thought Peiperová, as she pulled her jacket around her and looked for her assistant. You would not think it would be difficult to spot a small dark-haired woman with poor dress sense in a small park, but it wasn't easy … hang on, that figure on the bench looked familiar. But what was that beside her?

Peiperová walked round the path to the bench, resisting the temptation to march across the reseeded grass. 'What is that?' she demanded.

Jerneková paused in the to-and-fro motion she was making with her arm. 'What?'

'That!'

'It's a buggy, obviously. A sort of pushchair thing,' she added helpfully.

'I can see that. Why have you got one?'

'Make me fit in better. It was either this or jog all afternoon and I thought "Stuff that for a lark", so I borrowed a buggy.'

'There's no baby in it,' Peiperová objected.

'Of course not. They didn't have one of those in lost property. Even the worst mother doesn't usually leave a baby behind. Admittedly, my Granny left me outside a church once, but she was old and batty by then. And she was a bit annoyed that I wasn't a boy.' Jerneková leaned forward and adjusted the hood. 'Anyway, I've got the hood up to keep the wind off, so you can't see there's no baby inside.'

'And if we see Paulina Zechovská, how are you going to give chase with a pushchair?'

'Well, obviously I'll leave it and come back for it later.'

'You don't think it'll look a little odd for a mother to desert her child in a park?'

Jerneková considered this proposition, but only for a moment. 'No, because I don't give a toss what people think of me as a mother, seeing as I'm not one.'

The two detectives walked around the park a couple of times but saw no sign of Paulina Zechovská.

'You don't just stop running,' Peiperová complained.

'I would if someone might be lying in wait in a bush for me,' Jerneková replied.

'Well, run somewhere else then. Running is addictive. You hate not being able to do it once you're committed to it.'

'Is that right?' Jerneková asked doubtfully.

'Don't you feel the endorphins after a good run?'

'The what?'

'The endorphins. Brain chemicals that make you feel good.'

'Can't say I do. I run to keep fit enough to pass my medicals. Even then, it's bad enough having to run, let alone go outside to do it. I prefer to run on a treadmill, where at least I can listen to music or watch a television programme while I do it.'

'That's it!' said Peiperová. 'She's taken to running indoors. I'll bet she's going to a gym.'

'It sounds like her boyfriend works out, so maybe they're going to the same one.'

'Okay, let's get back to the office and make a list of all the gyms near here where she could be running on a treadmill.'

'Have you got space in the car for this?' Jerneková enquired immediately, indicating the buggy.

'Does it fold?'

'How should I know?'

'Wasn't it folded when you got it?'

'No. The desk sergeant put it up for me.'

Peiperová inspected the pushchair. 'There must be hinges somewhere. Push these rings up and press on the handle.'

The buggy refused to stay folded.

Jerneková drew her gun.

'What are you doing?' asked Peiperová.

'Just going to ease the hinges a bit.'

'Put it away. People will think you're shooting at your baby.'

'God, this parenting business is harder than you'd think, isn't it?'

After a few moments of careful thought, Peiperová located the catch that kept the buggy folded and they were able to load it into the car.

'If we could detour past Břevnov I can return the buggy and save us a trip later,' Jerneková suggested.

'What do you mean, us? You borrowed it.'

'But we're a team. You always say so.'

'Fine,' sighed Peiperová. 'Let's drop off the buggy.'

Jerneková smiled. 'I'll buy you a coffee,' she said.

Krob and Navrátil stood back to survey their handwork. Having drawn a timeline they had attempted to trace Kateryna Teslenko's movements on the fatal day, and by dint of painstaking interviewing they had done rather better than either had expected.

She had left work that Saturday morning at 04:50 or thereabouts. At any event, the doorman at the Dreamy Clouds nightclub had hailed a taxi at 04:45, this being established by the taxi log that would, eventually, result in the taxi firm being paid. The taxi driver had delivered her to the street door of her home in Černý Most at 05:15, which was reasonable given that it was twelve and a half kilometres away and there would be bored traffic police lining the road waiting for the chance to pull a car over.

The outfit she had been wearing was hanging on the back of the bathroom door, so their best guess was that she had taken a shower or bath, changed into some other clothes, and had something to eat. A large omelette pan was inverted on the draining board as if it had been washed and left to dry.

At some stage she would have gone to bed, but it was always difficult to place that for night economy workers. On the other hand, Krob had some experience of night shifts and argued that people who do them often do not go straight to bed on arriving home.

'After all,' he argued, 'you don't when you get home after a day shift. You have three or four hours together or do things you need to do, then you go to bed at the right time to get up and go straight to work. And the neighbours are clear that Kateryna was normally up and about at around five o'clock, ready to go to work in time for her evening starting around seven.'

But on this particular Saturday, she must have been disturbed by someone coming to the door. Forensic examination of the door lock was hampered by Navrátil having destroyed the door when he barged it in, but the technicians were clear that the lock was serviceable if not particularly sophisticated.

Someone with a lockpick could have entered relatively easily — except that Krob had noticed that there was a chain dangling freely at the back of the door that had not been cut. Clearly the assailant could not go out and then restore the chain to its closed position from the outside, but why would Ms Teslenko have a chain if not to use it? That being so, she must have taken the chain off, presumably because she knew her attacker. That part was a puzzle — unless, of course, the attacker was her boyfriend, Yeremenko. The issue there being that the said Yeremenko was adamant that he had been out of town doing some unspecified business. However, he had been expected home that day — it was to explain the delay that Yurii Chigulin had gone round to Kateryna's flat — so maybe she had left the door unchained so he could come in.

This was backed up by Yeremenko's friend Chigulin. His telephone records proved that he had rung Yeremenko at 19:12 that evening, exactly as Yeremenko had claimed.

'Why did Chigulin go there?' Navrátil asked.

'To check up on Ms Teslenko,' answered Krob.

'But why did Chigulin think she needed checking up on? Did Yeremenko ask him to keep an eye on her?'

'He didn't say so, but we can ask him.'

'He was only going away for the weekend. If he thought she was in danger, he'd ask this man Chigulin to drive her to and from work, surely.'

'There is something odd about his story,' Krob conceded.

'How so?'

'He said he heard that there'd been a murder and he wondered if it was Kateryna Teslenko, so he drove across. But he didn't try phoning her first. Wouldn't you have at least one try?'

'Assuming he has her number. The likes of Yeremenko may be too jealous to share their girlfriend's phone numbers.'

'That's true enough, I suppose. Anyway, he goes over there, and sees the place swarming with police. But by the time the news broke, there were no police outside. We'd got our people in the flat, but would you know that from walking along the street?'

'There'd be police cars somewhere.'

'Not right outside. You can't park there. It's not just the parking restrictions — it's not safe to leave a car there. The road is too narrow with people parked opposite.'

Navrátil added a couple of questions to their display. 'How did she get to work?'

'Metro. Easy enough at night, not so safe in the early morning.'

'There'd be plenty of people around at five o'clock on a Saturday morning. I wonder if she had some particular reason for taking a cab after her shift. Had she been followed or molested before? Let's ask her colleagues at work.'

'They're not very communicative to the police.'

'Let's ask Kristýna and Jerneková to speak to them. They may get more out of them.'

'There's also the curious matter of her alarm clock,' Krob reminded Navrátil.

Kateryna's alarm clock was set to ring at 16:30 but had been switched off. The small lever that did this had blood on it, but no fingerprints, suggesting that the killer must have done it; but did he do it when it rang, or did he turn it off so that it would not ring?

'The neighbours say that they heard her walking about but nobody has mentioned an alarm clock sounding, either on that day or any other,' Navrátil remarked.

'But somebody made sure it didn't ring that afternoon,' Krob insisted.

'Cool customer,' Navrátil replied. 'I'm not sure I'd have thought of turning the alarm clock off.'

'That's why you'll never make a mass murderer,' Krob smiled. 'But, with respect, that's not the point I'm making. We've said it's unlikely that the murderer was still in the flat at half past four; the forensics suggest that he had probably killed her about sixty to ninety minutes before you got there, suggesting a time of death between, say, 15:45 and 16:15. And the neighbour called at ten to five, having had time to think for a while about whether she should investigate the noise.'

'All true,' agreed Navrátil.

'So why does it matter if the alarm clock goes off? The killer wasn't going to be there anyway.'

'Maybe he thought he still might be.'

'I wonder if he just turned the clock off automatically, just in case?'

Navrátil turned this over in his mind. 'I suppose he can't have known how loud the clock's bell might be. It might disturb the neighbours and cause them to be looking out when he left.'

'Maybe…' Krob conceded. 'But can I make another suggestion?'

'Go ahead.'

'We're fixing on the time of death because we always do, but after she died he cut her head off and put it on the windowsill. That wasn't a frenzied attack. He did it very carefully. I have no idea how long that would take but given that he poured blood over the knives and over the floor as he left, I can't see that he could have been there less than fifteen minutes after killing her. So maybe he was still in the flat at 16:30 when it went off, and he had to run to turn it off and then lie low a minute or two to see if anyone responded.'

'So he was still in the flat when the woman came to the door to see if everything was okay?'

'And he left when she went to phone us for help.'

Navrátil scratched his head. 'Why is this important?' he asked.

'Because at some stage we're going to have to work on someone's alibi, and I don't want us to concentrate on the wrong times.'

CHAPTER 13

Slonský heard Navrátil and Krob out without comment until they had finished.

'Good work,' he said.

'You accept Krob's hypothesis?' Navrátil asked.

'Certainly not. Maybe he was there, maybe he wasn't. What I want to know is who the display was for.'

'The display?'

'The arrangement of the body. It takes time, it adds to the risk of capture, so it's clearly important to the killer. But why? Who did he want to see it?'

'Whoever discovered the body, I guess,' Krob suggested.

Slonský tapped his pencil on his teeth as he thought. 'It's a lot of trouble to go to if you're not going to stay around and see the reactions, don't you think?'

'You think they stayed to watch us?' Navrátil stammered.

'Not us — you. I was safely tucked up in my hospital bed. I don't know, lad, but it's a key question. Was it a message to Yeremenko for when he came home and next went round?'

'Does that mean Yeremenko knows who did it?'

'I think if he did, we'd have a second body on our hands already. He might have a list of possible names, but I doubt that he knows for sure. But I'm as sure as I can be that it's why Darmant has shown up. He doesn't seem to be close to his daughter. On previous trips to Prague he doesn't appear to have gone to see her or hasn't thought it worthy of mention to us. But if someone is sending a message to Yeremenko or Darmant they're not the sort of people to walk away. We'll have more blood yet, mark my words.'

'We need to talk to this man Chigulin,' Navrátil suggested. 'I want to understand why he went there and then telephoned Yeremenko. And, for that matter, how he heard that there had been a murder. After all, if he telephoned at 19:12 that's only two hours and a few minutes after I rang it in, and I didn't use my radio so nobody could have intercepted it. Even if he phoned straight after he got there he must need some time to drive out to Černý Most and find out what's happening.'

'You've got his number,' Slonský replied. 'Give him a ring and get him to come in.'

'He might run off if he has something to hide.'

'He might, but at least then we'll know he has something to hide.'

Navrátil picked up the paper bearing Chigulin's phone number and walked over to his desk to make the call.

'Do you think Chigulin could be our man, sir?' Krob asked.

Slonský rocked back in his chair and scratched his head. 'I don't think so. According to Dvorník, Yeremenko described him as a friend and immediately volunteered his number. He trusts Chigulin. And while criminals are generally almost as untrustworthy as our colleagues here, they've usually got a sharp sense of which people can be trusted not to cross them.'

Navrátil put the phone down. 'No answer.'

Slonský picked up his jacket.

'Are we going somewhere?' Krob enquired.

'I'm going to the canteen. My stomach thinks my throat's been cut. I don't know what you two are doing.' He clambered to his feet and sucked in air as he put weight on his knee. 'But I'll tell you what you *could* be doing. Yeremenko said Chigulin told him what was going on, but he clearly didn't tell him the gruesome details. I wouldn't mind betting Yeremenko gave him a bell as soon as I let him go.'

'You've let him go, sir?' Krob and Navrátil chorused.

'I had to. Having a girlfriend who gets murdered is not a criminal offence in the Czech Republic, unless the Parliament introduced it while I was in hospital. They've done dafter things.'

'But a lot of murders of women are done by their partners,' Navrátil continued.

'So they are, lad, and those partners often leave evidence that justifies holding them here. I hope you're not suggesting fabricating evidence, Navrátil. People who do that risk being fast-tracked to Colonel.'

'Of course not,' Navrátil replied, before trying another tack. 'I thought we'd agreed it was my case. I should be making those decisions.'

'Evidently not,' said Slonský, 'because you're talking about stitching someone up with dodgy evidence.'

Navrátil opened his mouth to protest but then he saw a twinkle in Slonský's eye. 'You've set Hauzer to follow him, haven't you?'

'Not exactly. Following someone like Yeremenko could be dangerous. No, Hauzer just gave Yeremenko a lift into town and told him he'll be watching him. We don't actually have to put our best man onto following Yeremenko so long as he thinks he's on him. After all, if Yeremenko turns suddenly he's not going to see Hauzer, which is exactly what he'd expect if Hauzer's as good at following people as I told Yeremenko he was. We don't need to waste Hauzer's time and shoe leather actually doing it.'

Slonský limped out of the door, pausing to turn and call back through the opening to Navrátil and Krob. 'I might write an article for the police newspaper about it. I'll call it Virtual Following, I think.'

People were so used to saying Technician First Class Spehar that it may not have occurred to some of them that those were not his given names, though very few people knew or cared what they were. What they did care about was that he was a wizard with technology and employed a number of others with outstanding skill sets. Many of them would never have found a job anywhere else, because it was widely agreed that those who worked for Spehar were misfits. One never took his anorak off; another ate yoghurt more or less non-stop, but apparently little else.

It was one of these who had walked up to Spehar's desk and shared a piece of information that struck him as strange, and if Ricka thought something was strange, Spehar was not going to argue, because Ricka was himself rather out of the ordinary.

A large man with hair like badly cut straw, Ricka was the technician who knew most about telecommunications. Spehar himself was good, but Ricka was exceptional. He had made contacts with the technical departments of all the major mobile phone networks in the Czech Republic, and then written some custom software that was regarded by the computing mavens as eccentric and untidy but which did exactly what Ricka wanted it to do.

Navrátil had asked whether they were able to determine where Chigulin was when he telephoned Yeremenko on the day that the body of Teslenko was discovered. This had not been quite as straightforward as usual, because Chigulin appeared to have been moving during the call, but his starting point was consistent with his being at or near Teslenko's apartment. What was slightly more puzzling was that when Navrátil's next request was made earlier that afternoon, to see where Chigulin was now because he was not picking up calls, he was right in the middle of town, and over two hours later he

— or at least his phone — had not moved a centimetre. That struck Ricka as odd.

'Maybe he's waiting for someone,' suggested Spehar.

'Could be,' Ricka conceded, 'but if he is he's waiting on the Charles Bridge, and in this weather there are better places to meet.'

'Could he have dropped his phone?'

Ricka chuckled. 'How long would an unattended phone stay on the Charles Bridge?' he asked.

Spehar inspected the printout Ricka had given him. 'How precise are your calculations?' he enquired.

'I'd say to within fifty metres, possibly less in the centre of the city where there are more phone transmitters.'

'If we go there, can we do better?'

'It's worth a try,' Ricka replied. 'We can try pinging the phone and see how it responds.'

'Good. Get your coat while I tell Lieutenant Navrátil what we're doing.'

It is safe to say that of the members of Slonský's team, Navrátil was the most likely to understand what Ricka was talking about. That did not, of course, mean that he actually did understand Ricka's explanation, just that none of the others would have come close.

'So what are you telling me?' Navrátil plaintively demanded.

'Do you see a phone within ten metres of here?' asked Ricka, pointing in a broad arc across the Charles Bridge.

'No, of course not.'

'Well, Chigulin's phone is here.'

'Now?'

'Yes. The battery is failing but it's very close.'

Navrátil looked about him. 'Where?'

Ricka jiggled a dial on a little silver box that looked simultaneously highly complex and clearly homemade. 'If you twisted my arm I'd say it's under us now.'

Navrátil glanced at his feet.

'He means it's in the river,' Spehar explained.

'Why would it be there?'

'You're the detective. But isn't the question really whether it's there with Chigulin or without him?'

CHAPTER 14

Slonský leaned over the parapet and studied the water carefully. 'I still think it's a waste of time,' he declared.

Navrátil disagreed. 'Surely we need to know whether Chigulin is down there?'

'Yes, we do. He isn't.'

'How can you be so sure?'

Slonský gestured to each side of them. 'Twenty-four hours a day people are going back and forth here. There isn't a busier place in Prague. Now, I know Praguers are often disinclined to co-operate with the police and they like keeping themselves to themselves, but I like to think that if someone was heaving another person over the side of a bridge one of them would at least mention it to the police. Think how many reports we get of people threatening to jump off.'

'So what do you think happened?'

'I think someone threw the phone away. It might be Chigulin himself, or it might be whoever is holding him. After all, if you kidnap someone you don't want anyone to trace where they are through their phone.'

'There's no evidence that he's been kidnapped.'

'No,' Slonský agreed, 'apart from the fact that nobody has seen him for a while and we can't find him. But when you put together the fact that Yeremenko's girlfriend has been murdered and then his best friend goes missing, it's hard to escape the conclusion that someone has it in for Yeremenko.'

'But why, sir?' asked Krob. 'Is Yeremenko that high up the food chain?'

Slonský shrugged. 'I don't know, but history tells me that when Number One is untouchable enemies go after Number Two. Think of the show trials here; Gottwald survives, his deputy Slánský doesn't.'

The look on his juniors' faces conveyed their incomprehension of Slonský's point, so he continued. 'This is all when I was a child, but Gottwald was Chairman of the Communist Party and Slánský was its secretary. Put it another way, Gottwald was top dog and worried that Slánský might want to be top dog. Hanging him was a good way of discouraging ambition. And it worked! Slánský never became Chairman once he'd been hanged.' He wagged his finger at Navrátil. 'Let that be a lesson to you, lad. Don't get any ideas about replacing me just yet.'

'I wasn't planning to. I've still got a lot to learn.'

Slonský wrapped a fatherly arm round him. 'Yes, you have. But you're doing all right.' He wrapped his other arm around Krob. 'And you're doing all right too. And so are the lasses. You're all coming along nicely. So any one of you could replace me in time, but not until I'm dragged kicking and screaming to the front door and chucked out into the street. What does it say in the bible? Something about weeping and wailing and kicking in someone's teeth?'

'It's weeping and wailing and gnashing of teeth,' Navrátil replied.

'Is it? I think my version reads better. If you want to convert a lot of people quickly that's the way to do it.'

'It's hardly consistent with a gospel of peace and love though, is it?' Navrátil pointed out.

'Perhaps not. But you're a member of the club, I'm just an interested onlooker.'

A wetsuited figure bobbed out of the water and demonstrated that his hands were empty.

'Should we call them off, sir?' asked Navrátil.

'As you keep pointing out to me, it's your case. But if Spehar says it's down there, it'll be down there. Whether we can find it on a grubby river bed might be a different matter. Try ringing it again to see if it lights up like yours does.'

The divers ducked under the surface again. The Vltava flowed very quickly under the bridge and they were tethered to the ironwork to ensure that they were not swept away, but this meant that they had to take care not to tangle each other's harnesses.

After a few seconds a hand triumphantly waved, followed by the rest of a diver who began to swim towards the bank. The three detectives went to meet him, though only Navrátil offered him a hand to clamber out, Krob being under orders not to risk further damage to his shoulder, and Slonský being keen not to get his feet muddy.

Krob dropped the phone into an evidence bag while Slonský crouched as best he could to interrogate the diver.

'Just out of interest, you didn't happen to spot a stiff down there, I suppose?'

'Nobody at all, sir. The phone had dropped between two large stones on the bed. If a body was thrown in it could be well downstream by now.'

'I feared as much. We'll just have to wait for it to surface if it's there. There's no prospect of searching a river this large. I was hoping they might have encased his feet in concrete so he would stay where he landed, but criminals are so inconsiderate these days.'

'I think even Praguers would be mildly curious if they saw someone being dropped off a bridge with their feet in a concrete block,' Krob suggested.

'You're probably right,' Slonský sighed. 'Unless the villains had the presence of mind to hand out free sausages in the middle of the bridge to distract people.'

'Wouldn't you wonder why anyone would give away sausages?' laughed Krob.

'Yes. But I'd eat the sausage first while I was thinking.' Slonský held out his hand for the evidence bag and looked at the phone closely.

'Is something puzzling you, sir?' asked Navrátil.

'No, lad. I was just thinking that the next time I need a phone I might get one of these. They're obviously well-made if they can survive a day or two in the river. Let's give this to Ricka and see what he can pull off it. Good work, you two. Now, I'm off to a local landmark.'

'Sightseeing, sir?' suggested Krob.

'No. There's a place down a side street that does the best sausage in the district. All this underwater activity has made me peckish.'

'I spy with my little eye,' said Jerneková, 'something beginning with ... T.'

'Trees,' Peiperová replied.

'You're on a hot streak.'

'Not really. Playing I spy in a park offers very limited options. What I'd really like is to spy something beginning with Z.'

'Zechovská?'

'Got it in one.'

'I think she's taken off. Skedaddled.'

'We could try giving her workplace a ring again to see if she has shown up.'

'They promised they'd call me if she reappeared. And her bank is going to let us know if her card is used anywhere.'

'When was it last used?'

'The day after she was attacked. She took some cash out but nowhere near cleaning out her account.'

'So it doesn't look like she was planning on going far. Maybe she's lying low with a friend.'

'I hope so, because the alternative is that the creep tried again and he succeeded this time.'

Peiperová acknowledged the truth of this proposition with a nod. 'The bit I don't understand is why she gave us a false address immediately after the incident. I could understand if she thought about it and did so later but it was as if her first response was to lie.'

'Maybe that's what she does. She lies to everyone,' Jerneková suggested.

'She doesn't want people to know where she really lives?'

'Or she doesn't want the attacker caught for some reason.'

'I can't see that. She was genuinely frightened.'

'Maybe she was embarrassed about her apartment. Perhaps she has underwear drying everywhere or she had to sell the furniture.'

'You saw the trainers she was wearing. The girl doesn't do economy,' observed Peiperová.

'Well, then, perhaps she doesn't want us there because someone she lives with doesn't want us there.'

'Her boyfriend?'

'Remember what Honza said? He didn't think the boyfriend wanted people to know about him. That's suspicious for a start,' Jerneková decided.

'When we get back I'll run a search on people with criminal records living in the neighbourhood. It might give us a lead.'

'Let's go to her workplace too. Someone there may know something.'

'Let's hope they're prepared to talk. Come on, we'll go now.'

'Can I drive?' Jerneková asked.

'Have you passed your driving test?'

'No.'

'Well, there you are then. We've been through this.'

'How do you expect me to get better if I don't practise?'

'Practise at the driving school, Lucie, not driving through the middle of Prague.'

Jerneková considered this advice. 'The problem with that is that when I pass —'

'If you pass.'

'— when I pass, I won't ever have driven in the city centre. The police driving school is too safe.'

'Lucie, you told me last week they had you driving at a hundred and twenty kilometres an hour.'

'Yeah, but on an open raceway with no-one else around. And I said I was driving at a hundred and twenty, not that they asked me to do it.'

'You went that fast off your own bat?'

'Well, the instructor told me to go up through the gears, so I couldn't hang around at thirty, could I?'

'Going well, is it?'

Jerneková did not want to overstate her competence. 'I sometimes get the gearstick and the handbrake confused, but apart from that it's coming along well.'

Peiperová wrapped her hand around the car keys. 'I think I'll drive this time.'

Slonský drained the last mouthful of his beer and looked wistfully at the bar.

'Better stop there,' he announced.

'We're working after all,' Navrátil reminded him.

'It isn't that. With this gammy knee I don't fancy the long walk to the toilet here. It's way out the back.'

Krob diplomatically blew his nose to hide his smile.

'Now,' Slonský continued, 'theories on what has happened to Chigulin and how we track him down. In your own time, begin.'

'Whoever got Ms Teslenko has kidnapped or killed him,' Krob suggested.

'Definite possibility,' agreed Slonský.

'He's in hiding because he thinks whoever killed Ms Teslenko will come for him next,' proposed Navrátil.

'Also possible, but why chuck his phone away? We can track him, but can criminals? Wouldn't he need it to keep in touch with Yeremenko?'

'Maybe he thinks Yeremenko killed her?'

'If he does then he's thicker than I thought. Why ring her boyfriend to tell him? Why not get a head start?'

'To throw Yeremenko off the scent?'

Slonský raised an arm to summon a waiter. 'It's no good. If you're going to make suggestions like that I'm going to have to have another drink. One of you may need to walk me to the back door later. The thing is that with a very few exceptions criminals are actually quite rational. Not smart, not as cunning as they like to think, but they have reasons for what they do. If they try to overthink things they come unstuck. Like that fellow in Suchdol who burned his house down to get the insurance money, only to forget that the policy was inside.'

'Didn't the insurance company have another copy?' enquired Krob.

'Yes, but he went back in to try to find it. Grisly business.'

'So you don't think Chigulin is clever enough to kill Teslenko and pretend to Yeremenko that he just turned up after she was killed?' asked Navrátil.

'Well, we don't know Chigulin, do we? But given what we know about Yeremenko, wouldn't it be a dangerous game to play? Does Yeremenko strike you as a soft touch? For that matter, even if Yeremenko doesn't tumble to your plot, Darmant is coming after you too, and that's a seriously nasty prospect. Get on the wrong side of someone like him and you're likely to get fed through a bacon slicer bit by bit. Then there's Kristoň.'

'How does he come into it?' Navrátil wanted to know.

'I know he's a grade A pain in the rear end of humanity, but he was a detective and he's not completely useless. He can't be, because Darmant can afford to buy any number of crooked policemen and he has settled on Kristoň. There's a fair chance that Kristoň will get some kind of lead before we do.'

'But we've got all that technology on our side,' Krob protested.

'Yes, but we also have rules to work to. We're not allowed, for example, to question a witness while pulling their teeth out one by one. Not these days, anyway. Getting a confession was a lot easier in the seventies.'

'You pulled their teeth out?' Navrátil gasped.

'Not personally. There were people who had been trained to do it. You have a stroll round any prison in the Czech Republic and look in the mouths of the old lags. Barely a tooth between them.'

'I thought that was just Communist-era dentistry.'

'It didn't help,' Slonský conceded. 'I've got a couple of fillings at the back that feel like they were made out of old tank components.' He rubbed his knee ruefully. 'Thank heavens this didn't happen in those days. They'd probably have made me a new knee out of a windscreen wiper motor and some lengths of barbed wire.'

The waiter arrived with another round of drinks. Krob had given in to temptation and had accepted a small beer, but Navrátil stuck to the lemonade.

'That stuff can't be good for you,' Slonský opined.

'I need to keep a clear head,' Navrátil countered.

'So do I, but look at those bubbles charging up the glass. If you swallow them they've got to keep going upwards, haven't they? And who wants bubbles in their brain?'

'I think they disperse in your stomach.'

'You hope. Trapped wind is a terrible thing. Remember Major Lukas rolling around on his office floor, and that was down to trapped wind.'

'It was down to an inflamed gallbladder,' Navrátil corrected him. 'The wind was just a symptom.'

Krob decided to intervene. 'Why aren't we following Yeremenko, sir? He might lead us to someone of interest.'

Slonský shook his head. 'He'll lead you to Darmant, and Darmant will tell him firmly to lie low until our trails have gone cold. He'll be pulling the strings now.'

'Do you think he cared about his daughter, sir?'

'I don't know, Krob. But he will care about any challenge to his authority. You don't muck around with crime barons in any country. And he can't afford to let anyone get away with this. It wouldn't surprise me if Chigulin was given a plane ticket and told to chuck his phone away and go and live on a Greek island for a while until Darmant gets to the bottom of it all.'

'Can Darmant do that before we do?'

'Well, lad, as you pointed out, we have access to all the high-tech sophistication of modern policing. We'd better use it well, because sheer brutality is a potent tool for getting to the bottom of things.'

'Nothing sleazy about this place, is there?' Jerneková commented, nodding in the direction of the mirrored walls and floor that surrounded the poles on the dance floor.

'We're not here to be judgemental, Lucie,' Peiperová replied.

'I'm not being judgemental. If women want to display every square centimetre to a bunch of lecherous men, why shouldn't they? It's just not a choice I'd make myself, that's all.'

Peiperová could not imagine that anyone would invite Jerneková to pole-dance, but the image became harder to shake from her brain when her colleague gripped a pole and tried launching herself sideways from it, an action that looked rather like someone trying to put a large bean bag in a skip. Jerneková tried once more, then picked herself up, dusted off her hands, and fell back in step with her boss.

'Harder than it looks,' she commented.

'Evidently so,' Peiperová agreed. 'I wonder where everyone is?'

'Anyone here?' bellowed Jerneková, at which there was a thump from behind the bar and a young white-shirted man with a wispy goatee stood up, rubbing his arm as he did so.

'Sorry. I was counting the stock,' he explained. 'Didn't hear you come in. What can I get you?'

'You can get us the manager,' Jerneková replied, peering over the bar to confirm her suspicion that he had been having a sly kip sitting on a crate.

'There's only me here,' came the answer. He looked the women up and down and jumped to a conclusion. 'Are you here about the job?'

'Might be,' Jerneková replied. 'What job?'

'The job as a … dancer,' he stuttered, having taken in the inherent unlikelihood that the short, dark one was cut out for such work.

'We're police officers,' Peiperová announced, producing her identification and motioning to Jerneková to do the same.

'This is about Paulina, isn't it?'

'Yes. Do you know her well?'

'Not that well. Not — you know — well.'

'No, I don't — you know — anything,' Jerneková chipped in. 'Spell it out for me.'

'Well, we didn't have anything going. We just worked in the same place. I saw her here, never anywhere else. She seemed a nice girl.'

'Seemed?' asked Jerneková,

'No, not seemed — was! She was a nice girl. Some of them haven't any time for bar staff and waiters, but she at least talked to us.'

'Did she do more than talk to any of you?'

'Come again?'

'Was she particularly close to anyone?' Peiperová explained.

'I wouldn't think so. She had a very jealous boyfriend.'

'So we've heard,' said Jerneková. 'Know where we can find him?'

'No, sorry.' He picked up a glass and gave it a leisurely polish with his cloth, oblivious to the fact that it had not yet been washed.

'Well, if anything occurs to you…' Jerneková began.

'Power Gloves!' he suddenly said.

'Power Gloves?'

'Sometimes he came in with a couple of guys wearing T-shirts from Power Gloves. It's a boxing gym about three hundred metres along the road on the left. Maybe somebody there knows something.'

'Thank you,' said Peiperová. 'Has he been in since Paulina disappeared?'

The waiter shook his head vigorously. 'Haven't seen him in a fortnight or more.'

Peiperová thanked him again and the two women ventured out into the daylight once again.

'What does he look like?' said Jerneková. 'That stupid little beard. I've got more hair than that on my —'

'Lucie!'

'Yes?'

Peiperová said nothing, but glared at her colleague.

'Oh. Right. Too much information. Again.'

CHAPTER 15

As part of his rehabilitation, Slonský was supposed to spend half an hour in the police gym two or three times a week. He had been putting this off, partly because he had a natural and lifelong aversion to exercise, but also because he was aware that he looked ridiculous in shorts. He certainly looked odd in the shorts that he had donned for his first workout, a pair that might once have been navy blue and were rather longer than the norm. He could have stepped out of a photograph taken in 1890, right down to the cord holding his shorts up since the elastic was no longer reliable.

He sat on a bench and gingerly inspected his scar before fishing in his pocket for the sheet of exercises he was expected to attempt. One of these was so baffling he turned the paper the other way up to see if he was misunderstanding the posture needed.

'Need any help?'

He looked up to see a pleasant-looking woman in a dark green tracksuit with POLICE emblazoned across the chest.

'Pertová, Jana,' she introduced herself. 'I'm one of the gym's personal trainers.'

'Personal…?'

'Trainers. I help to work out personalised fitness plans for officers.'

'How long have we been doing this?' Slonský mumbled.

'I don't know exactly. I've been here nearly two years now.'

'What happened to Čada?'

She looked away uncomfortably. 'He's gone.' She dropped her voice. 'He was caught with some banned substances in his locker.'

Slonský could have told her that. He had been one of Čada's customers briefly, when he needed to lose weight in a hurry to pass a medical and Čada had slipped him a few diuretic tablets that made him pee like nobody's business. To be fair to Čada, he had not asked for any money during the transaction, but then Slonský had not returned to the gym since. Maybe it was like those fellows who sold hard drugs under the bridge. They would give you a few doses to get you hooked, then put the bite on when you needed more. Still, when he thought of some of his colleagues in the past, what Čada had done seemed very small beer compared with, say, arresting people so that they could not vote in elections or taking a percentage to fail to solve a robbery.

'What brings you here?' Pertová asked, briskly changing the subject.

'I've had knee surgery,' Slonský explained. 'An injury sustained in the course of duty.' He turned half away as if he did not want to talk about it, all the while hoping that Pertová would ask so that he could recount the story again.

'May I see?' Pertová knelt and lifted Slonský's leg, gently rocking the heel back and forth and then rotating the lower leg slightly. 'Are you getting any pain?' she asked.

'I don't like to talk about it. I'm just lucky that the damage wasn't worse, I suppose.'

This performance was wasted on Pertová, who was unable to give him a medal or even a commendation. Suddenly she grabbed the kneecap and pushed her thumb into the side of his knee.

'Jesus Maria Mother of God!' Slonský yelped, gripping the bridge of his nose in an attempt to restore his equilibrium.

'Sorry — did that hurt?' Pertová asked.

'A bit,' gasped Slonský, thinking how fortunate it was that he had somehow resisted the temptation to kick her with his other leg.

'Has a police doctor seen this?'

'I've got an appointment for a check-up next week.'

'Wait here a moment.'

'Believe me, I'm not going anywhere,' Slonský replied, privately doubting whether he could still walk.

Pertová broke into a trot and headed for a small office where she could be seen gesturing towards Slonský to another man in a green tracksuit. They both looked at him, so he pretended not to have noticed and gently massaged his knee while wincing. The wincing was not an act. His knee felt as if someone had stolen his kneecap in his sleep.

When he looked up, Pertová was making a telephone call. A few minutes later she reappeared with a piece of card.

'They'll see you now if you can get to the medical centre. Have you got anyone who can take you?'

Slonský tried to recall where his staff were, only to realise that he had no idea. That was the trouble with developing their independence; they used it to do things without being directed to do so. 'I'm not sure.'

'Come on, I'll drive you there. It's only a couple of minutes. I can't stay with you but the boss won't mind me doing it in my break.'

Slonský collected his clothes, slipping his trousers over his shorts since they were leaving the building, and limped to the back door where Pertová was waiting in the smallest car he had ever seen.

'Compact, isn't it?' he said as he attempted to squeeze in.

'I'll push the seat back,' Pertová answered, suiting the action to the word and sending the seat back so quickly that Slonský, who was leaning on it, went with it. After a few moments he managed to restore his rear end to the seat and checked his palm for carpet burns.

'All belted in?' Pertová chirped.

Slonský nodded. He had no intention of driving anywhere with this woman without engaging every possible safety device.

They pulled out into the traffic, drove to the next corner, turned left and rolled into a courtyard.

'Is this it?' said Slonský. 'I could have walked.'

'I don't want you putting any weight on that knee until an expert has seen it. Come on, look lively. The surgeon is seeing you between appointments.'

Slonský clambered out and gingerly flexed his knee. Now that she mentioned it, he could no longer put any weight on the leg and limped heavily into the clinic where a convenient wheelchair stood just inside the door.

'I'll push you,' Pertová announced with a certain amount of resignation, and wheeled Slonský past the reception desk to a room with a nameplate in a holder fixed to the door. He had no time to read it beyond noticing a lot of letters after the name before she knocked, opened the door and rolled him in.

'This is Captain Slonský,' she announced.

The surgeon looked up and smiled. He looked about eleven years old, thought Slonský. Navrátil was fresh-faced but it must be 50-50 whether this lad's voice had broken.

'Come in, Captain,' he said pleasantly. 'My name is Stockner. Can you lie on the bench there and I'll have a look at this knee that Jana is worried about?'

So that's how it is, thought Slonský. Jana — not Ms Pertová.

'I'll leave you to it,' said Jana. 'See you later.'

The remark was probably addressed to Stockner, but Slonský answered 'Hope so' before heaving himself onto the couch.

'Would you mind removing your trousers?'

'Ah, of course.'

Slonský lay back and stared at the ceiling. It was quite restful, at least until Dr Stockner began probing the knee with his fingers.

'Does this hurt?' he asked.

'Only like hell.'

'And this?'

'Not so bad.'

Stockner closed his eyes and gently squeezed in all directions, running his hands across Slonský's hairy knee like a concert pianist relishing a slow movement.

'Right — let's take a look inside.'

Slonský was about to grab his trousers and hop to the door when he realised that Stockner was reaching for something like one of those scanner guns they use to see what you have bought in a supermarket.

'The gel will be cold,' he warned, before slapping it on Slonský's knee and spreading it around.

After a few moments Stockner began to move his gun across the knee while watching a small and rather boring television picture.

'Aha!' he suddenly exclaimed. 'I'm sure someone mentioned this before, but losing a few kilos would reduce the pressure on these knees.'

'You're right,' Slonský agreed. 'Someone has mentioned it.'

'Nothing too drastic,' Stockner remarked. 'Just the occasional salad instead of a sausage.'

'Salad?'

'You know, green stuff.'

Slonský had eaten a salad not too long before, when he inadvertently picked up the wrong sandwich. In his view, salad was great for rabbits, but if God had wanted us to avoid sausage He wouldn't have invented it. Admittedly Navrátil had questioned some aspects of this theology, and he normally knew about that kind of thing, but it seemed to Slonský that not eating sausage was unpatriotic in a Czech.

Stockner was pointing at the screen. 'There's your problem.'

Slonský could only see a number of patches in various shades of grey. 'What am I looking at?'

'Here. You see that shadow?'

'No.'

'Well, take it from me that it's there. And it shouldn't be. They've repaired your ligament very well, but there's a meniscal tear.'

'I take it from your tone that there shouldn't be one of those?'

'No, there shouldn't. How can I explain this in terms that you'll understand? The ends of your bones have a protective lining of cartilage. When it's torn, it can cause pain. In your case, there's the added problem that the torn part is stopping your kneecap moving freely.'

'Can you do anything about it?'

'Yes. Bit fiddly but very fixable.'

'Will I need another operation? I can't afford a long time off work. I need to be at my desk on the eleventh of November.'

Stockner glanced at his paperwork. 'Your birthday? Worried about missing cake?'

'Worried about being turfed out on my ear.'

Stockner smiled and clapped Slonský on the shoulder. 'Worry no more. No need for a prolonged recovery period. I can sort this through a keyhole.'

'You mean you're going to be out in the corridor?'

'Keyhole surgery. A tiny hole in your knee, perhaps two, and we put a little camera inside.'

Slonský had never seen a camera small enough to go inside a knee. Somehow the image of his grandfather's camera from the 1950's came to his mind.

'Then we slide miniature instruments inside your knee. If I can repair the tear I will. If not, we'll remove the cartilage and any debris, then smooth off the torn edge.'

Slonský remained uneasy about the idea of cameras and instruments inside his knee, but if it could remove his pain, he had no choice. 'When can it be done?'

'I've got to speak to the police's insurers to get them to cover the costs, but that should only take a day or two. Then I'll give you a call and you'll come in the next day. When we're done your knee should be a lot better. Just one thing — we'll do it as early in the day as I can schedule, but you can't have any breakfast because of the anaesthetic.'

There was a slight blip in Slonský's heartbeat. He could not remember the last time he went without breakfast. In fact, many days he had two, one before leaving home and another on arrival at work in case his energy levels had been depleted by taking the bus.

He returned to his desk in a daze and dropped heavily into his seat.

Peiperová had spotted him walking past and came into the office to get her expenses signed off.

'Are you all right, sir?'

'Hm? Oh, I've just been to see a doctor.'

'Sorry, sir. I didn't realise you had an appointment.'

This was a serious matter for Peiperová whose mental diary was stocked with birthdays, anniversaries, appointments and similar data.

'I didn't. I only went to do my exercises but they thought I should see a surgeon at once. One of the women even drove me there.'

Peiperová gulped. She had had no idea. As for Slonský, he stared into space, still shocked by the prohibition on breakfast on some unspecified future date.

'I'm sorry, sir. I shouldn't have bothered you with this.'

'What is it?'

'My expenses. But it can wait.'

Slonský grabbed a pen and signed the form without reading it. 'Best not. I could be gone in a few days.'

'Gone?'

'You know — not here.'

'Oh, sir!' Her hand flew to her mouth. 'It must have been a shock, sir.'

Slonský's mind was still reeling from the news about breakfast. He had not realised that such things were possible. 'I just wasn't expecting it, lass. But if that's how things are, I have to accept it. No point crying about it, is there?'

Peiperová gave an odd hiccupping noise and ran from the room. As for Slonský, he appreciated the fact that she was so moved by his plight.

'Maybe I should have a big dinner the night before?' he mused.

You had to hand it to the receptionist at Power Gloves, thought Jerneková. Somehow, she managed to balance the appearance of assistance with giving no possibly useful information away.

'Has he committed any actual offence?' she asked.

'We don't know,' said Jerneková, 'seeing as we don't know who he is. If we had a name we could type it into our computer and in no time at all I could answer your question.'

'I'd love to help,' the receptionist claimed, 'but unless criminality is involved I don't think I can give you any information about our members.'

'But he is a member, then?'

'I can't confirm or deny that.'

Jerneková hitched up her trousers by yanking her thumbs in the belt loops and jerking her hands upwards. It was a gesture that her colleagues knew meant that she intended to be business-like about getting her own way. When she was at her most belligerent one could expect some trouser-raising, and the more determined she was the more vigorous it would be. On this occasion her waistband moved a full five centimetres, a definite sign that she meant business.

'Let's look at this another way. If I were to go and get a warrant, you would give me the information I need, right?'

'If I had it. Which I'm not saying I have.'

'Understood. But you would respect the warrant?'

'Of course. We are law-abiding citizens here.'

'Good to hear it. And among the things that you definitely would be able to give me is a list of your members.'

'Yes, if the warrant required it.'

'Now we're getting somewhere. And would this list include the addresses of your members?'

'Yes, of course. If they pay their membership fees by bank transfer the banks require it.'

'Excellent. Do you see where this is going?'

'Not really.'

Neither do I, thought Jerneková, but it was vital to keep the upper hand. She did not know if she could get the warrant she was threatening, given that she did not have any real evidence to tie anyone to the Dreamy Clouds club, so why should anyone in authority issue one?

'You'd prefer that I didn't have the addresses, wouldn't you? I mean, only the ones I really need, not everybody's.'

'Of course.'

'So we could make a deal. If I mention a part of town, you can tell me how many members you have there, and then I could ask for just those names on the warrant, which would reduce your embarrassment.'

The receptionist's voice was beginning to falter. She was no longer sure who had the whip hand in this discussion. 'Well…'

'So if, for example, I said Holešovice, you could look at your database and save me a wasted journey and you the embarrassment of giving out more information than we really need.'

'I suppose…'

'Great. So let's try Bubeneč.'

The receptionist was doubtful, but consulted her list. 'There are five,' she said.

'Excellent. That saves a lot of your members any awkwardness.'

Jerneková marched towards the door to the gym.

'Where are you going?' screeched the receptionist.

'To ask if anyone in there is from Bubeneč, then I can exclude them from the warrant if they're not the man I want.'

'You can't do that!'

'Hot pursuit of a criminal. There are lots of things I can do if I'm in pursuit of someone I have reasonable cause to believe has committed an offence.'

'What offence?'

'Sorry,' said Jerneková, shaping her face into what she hoped might be an expression of regret, 'that's confidential. I can't just go telling members of the public.'

'I'll get sacked,' the receptionist wailed.

'That would be grossly unfair. I could ask my Captain to write a note to your boss in your defence if that helps?'

'It won't. I'll already be out on my ear.'

'That would be a shame. Tell you what. If you were to put those five names on your screen and then go and powder your nose you'd have no way of knowing what I'd done. And I'll be gone when you get back. How does that work for you?'

Wordlessly the receptionist tapped at her keyboard, then she grabbed her handbag and threw up the counter-flap to leave Jerneková alone.

Jerneková looked at the list, immediately spotted one name of potential interest, but took a photograph of the screen just in case. True to her word she then made for the door, carefully closing the hatch behind her.

CHAPTER 16

'Are you sure?' Navrátil whispered.

'It's what he said,' Peiperová insisted.

'Goodness!' said Navrátil, who was unskilled at strong language.

'He's being terribly brave, but the doctor said it could be any time. He might not be here next week.'

'That's awful,' Navrátil murmured.

'Do you think we should tell Krob and Lucie?'

'They're as entitled to know as we are, I suppose. But I can't imagine he wants this kind of news talked about, or he'd have told us he was going for an appointment.'

'He didn't know. He thought he was just going for some physio.'

Navrátil shook his head. 'Surely you don't die of anything they give you physio for?'

'I don't think it can be connected. They just found it by chance when he was there.'

Navrátil ran his hands through his hair and grabbed a fistful in each hand. His wife was coming to recognise this as a sign of great mental perturbation. 'If anyone ought to know, it's Valentin and Mucha,' he said. 'They're his oldest friends.'

'Who knows where Valentin will be? But Sergeant Mucha is downstairs now.'

'Can you have a quiet word with him? I'd do it but you know what was said.'

'I'll try. Just watch that the Captain doesn't decide to go down to the desk while I'm there. It could be really awkward.'

Mucha was used to standing all day. With no stool to flop on, he dropped forward and rested his head on his arms. 'That's awful,' he cried. 'Poor Slonský.'

'He's being very brave,' Peiperová assured him.

'It probably hasn't sunk in yet. That kind of news doesn't. And they say he could be gone any day?'

'That's what he said.'

'Maybe we can have a whip round and get him a second opinion somewhere? Or buy him something to make his last few days more comfortable.'

The swing doors opposite opened and Slonský walked into the lobby.

'Where did you come from?' Mucha stammered.

'I used the lift,' Slonský replied.

'You never use the lift. In thirty years I've never known you to use the lift.'

'That's because for twenty of those years we didn't have one and it was out of order for about five. Anyway, given my health issues I can't faff around with stairs.'

There was a clatter from the stairs and Navrátil burst in upon them.

'Captain Slonský is taking the lift…' he began, before drying up when he realised that his warning was too late.

'Why is everyone making a big deal out of my taking the lift? If I'd known it was going to cause such consternation I'd have made my way down by throwing myself out of the window.'

'Don't say that,' Mucha said. 'Just don't. Don't even think about it.'

Slonský looked around him. 'What is wrong with you people? You look like someone just died.' An awful thought occurred to him. 'Nobody has, have they? Major Lukas is still with us?'

'Yes, *he* is,' Mucha replied, then found himself overcome with emotion and turned away.

'Have I forgotten someone's birthday? Peiperová usually keeps me up to speed on those.'

Navrátil felt that, as the senior officer present after Slonský, he should take command, and stepped forward. 'Peiperová told me about your conversation earlier.'

'Oh, that!' Slonský replied. 'I suppose it wouldn't worry many people, but it seemed a big deal to me at the time.'

'It is a big deal, sir,' Peiperová insisted. 'For you and for us.'

'I don't know how we'll manage without you,' Navrátil admitted.

'Well, we always knew one day you'd have to,' Slonský told them. 'I can't go on for ever.'

'Excuse me,' Peiperová squeaked, and ran back upstairs, biting her sleeve as she did so.

Slonský followed her with his eyes, then fixed Navrátil with a meaningful gaze. 'Your wife seems very emotional lately,' he said. 'Is it a hormones thing?'

'She's just shocked,' Navrátil said. 'We all are.'

Mucha nodded. He could not speak, but Slonský could see that his eyes were red.

'They're not planning to let me go?' he whispered. 'Have you heard something?'

Mucha found his voice. 'Josef, you're a dear, dear friend and you know how much I think of you. You can be an aggravating so-and-so at times, but you don't deserve this.'

'They *are* letting me go! The bastards!'

'Not letting you go, as such,' Mucha explained. 'Just accepting the inevitable.'

'There's nothing inevitable about it,' Slonský thundered. 'I'm not going quietly. I'm going to fight this every step of the way!'

'That's the spirit!' declared Mucha, while Navrátil turned away and dabbed his eyes with an immaculate white handkerchief that he produced from his pocket.

Slonský was limping towards the lift again. 'If anyone wants me I'll be in the HR department giving them the arse-kicking of a lifetime,' he roared.

'What's it got to do with them?' Mucha enquired.

'They're not getting rid of me that easily. It'll be that little squirt of a lieutenant again.'

Mucha chased after him and grabbed him. 'Josef! That isn't going to help.'

'It'll make me feel better. Might hurt a bit, what with this knee, but I'm not being sacked just because I need another operation.'

'Another operation?'

'Yes. The specialist said he can fix my knee, but I'll need another operation. And I'll have to be put under, so I can't have breakfast. Would you believe it? All that guff about the wonders of medical progress and they still can't do a little operation and give me breakfast too.'

Mucha tried to compute what he had just heard. 'So — when you went to the gym…'

'Yes?'

'And they said you needed to see a specialist at once…'

'Yes?'

'And someone drove you straight there…'

'Yes — where is this going?'

'They were talking about your knee?'

'Yes. I told Peiperová all this. What did you think I was talking about?'

'Oh, nothing, nothing at all. Just glad your knee is finally going to be sorted out for you.'

'Navrátil, can you close your mouth before someone posts a letter in it?' Slonský demanded.

'I'll … I'll just go and see how Lieutenant Peiperová is doing,' Navrátil muttered, before taking the stairs three at a time.

'I worry about that boy,' Slonský said. 'I mean, we all know they're married, so why call her "Lieutenant Peiperová" all the time?'

Mucha patted him on the shoulder. 'They're just concerned about you. Best if you don't say anything to them about this, unless you want to turn the taps on again.'

'They're that upset about my knee?'

'Well, it's a very important knee,' Mucha lied.

'Fair enough,' Slonský replied. 'Anyway, I'm off to sort out HR.'

'You've got the wrong end of the stick,' said Mucha. 'They're not giving you the push.'

'Then why did you say whatever you said?'

Mucha realised he was going to have to give some sort of explanation. 'When you spoke to Peiperová, she got the impression you'd decided to resign.'

'Because of my knee?'

'Yes. We can all see how it's getting you down. She was just trying to find a way to tell you not to give in. But since they're going to operate, she'll be fine now that she knows something can be done.'

Slonský looked up the stairs as if he could see Peiperová running up them. 'The lass was that upset about my knee? I'm quite touched.'

'Are you getting sentimental in your old age?'

'Certainly not. And less of the "old age", you cheeky devil.'

In his teenage years Krob had been quite a formidable chess player. Not brilliant, perhaps, but very dogged, and known for his imperturbability. The problem was that his team-mates could never tell from his facial expression whether he thought things were going well or badly; he sat patiently looking at the board with an entirely neutral expression before finally making a move.

He no longer played regularly, but he had carried this impassivity into other walks of life, and was now sitting on a log ostensibly watching his son Marek play but actually turning over the question of Chigulin's disappearance in his brain, working out all the possible moves.

He was distracted momentarily by Marek's inability to apply the basic laws of physics to a see-saw, and rose to push down on the other end and lift his son gently from the ground. Taken by surprise, Marek tumbled backwards, and required some comforting before suggesting that ice cream might make the bump go away.

'There is no bump,' he assured his son.

'Not yet,' Marek agreed, 'but I bumped it so there will be a bump some time. Unless I have ice cream.'

Krob laughed and put his son down to walk with him to the little local supermarket. The traffic was not racing past as usual, and it took Krob only a moment to realise why. About eighty metres up the road a dark blue BMW was blocked in by a police car and the unhappy occupant was giving his details to the officers.

An idea sparked in Krob's head, so a few minutes later father and son were sitting on the log again, the latter holding a large ice cream and the former with his mobile phone jammed to his ear.

He was in luck. Berger was on duty. The two of them had worked together for a while when Krob was still with the City police. After a few pleasantries, Krob got to the point. 'I'm working on a case and a witness has disappeared. But he said he drove to the site of the crime, so he has a car, and I wondered if you'd ever picked him up.'

'I'll look him up. Name?'

'Chigulin, Yurii.'

'Stand by.'

The police computer did its thing laboriously. Some time ago the National Director of Police had commissioned a report on how the system could be modernised which had concluded that the architecture of the files was so weird that there was no easy way to transfer them to a new system. One of Technician First Class Spehar's team could have put them right on that, because he had worked out a way to download all the files and convert them to a standard format, but then he was not hoping to be awarded a lucrative contract for doing so.

Eventually the system disgorged its conclusion. 'Yes, we booked him for running a red signal about eight months ago.'

'Have you got the registration of his car?'

'Sure. Got a pen?'

Berger duly recited the registration mark.

'I don't suppose there's any way you could ask units to keep an eye out for it. No need to approach, just advise any sighting to me?'

'I don't see why not. For an old mate, eh?'

Jerneková had been drilled well. Despite her keenness to find Zechovská's boyfriend she knew that she must not go unaccompanied and therefore returned to base first to tell Slonský what she had discovered.

'How did you get this list, lass?' Slonský asked.

'I told them I'd get a warrant but if I had to go through all that I'd want everyone's details, or they could just hand over the ones in Bubeneč and save us all some grief.'

'And they did?'

Jerneková shrugged. 'The woman left me with the computer while she went for a whoosh.'

Slonský smiled. He knew his instincts had been right when he persuaded Jerneková to apply to the police. She might not have been the force's best thinker, but she was one of the best doers he knew. Somehow, she found a way; not always by the book, not always legally defensible, but she found a way.

'You'd best go with someone. Where's Krob?'

'Day off, sir.'

'Peiperová?'

'Muttered something about organising some flowers for someone.'

'And Navrátil?'

'Chased after Peiperová to tell her not to buy the flowers. Whatever it was must have been sorted.'

'So it's just thee and me, then?'

'Yes, sir.'

'And I can't drive because of my knee.'

'I'm taking lessons, sir.'

'How are you getting on?'

'Very well, sir. But I don't get any practice driving in the streets. I could do with some of that.'

Slonský reached for his coat. 'No time like the present. Let's get a pool car. It'll have to be in my name but you can drive once we're out of the compound.'

Once, Slonský had tricked old Dlouhý, the warden of the

carpool, into giving him a much better car than he had signed for. Not long after, Dlouhý had been pensioned off because his ability to read registration numbers and odometer readings was impaired, and the pool was now in the hands of one Sergeant Voyta, a man whose frame gave the impression that his little booth in the car park had been made to measure for him, since his shoulders seemed to touch both sides. Whatever the weather Voyta would be wearing a coat, his justification being that, in Prague, if it was not raining it must be about to rain.

'A car, sir?' he parroted.

'Yes. You know, one of those things with wheels that we're surrounded by here.'

'These are all spoken for, sir. I'll see what I can find.'

'Something with a bit of legroom would be good. If it has pastries in the glove compartment, even better.'

Voyta marched eight paces forward, executed a right turn that would not have been out of place on a parade ground, and stood surveying the options. 'Just the two of you, sir?'

'Yes.'

'Not planning to arrest anyone?'

'No.'

'Good. Some of these don't have proper locks on the back doors, you see. Terrible oversight, if you ask me. If I was in charge of purchasing…'

There followed around three minutes' discussion of Voyta's purchasing plan for the Police Service of the Czech Republic while Voyta ambled through the compound.

'If he doesn't get a shift on I'll be going through the change before we're out of here,' Jerneková hissed.

'Let the nice man vent,' Slonský advised, 'and it will all be worthwhile in the end.'

Voyta strode towards them with a set of keys in his extended arm. 'Will that saloon do, sir? Sorry about the bird crap on the roof.'

Slonský beamed and accepted the keys, showed his identification, signed the sheet and promised to return the car later that day or, at worst, the next morning, hobbled to the vehicle, climbed in and drove slowly out of the compound, into the road, and around the first corner on the right, where he pulled over.

'Right, shift over. If I can get over the handbrake and gear lever I'll sit there. You can walk round.'

In the event, Slonský could not manoeuvre himself into position.

'Are you having trouble getting your leg over?' Jerneková asked.

'I decline to answer that question,' Slonský replied. 'But I can't get it out from under the steering wheel. I'll have to get out of the door and go round.'

They took up their new positions.

'You don't think driving so slowly would make Voyta suspicious?' asked Jerneková.

'You're damn lucky I could drive it at all. Stop whining. You wanted to drive, so drive.'

Slonský had never been a religious man — he left that kind of thing to Navrátil — but after a few minutes he was ready to repent the sins of his past life and wished that he still had that St Christopher medallion his great-aunt had given him when he went off to Pioneer Camp back in his youth.

'It's just a thought, Jerneková, but the conventional thing is to signal before you take the corner, not afterwards.'

'I'd have to take my hand off the wheel though, sir, and neither of us wants that.'

'Can't you flick it with your little finger?'

'My little finger is too little.'

'I didn't notice any reluctance to take your hand off the wheel when you made that gesture to the taxi driver.'

'They think they own the road, sir.'

'Maybe,' Slonský conceded, 'but does the expression "right of way" mean anything to you?'

'Sort of. Which way now, sir?'

'Turn right here. No, the next road, Jerneková, not the Metro entrance.'

They careered through the streets. To Slonský's surprise they did not hit anything or anyone, though it was only as they drew to a halt in Bubeneč that he realised that the siren he had been able to hear for the last few minutes was coming from their car.

'How do you turn it off?' he asked.

'I don't know,' Jerneková replied. 'I didn't know I'd turned it on. Was it when I worked the windscreen washer?'

Slonský found a button that was in and clicked it out. The wailing stopped. 'It's that one next to the hazard lights button.'

'Ah, that's good to know.'

'Well, we won't be using it on the way back, will we, Jerneková?'

'No, I meant it's good to know that's the hazard lights. I wondered what that triangle sign was about.'

With a blissful disregard for her half hour of havoc Jerneková hitched up her trousers, zipped up her jacket and strode purposefully along the road, leaving Slonský to yell after her to slow down and have some consideration for a man with a dodgy knee.

Jerneková produced her list of addresses. 'I reckon these must be right because the banks use these addresses, so they wouldn't pay the subs for the men if they weren't accurate.'

'Good thinking. Which one is nearest?'

'A man called Ladra. Flat 5a.'

They discovered that they were standing outside number 9, so it was no great effort to find number 5, but it was only when Slonský explained that 5a might be accessed from the rear that Jerneková stopped scratching her head.

There was a staircase at the rear that led up to a white door. Slonský limped heavily up the stairs and knocked on the door, which was opened by a young woman with her hair tied up and a baby tucked under her armpit.

'We've got a bell,' she grumbled.

'We didn't want to wake the baby,' Slonský replied. 'Is Mr Ladra at home?'

'No, he's at work, isn't he?'

'And where might that be?'

Suddenly suspicious, the woman narrowed her eyes. 'Who wants to know?'

'We do,' said Slonský. 'By which I mean the Police Service of the Czech Republic, criminal department.'

The two police officers displayed their credentials.

'How do I know they're genuine?'

'Why would police officers have fake IDs?'

'You might be fake police officers.'

'Then we wouldn't have genuine IDs like these, would we?'

Despite Jerneková's unspoken reservations, this seemed to satisfy the woman, who recited the address of a metalworking factory where Ladra worked one of the metal presses. 'Has he done something wrong?' she asked, suddenly concerned.

'I don't know. Has he?'

'Well, why are you here?'

'To exclude him from our enquiries,' Slonský began.

Jerneková decided this spartan explanation needed some corroborating detail. 'Incident at the boxing club,' she said.

'Again? Honestly, men! They go somewhere to let off steam and finish up hitting each other anyway.'

The baby began to complain, possibly a response to having been held head downwards for a few minutes, so Slonský apologised for the disturbance and began the descent to ground level.

'Cross that one off, then,' he said.

'Why? Just because he's got a wife and kid doesn't mean he hasn't got a bit on the side.'

'I doubt he makes enough at the factory to keep two women in the manner to which they'd like to become accustomed, lass. And from the way you described her, I doubt Zechovská is chasing after a bit of rough.'

Jerneková nodded. 'I suppose not,' she said. 'Right then — on to number two.'

CHAPTER 17

Give Krob his due, when Slonský told him the nature of the enquiry he did not bat an eyelid, neither did he attempt to claim that the disappearance of Ms Linhartová's panties was not a matter for the criminal police, but merely wrote down all the details in his notebook, returned to his desk and thought for a while about how to tackle this one.

If this was to be his first solo investigation he needed to do it right, he thought. The motto of the police, "To Help and to Protect", surely applied to the underwear of Czech citizens too; or, indeed, he thought, foreign citizens temporarily visiting the Czech Republic. What would it do for the tourist trade if foreigners believed that their underwear might disappear during a trip to Prague? Although, he reminisced, during his time as a city policeman trying to control hen parties it seemed some western women chose to manage that risk by leaving their underwear at home.

He had the address of the laundry service, so he decided to start there. Not yet ready to trust his shoulder to allow him to drive safely, he hopped on a bus and twenty minutes later was standing outside a dull grey building in a dull grey part of town. There was no sign that this was actually a laundry, and every sign that it was an accommodation address. The ground floor belonged to a recruitment agency, but the floor above was occupied by a lawyer, so that seemed the best place to start.

Krob climbed the stairs and knocked gently on the open door. It was a warm day so all the doors and windows were open, which allowed Krob to see at a glance that there was the front office, a small kitchenette or staff room behind, and what was presumably the tiniest toilet in Prague at the back of that. The front office contained two desks and a chair for a visitor, and a row of filing cabinets, and one of the desks was unoccupied. Behind the other sat a woman who was printing off what appeared to be invoices for rent due.

'Can I help you?' she asked.

'I hope so,' Krob replied, and produced the business card Petra Linhartová had given them. 'I'm trying to find this business but I can see that they don't operate from this address.'

'No,' agreed the secretary. 'We do all sorts of things here but we don't take in laundry!'

Krob glanced at the nameplate on the other desk. 'Presumably Magister Moulis helps people to register businesses?'

'Yes. This is probably one of those. They keep this address so that legal papers can be delivered here and he can see that they are dealt with. At some stage the businesses grow to the point where they don't need us any more, or they fold.'

'I see. I don't suppose you have any other way of contacting them?'

'I'm afraid I can't give out that information, sir.'

Krob flashed his police identification.

'I see,' she gulped. 'Even so, Magister Moulis is most insistent that we maintain strict client confidentiality.'

'I completely understand,' Krob replied. 'But I'm not asking you to give me the address, just to confirm that you have one. Then I can get a warrant in the normal way and my colleagues and I can bring it here. Obviously, we'll try to keep disruption to a minimum as we go through the files looking for any other businesses the same individuals may have an interest in but it is a little compact in here, so we may have to take the files away for a short while.'

'That may not be necessary,' the secretary said. 'The address on the card is ours, but the telephone number isn't. You ring that number and they come and collect your laundry and then return it the next day.'

Krob smiled disarmingly. 'It sounds as if you've used the service.'

'I did, once or twice. But I don't now.'

'Oh?'

'Well, they were a bit careless. I noticed my parcel was missing one or two bits when it came back. I phoned them, but they couldn't find them. And it's not so cheap when you're having to buy new underwear each time, is it?'

After a little more chatting to the secretary, and a telephone call to Ms Linhartová, Krob had matching descriptions of the two young men who came to collect and deliver the laundry, and he had traced an address that corresponded to the telephone number that was used. Arriving at the building, he could see that it looked much more residential than commercial. Presumably the laundry was being run on a very small scale.

However, there was a black van parked outside. There was no signwriting on it but a clean patch on the door suggested that a magnetic sign may have been there recently. On a cursory inspection through the window Krob could see no definite proof of its use but there were plastic baskets in the rear compartment such as might have been used for laundry.

There was a controlled entry system on the door to the flats, so Krob either had to invent a reason for needing to enter or he had to wait for someone to come out. Being the man he was he found a convenient ground level windowsill and sat down to wait and watch.

Me and my big mouth, thought Slonský.

In a moment of unthinking weakness he had told Jerneková to put her foot down as they headed to the second address on her list. He had said it many times to Peiperová and Navrátil without much in the way of obvious effect, but Jerneková took him at his word. There was an entertaining moment as she debated which side of a traffic island they should pass, and the armrest on the passenger door might have needed some tightening after she took a right turn in fifth gear, but she had finally interpreted his cry of 'Jesus Maria!' as an instruction to reduce her speed and they were coming into the street they wanted anyway, so they came to a halt with Jerneková smiling ecstatically and Slonský expressing silent thanks that his bladder sphincter was in good working order.

'We may need to have a little tutorial on appropriate speeds,' he said, once he had regained control of his teeth.

'I know,' Jerneková replied. 'I overcooked that turn, didn't I? I should have changed down earlier.'

'I wouldn't say that,' Slonský said. 'Changing down at any time would have been a good idea.'

'I'll bear that in mind,' Jerneková said chirpily, opening the door and bounding out with all the exuberance of someone undergoing an adrenaline rush.

Slonský stayed put.

'Not coming out, sir?' she asked.

'Bit difficult,' he answered, 'seeing as you've parked next to this tree and I can't open the door.'

Jerneková made to climb back in. 'I'll reverse it,' she announced.

'Dear God, no!' yelped Slonský, in the grip of an extreme passion and desperate to live a little longer. 'I mean, that won't be necessary. You can go and handle this one yourself and just report back.'

Jerneková zipped her blouson jacket and trudged across the street and up a flight of steps to the front door of a house. There was a panel of buttons with names alongside at the side of the doorway, and she could be seen checking the names against her list before pressing the button third from the top. The door opened, she marched inside, and Slonský sat back and pondered whether there was a decent bakery anywhere nearby since the excitement of the drive appeared to have depleted his energy stocks.

Jerneková was gone for about ten minutes, but finally the door opened and she descended the stairs and walked back to the car.

'He's not our man,' she announced.

'No? How so?'

'Two reasons. First off, he's no oil painting. Zechovská can do a lot better than that little squirt. But mainly because he has a home gym festooned with pin-up pictures out of magazines, and when a guy does that it's usually because they've never had a real girlfriend.'

'You weren't taken with him, then?' Slonský asked.

'I know I don't have a boyfriend, sir, but frankly if he was the last male left in the world I'd still give him a miss.'

'Right. Cross him off the list.'

'Off to number three, sir?'

'In due course, Jerneková. Let's find somewhere for a coffee first.'

Krob waited until the lads had finished loading the van before he strolled forward and produced his police identification. 'I think you may know why I'm here,' he said.

'No idea at all,' said the taller one with a sideways warning glance to his colleague.

'Good. I like surprises,' Krob replied. 'We can do this here in full view or you can invite me inside and we can talk in privacy. Your call.'

The taller one licked his lips as if sizing up how much Krob already knew.

'Let's go inside,' he said at length.

'You first. And don't try slamming the door on me or I'll have a squad here in minutes and they won't be as polite as me.'

They led him up a flight of stairs and opened the door of a flat. There were baskets of laundry all round the kitchen with labels taped to the handles.

'We're just trying to earn an honest living,' the smaller one blurted out.

'I'm glad to hear that. The snag is that it doesn't seem that your customers think the same thing.'

'You won't find any complaints about our work,' argued the taller one. 'We're meticulous about our washing and ironing. That's why we've got all these customers.'

Krob walked slowly round the room reading the labels. 'You know, the interesting little nugget that nags at me is that a surprising number of these baskets have the names of single women on them. There are a couple of "Mr & Mrs" labels, but that's all. You seem to specialise in doing the laundry of women on their own.'

The taller one shrugged. 'Married women mainly do their own laundry. We specialise in professional women who don't have time for that.'

'Shame you don't specialise in professional women who don't like wearing underwear.'

Small shot a haunted look to tall.

Krob lifted a basket on the kitchen worktop. 'You see, this basket doesn't have a name on it.'

'It must have fallen off,' said the tall one.

'That's a pity,' said Krob. 'You'll have a disappointed customer if you can't return this lot. It shouldn't be hard to trace who this is from your records, though, since she appears to wear only knickers and seems to need three different sizes.'

'Probably a woman and her daughters.'

'Maybe,' said Krob. 'I can't help noticing none of these have been washed, by the way. Oh, and here's a bit of luck! This pair have a name label in them. It should be quite easy for us to call this woman in and she can tell us which are hers and which are her daughters'. But for the time being I'll impound these as stolen goods and if anyone wants them you can refer them to us.'

'You can't do that!' protested the small one.

'I've just done it. And the two of you can report to police headquarters tomorrow to answer some further questions. The address is on this card. Now, if you'll just show me your citizens' ID cards I can make a note of your details and ensure you don't do anything daft like trying to leave the country.'

It was only as he left that it occurred to Krob that he had better ask for a car to pick him up, since he could hardly take a plastic basket full of women's panties on public transport, so he called Mucha and asked him to arrange it.

Navrátil answered Krob's phone extension when it rang and immediately realised the importance of the information he had been given. Since there was nobody else in the office to share it with he went next door to see if Peiperová was at her desk.

'They've found Chigulin's car,' he announced.

'Where?'

'In Teplice.'

'Do they know when it got there?'

'They're checking for any video footage but he paid for six hours' parking early on Sunday.'

'So less than a day after he found Teslenko's body?'

'Not to split hairs, but I actually found the body.'

'So is he running because he's guilty or because he's scared?'

'That's the key question, of course. But at least it tells us he's alive.'

'No, it doesn't. It tells us somebody drove his car to Teplice. It doesn't prove that was Chigulin. We need the video for that, and someone who knows what he looks like.'

'Why Teplice, do you think?'

'Isn't that the quickest route out of the country from Prague? Pretty well due north, and then he can get a bus or train to Dresden.'

Navrátil gripped his hair again. 'I'd better ask the German police if they have any way of tracing him. I'm just not getting anywhere with this enquiry.'

'I know. You're tense. But you'll get there.'

He stroked her cheek tenderly. 'Thanks.'

'You're welcome. Now, back to work.'

'Of course,' he replied, reddening slightly at the thought that she might have anticipated anything improper happening during working hours.

Slonský felt refreshed. There was nothing like a good cinnamon bun to restore the inner man, so now he felt restored three times over. Jerneková had ordered a thing called a smoothie which, so far as could see, involved mashing up some green stuff with some berries and was to be avoided at all costs. Jerneková assured him that drinking those things would make him live longer; he could certainly see how time would drag if that was all the pleasure you had in life.

'Right, lass, who's next on the list?'

Jerneková consulted her sheet, dog-eared as it was becoming, and pointed down the road. 'About two hundred metres that way. Shall we walk?'

'No, Jerneková, we'll take the car. Or you can walk and I'll get a taxi.'

They resumed their seats in the car and Jerneková carefully consulted the rear-view mirror before pulling out without a signal and earning a loud honk from the car behind them.

'I'm not a qualified driving instructor,' said Slonský, 'but this experience is giving me much greater respect for those who are.'

'Sorry. Didn't see him there. Anyway, he was a good fifty metres back.'

'How do you know if you didn't see him?'

'I didn't see him before I pulled out. Once I was out I could see him clearly. This is the place.'

There was a clunk as the wheels mounted the kerb and the car came to a halt just before it met a lime tree.

'Never park under a lime tree,' Slonský advised.

'Why? Is it unlucky?'

'No, but you get sticky stuff all over the car and it's a so-and-so to get off.'

Jerneková turned this over in her mind before zipping her jacket again and leaving the car where it was. 'It's not our car,' she said. 'Somebody else's problem.'

Slonský levered himself out of the passenger seat and hobbled behind her as they followed the path to the door of a smart villa. The front garden had been largely ripped up to accommodate a much larger drive, suggesting a number of cars ordinarily parked there, but there were none that day.

Jerneková was about to hammer on the door when Slonský stopped her.

'Just a minute. I've got a bad feeling about this. Let's go round the back first.'

The two detectives walked slowly round the side of the house. There was nobody around, so they looked in the windows for any signs of life.

'What now?' asked Jerneková. 'Do we kick the door in?'

'It's tempting, but let's do things legally. I might be wrong, of course. It happened once in 1998.'

Jerneková drew closer to him. 'What am I missing? What gives you the heebie-jeebies about this?'

'A bulging mailbox. No cars in a drive built for several and, to judge by the marks on the concrete, used by several. But there's an open carton of milk in the kitchen. They've done a runner in a hurry, I reckon.'

'Why would they do that? If he's Zechovská's partner, why would someone attacking her in the park freak him out?'

Slonský wiggled his tongue around to extricate a sliver of bun that had lodged between his teeth. 'Because he knows why she was attacked. And he doesn't think it was the usual pervy thing. What was his name again?'

'Stanislav Polášek.'

'Let's get some details on him. Bank records, credit card usage, phones, vehicles, recent movements.'

'I'll go back and get right on it.'

'No, ring in and ask one of the others to start it rolling. You and I have three more important things to do.'

'Which are?'

'Visiting the last two on your list. And then it will be time for lunch. You can't detect on an empty stomach.'

CHAPTER 18

Jerneková paused in her consumption of a mid-afternoon pickle to ask Krob the question that had been nagging at her for an hour or more. 'Why have you brought your wife's washing to work?'

'It's not mine. It's evidence. I have to catalogue it, for which I have to describe it, for which I could do with some help if you've got a minute.'

'How do you mean, describe it? They're pants, end of.'

'Yes, but I have to count them and describe their colour, size and any ownership markings.'

'Doesn't the police have a Ladies' Underwear Identification Team?'

'I wish.'

'Surprises me. They seem to have all kinds of other useless squads. Well, let's give it a go.' She fished in the basket. 'Pants, cotton, white, small. No owner. Pants, cotton, dark blue, stupid little bow on the front, manky gusset. Hang on, none of these have been washed.'

'That's the point, isn't it?'

'How do you mean?'

'These two set up a laundry company. They made some money out of doing other people's washing. But they made much more money by stealing worn women's knickers and selling them online.'

'Filthy bastards.'

'The business only exists to give them access to women's underwear.'

Jerneková chewed her lip in thought. 'How much did they make?'

Krob pushed the underwear aside to reveal a printed spreadsheet. 'I'm guessing, because I'm questioning them tomorrow, but I think these regular Friday deposits are the legitimate takings, and these online ones are from the sale of clothing.'

Jerneková ran her finger down the list but stopped at one entry. 'People paid that much?'

'I imagine that's for a few pairs.'

'Look at these!' Jerneková remarked, raising a filmy pink shred of cloth to eye level. 'If I tried wearing these I'd do myself a mischief. To my mind, bras and knickers are there to keep everything that should be in well and truly in. With this thing half my whatsit would be on view.'

Krob was trying, unsuccessfully, to concentrate on his list, but was saved by Peiperová entering the room.

'Ah, there you are, Lucie! Your file has come up from records.'

'It's all lies. I was stitched up.'

'I mean the file you asked for.'

'Oh. Thanks. I was joking about my own file, by the way,' she said uncertainly, as if trying to convince herself.

'I'm sure you were,' replied Peiperová, who had actually seen Jerneková's file and was satisfied there was nothing in it dating from her adult life, though the early teenage years had been a bit exciting.

Jerneková flicked through the pages. 'We've got a wrong 'un here,' she pronounced. 'A bunch of aliases, a bit of time served for actual bodily harm, and — wouldn't you know it? — Polášek isn't his real name. It turns out he's an asylum seeker from Belarus.'

'If he's got a criminal record why hasn't he been deported?' asked Krob.

'Because he was deprived of his Belarusian passport for "anti-state activities",' Peiperová replied. 'He can't go back there.'

'Real name is Denis Polstrelov,' said Jerneková. 'No cars registered to him so presumably he leases one or has the use of someone else's. No mobile phones registered in his name, so he has the use of someone else's. Bank account last used on Monday.' She whistled. 'Well, look at that! He took money out at a cash machine in Teplice.'

Slonský thought the best way to stay up to date on the inquiries his team members were processing was to have regular team meetings, so he called one for half-past four that afternoon.

'Right,' he said to the waiter, 'that's a beer for me, a cranberry spritzer for the blonde one, a hot chocolate with a shedload of marshmallows for her, a small beer for Krob and a sparkling water for Navrátil. It's all right, if he gets loud we'll take him outside.'

They were at the café on the corner which Slonský had previously disparaged on the grounds that he didn't like many of the customers. Judging by the number of police uniforms on view, Jerneková could see why.

'Now, we're in a public place so pay due regard to confidentiality. There's folk in here with big ears and no morals. Oh, look, there's Major Klinger in the corner.'

All eyes were turned to look at the head of the Fraud Squad, who was rarely seen in there because public places were full of germs, but he was in conversation with another man whom Slonský knew vaguely.

'Isn't that typical? My informants are sleazy characters in torn overcoats. When you're in the Fraud Squad they're deputy directors of the National Bank. Sleazy characters in sharp suits.'

'Sir,' Peiperová hissed, 'you're being a little louder than you realise.'

'I know how loud I'm being. Anyway, here are our drinks. Got any cash, Navrátil? I seem to have left my wallet in my coat.'

'You didn't wear a coat today, sir,' Jerneková helpfully reminded him.

'Didn't I? Well, it must be in my desk then. I'll pay you back when we're in the office.'

Navrátil produced a banknote from his pocket.

'Now, first things first,' said Slonský, and took a large slurp of his beer. There was a period of silence as he rolled it around the inside surfaces of his mouth and swallowed. 'God, that's better! I can feel the little grey cells pinging back into life. Who's going to start?'

'I think Officer Krob should,' Jerneková suggested, 'because if people are going to eavesdrop, this is the one they'll want to listen in on.'

'Really? You intrigue me. Speak on, Krob.'

Krob composed himself before speaking. 'This is to do with the woman you saw who complained her washing was going missing,' he began.

'Specifically, her drawers,' Jerneková glossed.

'Oh, I remember her. Good-looking woman in her forties. Linka-something-or-other.'

'Ms Linhartová. The address the laundry uses is an accommodation address, a lawyer's office. The secretary there wouldn't give me any other address, but she volunteered the information that she was also a disappointed customer and that the phone number on their business card was theirs and not the lawyer's office.'

'Well, it would have to be, wouldn't it?' said Slonský. 'You wouldn't want to go to get your will done and find the lawyer surrounded by other people's washing.'

'Indeed,' agreed Krob. 'I did a trace on the number and found their place. It's not a commercial laundry. They're doing the washing in an ordinary washing machine in a flat. But I noticed one basket didn't have a customer's name attached and appeared to be full of unwashed items.'

'Specifically, women's knickers,' Jerneková explained.

'Yes, we get the picture, thank you,' Slonský replied. 'Continue, Krob.'

'The underwear was in a range of sizes and some had an owner's name inside. I formed the opinion that these had been abstracted from the other baskets for a criminal purpose and…'

'What possible criminal purpose can require ladies' pants?' Slonský mused aloud. 'Bank robbers usually cover their faces with stockings, and I don't think a pair of knickers would work for them. Oh, sorry. Keep going.'

'I think they're selling the pants online. The Vice Squad found that telephone number on a small ad in some magazine they have, offering items for sale.'

'I hope they're not thinking of taking over the case?' Slonský interrupted.

'I think they've got bigger things occupying their time, sir,' Krob answered.

'Thank goodness for that. We've got to keep our crimes solved percentage up. Excellent work, Krob.'

'They're coming in tomorrow with their lawyer. I'll charge them and hand it over to the public prosecutor.'

'We'll probably find he's one of their best customers,' Slonský sniffed. 'But we've done our job. Keep Linhartová informed, would you?' Slonský picked up his glass and looked disappointed. 'This glass must have a leak. I'll have another of those, waiter, but in a different glass, please. Anybody else need a top-up?'

Heads were shaken all around.

'Just the one then, thanks. Navrátil, would you mind?'

'Shall I run a tab, sir?' the waiter asked.

'It may be best,' conceded Slonský. 'We'll be here a while yet. Police work is thirsty business. Who's going next? Ladies first?'

Peiperová gestured to Jerneková to take the lead.

'We've got a woman jogging in the park who gets attacked. The attack was frustrated by a little yappy bitch. That's a dog, by the way, not a passer-by. So we take details and discover she's given us a false address like she doesn't really want us investigating, despite the fact that she was clearly rattled at the time. Anyway, we can't find Paulina Zechovská since. But we got a lead on a potential boyfriend, a man called Denis Polstrelov, no known employment but a nice house out at Bubeneč, presumably paid for by the same kind person who lends him a car and mobile phone. Polstrelov seems to have done a runner. He was last heard of in Teplice, which is interesting for reasons Lieutenant Navrátil will no doubt explain.'

Navrátil picked up his cue. 'It's also where we last have Yurii Chigulin using his bank card.'

'Or someone else using the bank card,' Slonský pointed out.

'I'll ask if the bank has CCTV on the machines,' Navrátil said, scribbling a note to himself in his notebook.

'Do we know what Polstrelov looks like?' asked Slonský.

'No, but given that Polstrelov has a criminal record there'll be a photo somewhere on file.'

'Get Mucha onto it,' Slonský advised. 'If there's a file with Polstrelov's name on it he'll track it down.'

It was true that Mucha seemed to be able to find files even if they were not correctly indexed. This was not the result of magical powers, whatever Slonský thought, but the inevitable consequence of spending far too many hours over the years filing the wretched folders in the first place. Even though the money available for indexing the back records had run out, Mucha was able to remember where things were likely to be and how they were filed.

'I have to admit,' said Navrátil, 'that I'm disappointed with our progress. There's not much in the way of forensics and a major witness has run off before we could speak to him.'

'The fact that Chigulin has ditched his car and phone suggests that he doesn't want anyone to find him,' Slonský responded, 'so don't feel too bad about not having done so.'

Krob asked a pertinent question. 'What is Darmant up to? We know he came to town and we know he wants to know what happened to his daughter. Shouldn't we be following him in case he's found something we don't know?'

'There are lots of things we don't know,' counselled Slonský. 'Things like why prawns change colour when you cook them and what Slavia's chances of winning the hockey league are. If Darmant finds something he'll move, and we'll know.'

'How?' asked Navrátil.

'When did you last see Hauzer?' said Slonský.

'But you told me Hauzer wasn't going to be following Darmant.'

'No, I told you he wasn't going to follow Yeremenko. He couldn't, because he was already following Darmant.'

'Couldn't that be dangerous?'

'I don't think so,' Slonský replied. 'Darmant will expect to be followed. He always is. And he won't want trouble from the local authorities. I expect he'll keep his hands clean as long as he can.'

With the meeting finished, Slonský decided to track Valentin down in his regular drinking hole. It took a moment or two for Slonský's eyes to adjust to the gloom, but eventually he was able to pick out a miserable figure wrapped in an overcoat sitting in one of the booths with a half-drunk beer in front of him. 'Drink up and I'll get you another,' he said.

Valentin eyed him balefully. 'Oh, you've finally remembered I exist, I see. Where have you been?'

'Busy. Criminals have been doing criminal things again. I ought to get the Police's communications team to put a notice in the papers asking them to stop.'

'You've come looking for me. You must want something.'

'Just the pleasure of your company.'

A waiter was hovering over them.

'Catheterise the cat again and fill this for my friend, and I'll have the same.'

'Thanks. I'm not sure I want to drink it given that image.'

'When did you last turn down a free drink?'

Valentin dredged his memory. 'There was that time in 1959.'

'When your granny caught us with the vodka in the tree house? Happy days. I wish I was eleven again.'

Valentin shook his head. 'No, I wouldn't want to go through all that again. I'll just grow old gracefully.'

'What is bringing on this morbid line of thought?'

'Have you forgotten? It's my birthday in a fortnight.'

'Of course I haven't forgotten,' said Slonský, who had completely forgotten and was now trying to remember whether it was on the 4th or 5th. 'But it's not a landmark one, is it?'

'You should know. You're the same age.'

'Yes. Right. How old am I again?'

'You'll be sixty-one in November.'

'Ssh! I'm trying to persuade the HR department that I'm fifty-nine.'

'Give it up. You've failed once.'

'Ah, yes, but for quite a while I succeeded.'

'That's like saying you were completely unscathed for nearly the whole war, until you got shot in 1945.'

'Yes, but still true, isn't it? I'll just have to think of some other wheeze, that's all.'

'If you can pass yourself off as Peiperová you'll be good for another thirty-odd years.'

'I don't think I want to go that far.'

'How's the belt?' asked Valentin.

'Fine. No risk of involuntary indecent exposure at all.'

'Good. That's a hundred and fifty crowns you owe me.'

'A hundred and fifty? Is it a family heirloom?'

'No, it's an emergency purchase from the nearest store that sold belts.'

'I'll have to square up with you later. That reminds me. I owe Navrátil for a round of drinks.'

'He doesn't learn, does he? He'll never see that again.'

'I'll pay him first thing in the morning. Hang on, no, I won't, because he and Peiperová are off to Teplice.'

'I thought he worked with Krob.'

'He does, but Krob is interviewing a pair of women's underwear thieves.'

'Shouldn't a woman do that?'

'It might have been better,' Slonský conceded, 'but it was his case. When it came in Peiperová was busy and Jerneková was … well, being Jerneková. I couldn't risk letting her loose on a discreet enquiry.'

Valentin shuddered. It didn't bear thinking about. 'Anyway, why are the lovebirds off to Teplice?'

'I can't discuss confidential details of an active enquiry! I'm shocked you should think I might.' Slonský took a pull of his beer. 'They're going to look at security cameras to see if they can find two men we're after who were last seen there. Or not, because they might be the same person. Or possibly neither of them,' he added.

'You speak in riddles. I assume you're not suggesting that Navrátil and Peiperová are the same person, so the "they" is presumably the two villains.'

'Correct.'

'One person with two identities?'

Slonský eyed his friend suspiciously. 'Why aren't you a detective?' he asked.

'Too many brains.'

They drank in silence for a few moments.

'Anything I can do to help?' asked Valentin.

'Well, it's funny you should mention that,' said Slonský, 'because there might be…'

CHAPTER 19

Krob was reading the morning paper when Slonský arrived.

'You're in bright and early, lad.'

'Same time as always, sir. Have you seen this?' He pointed to a small box on the front page which Slonský read aloud.

'The Prague police are keen to trace Stanislav Polášek, believed to be travelling in the Teplice area, for whom they have some important news.' He handed the paper back.

'Did you get that put in, sir?'

'I did. Valentin must have worked quickly.'

'But surely Polstrelov or Polášek isn't stupid enough to give us a call?'

'It's highly unlikely, I grant you, unless he's cocky enough to tease us that we can't trace him. But his friends may be stupid enough to tell him.'

'But we don't have any idea of his phone number.'

There was an awkward pause.

'Well done, lad. I was wondering who would be the first to notice that.'

Later that morning, Dr Novák delivered his post-mortem report on Kateryna Teslenko in person. 'No sign of sexual interference so far as I'm able to tell, but given the mutilations I'm not sure I can guarantee that,' he said.

'Any clues as to the perpetrator?' Slonský asked.

'No, but a slightly odd finding. There are two different blood types in that room.'

'The murderer cut himself?'

'Possibly. But the second blood type is confined to a small area by a radiator. Plainly any conjecture on my part is exactly that — guesswork. But it would be consistent with a second person being tied to the radiator and trying to free themselves.'

'There was an unwilling observer?'

'Certainly looks that way.'

Slonský was intrigued. 'But that surely can't be Yeremenko. He wasn't in the district and even if he had been I can't imagine that he wouldn't have told us what he'd seen.'

'The desire for personal revenge is very strong in some people.'

'You mean he'd want to sort it out for himself? Maybe. And he could soon round up some mates to help him. It would help if I knew what Chigulin was up to.'

'Who is Chigulin?'

'Friend of Yeremenko. Allegedly told Yeremenko what had happened, then dumped his phone and car and disappeared.'

'Probably terrified.'

'And with good cause. These gangs don't play by any rules. I'd be much happier if we could get shot of them all. And the name Darmant keeps coming up, but we don't know how far he is involved. He's too clever to get his hands dirty. He might be pulling the strings. And he has deep pockets and plenty of contacts. If Yeremenko is plotting revenge for his girlfriend's killing he could probably go to Darmant and get anything he needed to make it happen.'

Novák stood. 'You'll see Navrátil gets my report?'

'Yes. It's his case.'

'Where is he?'

'He and Peiperová have gone to Teplice to see if they can discover who dumped the car and used the bank cards. At least now they're married I don't have to worry about them being pulled over in a lay-by somewhere.'

Novák chuckled. 'I don't think that idea would ever have occurred to Navrátil.'

'No, but it might have occurred to Peiperová. And she can be very persuasive.'

Navrátil was frustrated. 'No video of anyone parking the car. I was hoping there might have been.'

'There may be some somewhere,' Peiperová insisted. 'Maybe a traffic camera the car drove past, or a shop they drove past. Don't give up on it.'

'I know you're right, but we don't have time to chase that down now.'

'There's always time to find a criminal. You know that.'

'Let's head for the banks and see if they can give us anything.'

They drove to the first and parked up. The cash machine was not, in fact, inside a bank, but an ATM in the street. To their disappointment there was no immediately useful video footage, but across the street there was a block of offices with a door entry system and a security camera.

'Bingo!' said Navrátil. 'Right time, right place.'

'It's a good view of his back,' said Peiperová. 'Let's see if we can see him when he turns.'

The security guard worked the controls.

'Bother! A truck goes by at just the wrong time,' Navrátil complained.

'I'll copy this off for you,' said the guard. 'But it could be worth asking at the jeweller's up the street. They have cameras in their window, and you know what he's wearing from these pictures.'

The two detectives thanked him, waited for the DVD that he made, and went off in search of the jewellery shop. It was easily identified by the expensive watches in the window and the two very visible cameras directed at the passers-by.

The jeweller, though disappointed that they had not come to buy matching wedding rings, was extremely helpful. He found the relevant recording and set it to play for them before excusing himself to deal with a customer.

Peiperová rolled the mouse along the timeline. 'Okay, so this is the moment when someone is using the ATM. Let's watch from here for fifteen minutes.'

Navrátil bent over her to lend a second pair of eyes. 'Too many men wearing jeans for my liking,' he said.

'Forget that. The tan leather jacket is a better thing to fix on. And we know whoever it is has blond hair thinning on top.'

'Pause it!'

They looked closely at the man in the picture.

'The jacket is the wrong colour,' Peiperová remarked. 'And our man didn't have a plastic bag.'

'He might have picked one up on his way up the street,' Navrátil suggested. 'But I agree about the jacket. This is like looking for a needle in…'

'There!' Peiperová exclaimed. She called up a photograph on her phone of the back of the man at the ATM for comparison. 'Same shoes, same jacket, same coloured hair.'

The person in question was walking quite quickly on the far side of the street and took only a couple of seconds to stride across the image.

'Great,' said Navrátil. 'Let's get copies and then we'll see if Yeremenko can identify this man as Chigulin, or anyone else for that matter.'

'It's Chigulin's card and whoever it is didn't seem to need to check anything written down to know the PIN, so surely the odds are that this is Yurii Chigulin.'

'Probably. But let's dot the i's and cross the t's. Let's look at the other camera just to see if there's a better angle.'

The other camera was directed up the road, away from the ATM, so it was more likely that it would show the ATM user's back, but Navrátil was known to be thorough, so Peiperová did as she was asked.

She found the same time point and began running the video. The man walked across the picture once more, then stopped briefly and turned slightly left.

'Can you zero in on that man outside the café?' Navrátil asked urgently.

The man jumped up as the ATM user approached and it looked like they were going to walk together out of town.

'That's the best I can manage,' Peiperová answered. 'Do you know him?'

'Oh, yes. That's Oleg Yeremenko.'

Krob and Jerneková were leaning against the wall outside the interview room. Not for the first time, Jerneková was wondering where they got that shade of cream paint that only ever seemed to be used on state buildings, not that she would have wanted it in any place of her own. Who knew what Krob was thinking? Impassive as ever, he leaned back and waited for the client conference between the underwear stealers and their lawyer to finish.

'What are you thinking?' enquired Jerneková.

'Me? Nothing. Just waiting.'

'How can you do that? How can you think about … nothing?'

'I'm not thinking about nothing. I'm not thinking at all. I'm resting my brain. Clearing out old junk that clutters it up. Trying to put aside the stuff that nags at you and stops you sleeping.'

Jerneková frowned. 'How do you do that then?'

'Ask yourself whether you can do anything about what is bugging you. If you can, do it. If you can't, let it go.'

'Simple as that?'

'Simple to say. Not always simple to do.'

The door opened and the lawyer appeared.

'Could I have a word before we start?' he asked.

'Of course,' Krob replied. He had shared the evidence they had with the lawyer who could see that a plea of not guilty had as much chance of success as an elephant walking a tightrope. This, he hoped, would inform the client consultation.

'My clients recognise that their activities were not, perhaps, as victimless and trivial as they had previously believed. However, they feel that a custodial sentence would be disproportionate and would want me to press for some alternative sanction.'

Krob had prepared for this. 'The difficulty we have is that a number of women have been deprived of property. If there were some means of restitution available I would find it easier to recommend leniency to the public prosecutor. You will know, of course, that the prosecutor has the final say on this. I cannot bind his hands.'

'I believe you are holding some items as evidence that could potentially be restored.'

'Indeed, though there will be some work in pairing owners with items. Your clients could help with that.'

'I am sure that they would wish to give any assistance they could.'

'Do they still have any of the proceeds of crime?'

'There is some money in their bank account. I have the figure here.' The lawyer brandished a bank statement.

'There is no doubt that there are victims who have not yet come forward out of embarrassment or ignorance,' Krob pointed out. 'I don't yet know how far that sum would go. But if your clients' co-operation extended to sharing the contact details of all their female customers, then we might begin to reduce the gravity of the charges against them.'

The lawyer smiled. 'Will you excuse me while I consult them again?'

When he had gone Jerneková rounded on Krob. 'You're letting those scumbags off?'

'No, they'll still be charged. What do the women want?'

'They want their pants back. And they want those guys to pay for what they've done.'

'We're achieving the first objective. As for the second, to get that the complainants have to stand up in court. Every newspaper is going to run that story. Would you want that?'

'Every woman who has been sexually assaulted has to go through that.'

'I know. I don't like it, but I know it's true. But if that's what it takes to get justice many brave women do that. Would they want to do it just to get underwear back?'

'I suppose not.'

'I'm not belittling this crime, but it would be good to wrap this up so we can help Jan with that awful mess at Černý Most.'

'I can't argue with that. He's struggling and I'm surprised Captain Slonský isn't doing more.'

'He says it's Jan's case and he doesn't want to take it off him.'

'But surely the point is to arrest the killer and it doesn't matter who does that.'

Slonský stirred his coffee, slowly scanning the room. 'Thanks for joining me,' he said. 'I assume those two in the leather jackets by the door are here to keep an eye on us.'

Daniel Kristoň did not turn around, but lowered his voice slightly. 'Think of them as insurance for my client.'

'Of course. Trust is in short supply in his circles.'

Kristoň smiled. 'Almost non-existent, I'd say.'

'I thought it might be useful for us just to compare notes. There may be areas where you could set my mind at rest.'

'My client would always want to support the police.'

Slonský almost choked on his coffee. 'I'm sorry. For a moment there I thought you said Darmant always supported the police.'

'I did,' said Kristoň, and slyly winked.

'We appreciate his assistance,' Slonský replied a little louder to make sure the goons heard it.

'I'll tell him that,' said Kristoň, who was struggling to keep a straight face.

'Do you have any idea what has happened to Yurii Chigulin?'

'Chigulin? No, none at all. Is he missing?'

'He informed Yeremenko of the killing, and therefore, indirectly, your client. Shortly afterwards his phone disappeared into the Vltava and his car turned up in a car park far from Prague.'

'Really? Where?'

'I think I'll keep that to myself if you don't mind.'

'I don't think we know anything about Chigulin's movements, but I'll ask my client.'

'Ms Teslenko's body will be released for burial very soon. As we can't get hold of her mother, Mr Darmant could claim custody of her.'

'Thank you. I'll inform him.'

Slonský drained his cup. 'Now, I've given you some info. What have you got for me? Who did it?'

'I really don't know. Clearly, my client has some business enemies, but this is an extreme step. I've tried to find out whether Yeremenko has upset anyone but nobody is very forthcoming on that. As for Teslenko herself, she seems completely blameless. Nobody can suggest any motive for killing her except to annoy Darmant or Yeremenko.'

'I know you know this, but I'll say it anyway. At least one of those two knows what this is about. It's hampering my enquiry that I don't. It would be good if I did.'

Kristoň swilled the contents of his cup around as he thought. 'I honestly don't think Darmant knows. He's made quite a few phone calls to people. Obviously I don't know who he's calling, but he seems to be as baffled as you are.'

'And Yeremenko?'

'Mr Yeremenko is not my client, of course. I have no privileged information. He's not a very talkative person.'

'Meaning you don't know?'

'Exactly so. If either of them knows, I'm sure it's him. But he has said nothing in my hearing and I don't believe that he has told Darmant either.'

Slonský put his coat back on. 'I would have thought that keeping Darmant in the dark was unwise.'

Kristoň finished his coffee and smiled thinly. 'It would certainly be a high-risk option.'

Navrátil and Peiperová were also having a coffee break. For Peiperová their trip to Teplice was already a success, because she had seen a vase in one of the shops they had walked past and it was now in a carrier bag at her feet. Navrátil was still trying to put together what they had discovered.

'So it looks likely that the blond-haired man is Chigulin, and he drives here, dumps his car, and meets Yeremenko.'

'Or Yeremenko meets him and kills him so that he doesn't pick up his car again,' Peiperová suggested.

'Either way, Yeremenko knows where Chigulin is.'

'Not necessarily. He knew where he was on that day. They could have separated again.'

'Let's see if we can find out where Yeremenko went straight after meeting up with Chigulin. Maybe he used a bank card somewhere.'

'I'll get Lucie onto it.'

'But how did Yeremenko know Chigulin was here? It can't be just chance that the two of them arrive in the same street in Teplice.'

'Yeremenko said he was out of Prague when Kateryna was murdered. Maybe he was already in Teplice, and Chigulin came here to report in person.'

'And then Yeremenko tells him to lie low because he may be in danger?'

'Chigulin knew that when he left Prague. That's why he dumped his phone, so people couldn't trace him. He buys a new phone, copies his contacts over, rings Yeremenko to give him his new number and throws away the old one.'

'But if he bought one, why can't we find one in his name? He must have been given it.'

'It's a long shot, but if the gang bought a batch of phones they may have similar numbers. Let's see if Lucie can run an ownership check on the numbers around Yeremenko's to see if one has recently been activated.'

CHAPTER 20

Lieutenant Dvorník was not made for running. It was a matter of some astonishment to his colleagues that he passed his fitness tests, given that a man of his height would usually have been around sixty kilograms lighter and considerably less spherical. It was therefore an axiom within the Czech police force that if something made Dvorník run, it was important.

He skidded as he reached Slonský's office. The door was, as always, open, which was just as well because he could not have stopped if it had been shut.

'What is it?' asked Slonský.

The effort had left Dvorník breathless. 'Phone … my office … another body…'

'Another woman?'

Dvorník nodded. If Peiperová had been there she could have told Slonský how to pick up a call from another extension, but in her absence it was his turn to demonstrate an inability to sprint. His knee did not appear to impede him as he made for Dvorník's desk.

'Captain Slonský here. Tell me more.'

It was a City policeman.

'We got called to a house after the gardener said he wasn't getting any reply at the door although he had a booking to mow the lawns. He noticed a lot of flies on one of the upstairs windows. I've just climbed up to have a look, and there's a body there. It's a naked woman and she's been beheaded. It sounded like that case at Černý Most you're dealing with, so my sergeant said I'd better report it to you directly.'

'I'm glad you did. Are the pathologists on their way?'

'I called you first, sir.'

'No problem. I'll do all that. You just stay there and keep people out. And don't enter that room.'

'Don't worry, I won't.'

Dvorník had driven Slonský and Jerneková to the house concerned and stayed to help with the investigation. Krob was tied up dealing with the underwear thieves so Slonský was glad of Dvorník's assistance. Although Slonský regularly disparaged his colleague, he knew that Dvorník was an experienced officer, not to mention being one of the few police officers he trusted with a gun in his hands. Dvorník belonged to a gun club and was a noted marksman, though he preferred his own rifle to any police issue weapon. While Slonský apprehended no immediate danger, there was a certain comfort in being in the company of a man who could shoot the private parts off a rabbit from thirty metres.

The local policeman, whose name was Buček, had rustled up a ladder from somewhere by means of which Slonský was able to view the bedroom where the body was. There was no doubt that it looked uncannily like the crime scene photos from Černý Most.

'It seems we've got a serial killer on our hands,' remarked Slonský as he regained the ground.

'Does that mean it's got nothing to do with gangs and that sort of thing?' asked Jerneková.

'I wouldn't say that,' Slonský replied. 'All things are possible. But maybe Teslenko was just a random victim.'

'So we've been barking up the wrong tree all along?'

'Don't rub it in. It was just a working hypothesis. Which now needs revision in the light of new information.'

'I wasn't being snide,' protested Jerneková. 'Just getting things straight in my head.'

A white van pulled into the driveway and the scenes of crime team clambered out.

'Is there an entry point?' asked their chief.

'Isn't that what the front door is for?' replied Jerneková.

'I meant one accessible now. Have you called a locksmith?'

'No. I could kick the door in if you want.'

'It might have evidence on it so I'd rather you didn't.'

Slonský was sure that he heard Jerneková mutter "make your mind up" but nobody reacted to the comment.

The chief technician scaled the ladder to look into the room. 'Can we get some photographs from here, then we'll move the ladder to that other window and see if can gain access there?' he said.

Slonský fished in his coat pocket for something. 'Jerneková, I don't want to be disturbed for a minute. Fend off allcomers for me, would you?'

He walked over to the front door and produced a small object from his pocket. He selected an attachment and began wiggling something. After a little while the door sprang open. Slonský walked away, resumed his place beside Jerneková, and said nothing.

It took a minute or two for the technicians to notice that the door was open.

'Does anyone know how the door came to be open?' asked the chief technician.

'Can't have been properly locked,' suggested Jerneková.

Within moments the team were swarming around the house looking for bloodstains and fingerprints. Slonský, Dvorník and Jerneková donned gloves and shoe covers and waited for permission to stroll into the hallway.

'Do you think she was dead when we came here…' Jerneková began.

'Not now, lass,' Slonský replied, but Dvorník's ears had already pricked up.

'You've been here?'

'We were looking for a man named Polstrelov. His girlfriend went missing after reporting a crime.'

'Could that be her on the bed?' Dvorník asked.

'Time will tell. But it wouldn't surprise me.'

Dr Novák had arrived and waved to Slonský before seeking out the chief technician. After a few words he came over to the detectives.

'They're going to be another quarter of an hour or so in the doorway to the room. There's no rush. She's not going anywhere and I understand there's no need to confirm that she is dead.'

'Not unless you can survive having your head lopped off and put on a windowsill,' Slonský replied.

'Doubtful,' agreed Novák. 'Same perpetrator?'

'Certainly looks that way.'

'Any idea of the victim's identity?'

'We were here looking for a man whose girlfriend had reported being molested in the park. It could be the woman, I suppose, but they were reported to be on good terms.'

Jerneková detached herself from the group and climbed the ladder. 'We can stop looking for our missing jogger,' she said. 'That's Paulina Zechovská. At least, the head is.'

By the time Navrátil and Peiperová arrived back in Prague, Dr Novák had provided a preliminary report and Slonský, Dvorník and Jerneková had been admitted to the crime scene.

'Did you find anything useful?' Navrátil asked.

'I didn't go to the first crime scene,' said Slonský. 'You may remember that I was holed up in a hospital bed following a grievous injury sustained in the course of duty. And unfortunately you didn't go to the second one because you were following a lead in Teplice. How did that go?'

'We found evidence that a person who may be Chigulin used his bank card and then met up with Yeremenko.'

'You don't say? That's interesting,' said Slonský. 'And where did they go after that?'

'We don't know where Chigulin went, but we know Yeremenko came back here, because we arrested him a day or so later at the airport. We found out that the last time Polstrelov's card was used was at 11:37, but we don't know who by. It wasn't used by Yeremenko. It could be Polstrelov, but since we don't really know what he looks like, we can't be sure.'

Krob slid a picture across the table. 'Taken from his prison record.'

Navrátil and Peiperová looked at it in turn.

'Given that this must be five or more years ago, and his hair is longer now, it could be him,' Peiperová said.

Navrátil had found the blurred still image from the security camera at the bank. 'I think you're right. We can't be sure given the poor images we've got.'

Slonský waved to Dumpy Anna behind the canteen counter. 'Are these cups getting smaller? Another of the same, please.' He took an enormous mouthful of ham roll, chewed a bit, and then tried to speak. 'The question is — hang on, mouth full — the question is, what spurred Polstrelov to go to Teplice? That seems a bit too much of a coincidence.'

'Did he follow Yeremenko?' asked Jerneková.

'No, because Yeremenko wasn't in Prague to be followed.'

Krob wanted to look at a different angle. 'Yeremenko told us that Chigulin rang him from outside Ms Teslenko's flat. But thanks to Dr Novák we know that someone else was in the flat. He found their blood. Let's suppose that person was Chigulin. Why would the killer leave him alive?'

'Presumably he wants someone to tell Yeremenko who did it. It's an attempt at intimidation,' Navrátil replied.

'So when he's done that, Chigulin now becomes a threat because he could tell *us* who did it.'

'And that's why he runs,' Navrátil concluded.

'Why not to us? We regularly keep people safe, don't we?'

'Don't overestimate the difficulty of giving someone a new identity, particularly if they're not very bright,' Slonský interjected. 'Very few people are happy not to make contact with family or friends. And when they do the first thing they say is "Oh, by the way, I'm now called…" and give the game away. But, yes, we could have given him a new start. So the fact that he doesn't come to us tells us that either he was specifically warned off, or someone gave him a better idea. And the one person we know he spoke to is Yeremenko.'

'So Yeremenko told him to run?' Krob persisted.

'Almost certainly. Not only that, he told him where to run. Yeremenko must have been in Teplice, and it's clearly too dangerous to come home because it sounds like a trap is waiting for him, so he tells Chigulin to join him there. And to make sure nobody can track Chigulin through his phone he tells him to chuck it away and get a new one.'

'Can we come back to these poor women?' asked Peiperová. 'After all, this is a murder case.'

'Too right, sister!' cried Jerneková, then, when everyone looked at her she added, 'I mean, yes, Lieutenant.'

'You're right, of course,' said Slonský. 'Well, Paulina Zechovská is an associate of Polstrelov, she's found in his house and there's no sign of forced entry, so on the basis that most women are killed by someone they know, he has to be the prime candidate.'

'So, given the identical modus operandi, he also has to be the prime candidate for having killed Kateryna Teslenko,' Navrátil opined.

'It looks that way,' Slonský agreed.

'Then we have to go all out to find Polstrelov.'

Dumpy Anna arrived at the table with a tray bearing a coffee and another ham roll.

'Why a ham roll?' asked Slonský.

'You said another of the same so I repeated your order. Coffee and a ham roll.'

'I only meant the coffee. However, since you've gone to the trouble of making it…' He took the ham roll and bit into it.

The group began to break up to return to their work, leaving Slonský and his ham roll in peace, which did not last for long, because Mucha appeared.

'Ah, the elusive Scarlet Pimpernel is here!'

'Hush, I told you that's a secret.'

'You know how long secrets keep in this place.'

'Especially with you around.'

'Hey! I see it as my role to keep you informed. I can stop and start tipping off Dvorník instead.'

'If you do I'll ring your wife's sister and tell her to come for Christmas and New Year.'

'You know, if you put your mind to it I reckon you could be a grade A bastard.'

'Thank you. I've been practising. Was there anything in particular or were you coveting my ham roll?'

'Good question,' Mucha replied, tearing the end off the roll in answer and popping it in his mouth. 'Have you been chatting up Dumpy Anna again? There's the best part of a pig in here.'

'She likes to mother me. She's worried I might be fading away. I lost three kilos in hospital, you know.'

'Have you looked down the back of the sofa? That's where I usually find things I've lost.'

'I'll look there for your marbles when I get home. What was it you came for?'

'Phone call from the clinic while you were out. They want you there at seven-thirty tomorrow morning.'

'I can't possibly do that. I've got three cases on. Which have turned out to be two, because two of them are linked.'

'And I hear tell Krob has solved the other one, so you've actually got one, which is Navrátil's case anyway, and they won't miss you for a day. Besides, have you forgotten your date with destiny on 11th November?'

'Don't remind me. My birthday, and I have to be here, complete with functioning knees.'

'Right. So it's in your interest to get them sorted. Half seven tomorrow morning. I'll get a car sent round to take you there. It'll pick you up at seven o'clock.'

Slonský inspected his roll. 'And no breakfast. This is going to have to do me until then. And they say the condemned man ate a hearty supper.' He waved to Dumpy Anna once more. 'Have you got anything more substantial?' he asked.

She inspected the contents of the chiller cabinet. 'A bit of liver sausage, some more ham, cheese.'

'That'll do. Bung them in a bun and send them this way.'

Mucha was slowly shaking his head.

'That'll keep me going until supper time,' Slonský explained.

CHAPTER 21

The alarm rang and Slonský greeted the day by giving the clock a good clout on the top. He rolled out of bed, flexed his knee, winced, and had a good scratch. He shaved and cleaned his teeth, carefully swallowing a little of the water on the basis that he could pretend it was accidental if challenged about it.

At seven o'clock a police car pulled up outside and Slonský climbed in. There was a strong smell of coffee, largely because the non-driver was cradling a drink and munching on a pretzel. The drive was only a quarter of an hour long at that time of day, but by the time they arrived at the clinic Slonský's stomach was growling like a grizzly bear prematurely woken from hibernation.

They swiftly found him a cubicle and gave him one of those special gowns hospitals have for operations that ensure that the surgeons can always see your backside, whatever they are meant to be operating on. In Slonský's case it was short as well, so he kept pulling it down at the front to ensure that none of the nurses fainted with shock.

Dr Stockner put his head round the curtain, having first called 'Knock, knock!'

'Why do you do that?' asked Slonský. 'You don't knock on a curtain.'

'Tetchy and tense this morning, eh?'

'No more than usual. Are you always this cheerful, because let me tell you, it's really irritating.'

'Take these and I'll leave you in peace.'

'What are they?'

'Muscle relaxants. They'll ensure your knee is nice and floppy before we start. And given that you'll be awake, we want you relaxed, don't we?'

'Do we? Shouldn't you be relaxed too?'

'I will be, but I don't need tablets to achieve that.'

'Then neither do I. You can take these and shove them anywhere you think fit.'

'If you're sure. They'll reduce the risk of complications afterwards.'

'In that event, give them here. They're the only solid food I'm going to get this morning.'

'I'll leave you for about fifteen minutes while we get the theatre ready for you. I'll see you later.'

'Not if I see you first,' muttered Slonský.

Navrátil was feeling much more positive. At last he felt that they were getting somewhere. 'Is it likely that the person who attacked Paulina Zechovská in the park is the same one who killed her?' he asked.

'If it isn't she's been incredibly unlucky,' Jerneková suggested. 'Molested one week and decapitated by someone completely different the next.'

'We can't ask Zechovská, but we could try showing pictures of the suspects to that librarian with the yappy dog,' Peiperová proposed.

'Let's do that, please,' Navrátil said.

'You'll never get a top job here if you can't shake this habit of saying please,' Jerneková observed.

'I don't know about that,' said Colonel Rajka, who was standing in the doorway. 'Please would you explain this photograph I've been sent by the traffic directorate. It's been captured by a city centre camera and it shows a police car speeding. Sixty-two kilometres per hour, it says here. And you're driving, Jerneková.'

'Yes, sir.'

'Whereas it was Captain Slonský who signed the car out.'

'Yes, sir.'

'So he should have been driving.'

'Yes, sir.'

'Added to which, I haven't yet seen a pass certificate from the driving school.'

'No, sir.'

'So you're driving a police car, at speed, without any warning that you're a learner driver?'

'That's about the sum of it, sir.'

'And your explanation for this?'

'Captain Slonský's knee was hurting, sir, so I asked if he wanted to swap places.'

Rajka took a deep breath to compose himself. 'Where is Captain Slonský?'

'At the clinic having his knee fixed, sir,' Navrátil chipped in.

'He hasn't requested leave.'

'He only heard about the appointment yesterday afternoon, sir.'

Jerneková was pleased that Navrátil had decided to take on the speaking duties.

'And when is he expected back?'

'This afternoon, sir.'

'I see. Perhaps, Lieutenant, you'd ask him to find some time in his busy schedule to drop by my office at his earliest convenience.'

'I'll pass it on, sir.'

'Good. See that you do. Good morning, all.'

Stockner could not help feeling that Slonský was a lot more compliant when he had a good belt of tranquilliser in his veins. The diazepam Slonský had been given was a muscle relaxant, so he had not really lied, but the mean reason for giving it to the detective was to stop him getting up and walking out halfway through. As it was, Slonský was lying back in the pillows, on the verge of sleep, but still able to grumble at intervals and ask how long it would be until he could have a bite of something.

After what seemed to Slonský to be two lifetimes, Stockner declared that everything was finished. Slonský was taken to a recovery room and given a drink and a cookie. Under normal circumstances he would have rejected the cookie outright but at that moment he was looking for anything edible that could follow it.

'It'll be sore for a week or two,' said the nurse, 'but after that it'll be much better. Try to keep the weight off it. How long have you got off work?'

Slonský glanced at his watch. 'About two more hours.'

The nurse was shocked. 'Have you got a desk job?' she asked.

'I've got a job, and I've got a desk, but I spend as little time at it as I can.'

'Well, don't put any strain on that knee. Sit down as much as you can. Do the exercises on the sheet I gave you to speed your recovery.'

Much as Slonský disliked this advice, he acknowledged the greater good of getting his contract extended. 'Yes, miss.' He hoped that she had not seen his fingers crossed behind his back.

Slonský took a taxi back to work; which is to say that he took a taxi to the street that his office was in, but then alighted outside a bar where, by prior arrangement, Valentin had secured a table near the door and quickly lined up a half-litre of something restorative and a plate of steak and potatoes, to which Slonský requested the addition of some fried onions and a spoonful of cabbage. Oh, and a couple of those bread rolls while he was waiting. In fact, leave the basket, he said.

'That's better,' he pronounced around twenty-five minutes later. 'I could see my life flashing before me.'

'Surely you go without food for that long during the night,' said Valentin.

'Yes, but I'm asleep, so I don't know I'm hungry.'

'So if you can't sleep, do you get hungry?'

'I don't know. I can't remember not being able to sleep.'

Valentin was in a cheerful mood. 'So can I tell our readers they can sleep safely in their beds because the Černý Most murderer is under arrest?'

'Of course you can. It won't be true, but when has that ever worried your editor?'

'You've got a sharp tongue, Josef Slonský.'

'Are you telling me I'm wrong?'

'No. Just saying you don't have to be so cutting about it, that's all.'

Slonský pushed his plate away and drained his glass. 'Do you want another?' he asked.

'I'm working.'

'So am I.'

'Just a large one then.'

Slonský summoned a waiter and gave the order.

Valentin's curiosity got the better of him. 'Apart from not being a success, how is your case coming along?'

'It's complicated,' said Slonský. 'I'm not sure I can explain it.'

'Try.'

Slonský took a deep breath. 'Right. There's a woman called Teslenko living out at Černý Most. Her boyfriend is a hoodlum called Yeremenko. Got that so far?'

'It's really not that difficult.'

'There's another hoodlum called Polstrelov who lives with his girlfriend Zechovská in Bubeneč. Zechovská comes to our notice when an unknown assailant tries to molest her in a park. Despite, apparently, being frightened, she gives a false address and Peiperová and Jerneková can't find her again.'

'That's odd. Why do that when she's scared? Did she know her assailant?'

'We don't think so. Our best guess is that she went to her boyfriend for the kind of protection we can't give. Anyway, for some unknown reason, Polstrelov and Yeremenko fall out. Polstrelov decides to kill Teslenko to teach Yeremenko a lesson.'

'Why doesn't he kill Yeremenko?'

'Too risky, I suppose. Plus if he kills Yeremenko, he'll only suffer for a while. Kill someone he loves and the hurt lasts much longer. Standard Security Bureau tactics forty years ago. Dissidents don't mind suffering themselves, but they hate the idea that their loved ones will suffer if they do something.'

'Okay.'

'But it's not enough for him to kill Teslenko. It's important that Yeremenko should know who did it, so Polstrelov kidnaps a mate of Yeremenko called Chigulin and makes him watch it all.'

'Why doesn't he just leave a note? You know, I did this, suck it up.'

'Because a note might get to the police. Chigulin is useful until he tells Yeremenko. Then, in an ideal world, he gets rubbed out before he can tell anyone else. Only Yeremenko knows this game and tells Chigulin to get the hell out and come to join him in Teplice, having first thrown his phone away to make him difficult to trace.'

'Why Teplice?'

'Presumably that's where Yeremenko was, because we know he wasn't in Prague. Will you stop interrupting?'

'I'm not interrupting. I'm seeking clarification of a confusing narrative.'

'Well, it sounds like interrupting. So, where was I?'

'On your way to Teplice without a phone.'

'Ah, yes. Now, this is where it gets complicated.'

'You mean it wasn't before?'

'I'll ignore that. We know what seems to have happened, but we don't know why. Polstrelov, having murdered Teslenko in a particularly unpleasant way, then does the same to his own girlfriend. Somehow, he seems to know that Yeremenko and Chigulin are in Teplice and heads up there looking for them.'

'Presumably he hasn't yet found them, since we're not hearing about body parts found in the street.'

'You'd think so. Though we know that Yeremenko is now back in Prague.'

'How?'

'We arrested him.'

'So he's in jail?'

'No, we had to let him go. No evidence.'

'Couldn't you make some?'

'Stop living in the past. We don't do that anymore. Not often, anyway.'

Valentin turned this story over in his mind. 'That makes no sense. Why would Polstrelov kill his own girlfriend?'

'She annoyed him. She ironed his boxer shorts the wrong way. She didn't want to watch another of his martial arts films. Who knows why men kill women?'

'Yes, but you said she went to him for protection. That was pretty dumb if he was behind the attack in the park.'

'Obviously that would mean she didn't know he was behind the attack.'

'Presumably he's had months to kill her if he wanted to. Why do it now?'

'Maybe after killing Teslenko he developed a taste for it.'

'But why Teslenko first? Isn't it more logical that he'd practise on his girlfriend because she wouldn't be expecting it before he tackled the more difficult one?'

'No, Novák is clear that Teslenko died a few days before Zechovská.'

Valentin scratched his head. 'It still makes no sense to me.'

'I think if you're expecting the acts of psychopaths to make sense, you're putting too high a value on reason, my friend.'

Dr Novák was looking at the evidence at that very moment. He circled the table and directed the lights on the lower end of the breastbone, just where the murderer had cut into Zechovská's abdomen, and followed the cut round to each side.

He frowned and repeated the exercise before frowning again. He fetched his notes on Teslenko's post-mortem examination from his filing cabinet and compared the two. Finally he picked up the telephone and called Navrátil.

'Have you got a moment this afternoon?' he asked. 'I want to show you something.'

Navrátil had passed on Colonel Rajka's message, so Slonský hung up his coat and began the walk to the executive corridor where his boss had an office. To his surprise, Rajka met him on the way.

'I asked Sergeant Mucha to ring me when you arrived,' he said. 'I thought I might save you an extra walk.'

'Very considerate of you, sir,' said Slonský, all the while thinking that it was more likely that Rajka had come up to make sure that they met by denying Slonský any opportunity to slip out the back way.

'Shall we find a quiet corner somewhere?' Rajka said, nodding in the direction of Slonský's office.

Slonský liked Rajka. The colonel was straight-talking, a good cop, honest as befits someone who had previously been in charge in internal investigations; he was also able to tear telephone directories in half and could pick up a water cooler under each arm. Somehow even after he gave up competitive wrestling he had remained in great shape, his crisp white shirt clinging to his abdominal muscles like a wet sheet on a draining board. But he was no soft touch, and Slonský feared that he must be about to give him some bad news, judging by the pulsing vein in his neck and the voice that was slightly louder than usual.

They entered the room and Rajka motioned to Slonský to sit at his desk, while he brought another chair over.

'Krob, would you mind giving us five minutes?' Rajka said.

'Of course, sir,' Krob replied, closing his notes file and making for the door. Slonský was so subdued he did not even ask Krob to bring him a coffee from the canteen.

'Do you know what this is about?' asked Rajka.

'No, sir, but I'm sure I will in a minute.'

'Too damn right you will.' Rajka laid the traffic photos across the desk, quite a balancing exercise given the number and variety of piles of paper there. 'How do you explain this?'

'The traffic police must have some cameras, sir.'

'They have. And they've been trying them out as you drove past. Let's look at this one, the first they took. Sixty-two kilometres per hour in a built-up area.'

'That's over the speed limit, sir.'

'Indeed it is. And do you recognise the driver?'

'It's not a great picture, but it could be Officer Jerneková, sir.'

'A promising officer with some definite good points, but a valid driving licence isn't one of them. Did you know that when you let her drive?'

'Yes, sir.'

'She tells me that you intended to drive, but your knee was too painful.'

'That is correct, sir.'

'Why didn't you turn back?'

'I thought it was a good opportunity for Jerneková to get some practice in, sir. Plus it didn't occur to me.'

'This could have had serious consequences, Slonský. Imagine the headlines if she had caused an accident. What would you have done if she had run over a cyclist?'

'Lied, probably.'

Rajka leaned back with his arms behind his head and took a very deep breath. 'Don't do this to me again. You're lucky you had the sirens going. At least people had some warning to get out of your way.'

'Yes, sir. How do you know about the sirens, sir?'

'Because I was about to exercise my right of way to turn left into the street outside when you went racing past.'

'Ah.'

'Ah, indeed.'

'So it wasn't to do with the photos, then.'

'Yes, it was. I can ignore what I see with my own eyes. I have to give some kind of answer to the traffic police who, fortunately, do not know that Jerneková is a learner driver nor that you were not in hot pursuit of a criminal, so I will fob them off this time.'

'Yes, sir. Thank you, sir.'

'This is probably a futile hope on my part, Slonský, but don't let it happen again. See if you can get through to retirement with a clean sheet.'

'Retirement? You haven't heard…'

'Relax. I haven't heard anything and now that you're back here I expect to keep you for at least another year. But just think — one of the casualties could have been you. And if you're back in hospital you can kiss goodbye to a contract extension.'

Slonský could feel his hands getting clammy. 'Yes, sir. Thank you, sir.'

'How is your knee? I understand they operated again today.'

'Just a bullet hole operation, sir.'

'I think you mean keyhole. Successful, I hope?'

'They're very confident, sir.'

'Good.'

Rajka stood up, so Slonský did the same.

'Well, I'm glad we understand each other. We *do* understand each other, don't we?'

'Oh, yes, sir. We're as one.'

'Pleased to hear it. Any news on the case?'

'I haven't seen Lieutenant Navrátil recently. It's his case.'

'I've got a bad feeling about this, Slonský. Young women being eviscerated isn't good for tourism, so you can be sure the Mayor's office is bending my ear. Do me a favour and solve it for me, would you? There's a good man.'

Given that I've just been let off, I don't have much choice, thought Slonský.

CHAPTER 22

Navrátil knew his duty. He was a lieutenant in the detective section, and therefore had to attend the post-mortem examinations of murder victims, and he would not flinch from that duty even though he was quite squeamish and feared that he might faint at any moment.

He managed his discomfort by looking away whenever he could, fixing his gaze around half a metre outside the mortuary slab so that it looked as if he was watching, but actually he wasn't.

This stratagem was about to be tested to the full, because Dr Novák wanted to show him something on the body of Ms Zechovská and was apparently expecting him to look closely at her breasts, something that Navrátil would have considered improper in any circumstances but especially when he and Ms Zechovská had not been properly introduced. Suddenly the room seemed very warm despite the fans whirring overhead.

'I'll tell you what I think,' said Novák, 'then you can see if you can make any sense of it.' He opened a folder and spread out some photographs. 'I haven't brought Ms Teslenko's body out again. We can work from these photos, I think. Now, the murderer used Teslenko's own knives to attack her, and we've been able to work out which particular knives were used by careful examination of the wounds, although we know at least some of the wounds were inflicted by another knife. For this woman, so far as I can see, he only used one knife which, one assumes, he brought with him. It was found in the room where the body was, but it doesn't match any of the other knives in the building.'

'Can we find out who bought the knife?' Navrátil interrupted.

'You can try, but it's an ex-military knife, I think, probably bought on a stall somewhere. It was actually a little bit short for his purposes, so it looks as if he had to move some of the internal organs to get the female reproductive organs out. There are some torn tissues as if he lifted the womb violently.'

Navrátil bit the inside of his cheek. The pain stopped him keeling over.

'But if we look at the point where he started, which seems to be here, just under the end of the breastbone, the cutting technique is quite different. In the case of Ms Teslenko the murderer makes a big bold cut; with Ms Zechovská it is more tentative — he saws at the tissue rather than swiping the knife through it.'

'Hang on,' said Navrátil. 'Are you saying the murders were committed by two different people? Not a serial killer at all?'

'That's what it looks like to me. It's not conclusive, just suggestive.'

'But the killings are so similar.'

'Copycat killings are not uncommon.'

'But we haven't released any details to the press. The only person who could know what injuries were inflicted on Ms Teslenko and repeat them on Ms Zechovská was the murderer.'

'Or someone who watched him.'

'The man tied to the radiator? Chigulin?'

Dr Novák pursed his lips. 'Or there was someone else who was watching. But usually serial killers get more proficient with each killing, unless they're frenzied. There's no sign that either killer was particularly rushed. And yet he does a more tentative job the second time than he did the first.'

'And we know the deaths were definitely in that order — Ms Teslenko then Ms Zechovská?'

'Oh, yes. The science is irrefutable on that point. Probably thirty-six to forty-eight hours apart. Slightly complicated because we don't know what the temperature of the rooms was, but the sequence is certain.'

Navrátil's heart was skipping around his chest, and not in a good way. It was bad enough trying to find one vicious murderer, and now, it seemed, he had to find two.

'Well, that's a turn-up for the book,' was all Slonský said when Navrátil told him.

'I suppose Dr Novák could be wrong,' Navrátil pondered.

'I doubt it,' said Slonský. 'Don't tell him I said so, but he knows his stuff. I wouldn't trust his opinion on hockey, since he's a Sparta supporter and I'm a Slavia man, but when it comes to dead bodies, he's one of the best. Certainly better than his predecessor, Hanč. He regularly got things wrong.'

'How did he keep his job?'

'I don't know. It certainly had nothing to do with his sister being the wife of a government minister, because that was just scurrilous and ill-informed gossip. Of course, he knew he was useless, so he would steady his nerves with a glass or two of vodka before he started an autopsy, which didn't do much for his accuracy, especially if he was doing four or five in a day.'

'That's scandalous,' Navrátil said.

'No, just our country's history. People in power too plastered to do the job properly. It's the Czech way, lad. Anyway, it makes it more important than ever that we should find Chigulin, since he's the only person we know who could have watched Polstrelov at work.'

'Unless Polstrelov had an assistant.'

'Only Chigulin can tell us that. But it does solve one problem. Why would Polstrelov kill his own girlfriend whom, it seems, he'd hidden away to keep safe? Answer — he didn't. Despite his efforts, somebody got to her. We've got a nasty bit of tit for tat going on here, my boy.'

'You mean Polstrelov kills Yeremenko's girlfriend, so Yeremenko kills Polstrelov's?'

'I don't know that he did it personally, but he — shall we say — had it done?'

'Where does it end?' Navrátil sighed.

'Where gang warfare usually ends. With an awful lot of people lying dead in a warehouse.'

Valentin was already in his place cradling a beer and looking sadly at his empty schnapps glass when Slonský arrived.

'I've been thinking,' Valentin began.

'I've warned you about that. It'll end in tears. Stick to what you're good at.'

'In that case, I'll have a pear brandy and a beer, thank you.'

'I asked for that. Anything to eat?'

'I've had dinner.'

'So have I, but that isn't what I asked you.'

'No, I'm full, thanks.'

'I might see if they've got any sausages.'

The waiter took their order and left them alone.

'Now, you mentioned you'd been indulging in an unnatural practice,' Slonský prompted.

'If you're going to bring that up again — oh, you mean thinking.'

'Nailed it in one.'

'I don't think Polstrelov did it.'

'Look, which of us is the detective here?'

'You are, of course. I'm just trying to stop you making a big mistake.'

'And your qualifications for that are…?'

Valentin took cover behind his glass and spoke quietly. 'The butcher out at Dejvice.'

Slonský paused in mid-slurp. 'You always bring that up, don't you?'

'You asked me a question. I answered it.'

'I admit I was wrong about that.'

'And?'

'And you were right. But it was his own fault. He swore that nobody else had access to his cleavers.'

'Which we discovered wasn't true because…'

'Because you went to his shop while he was in custody and one of the cleavers was being used by his assistant,' Slonský reluctantly admitted.

'Who had made himself a duplicate set of keys. I rest my case.'

'But this case doesn't depend on a duplicate set of keys.'

'No, but think of human nature. Or, in the case of Prague hoodlums, subhuman nature. If you hit one of these guys, what do they do?'

'Hit you back.'

'Exactly. Even if they get run in for it, they hit back. So isn't it much more likely that Yeremenko responded to Polstrelov killing his girlfriend by attacking Polstrelov's girlfriend in return?'

'Have you been talking to Dr Novák?'

'No,' said a bewildered Valentin. 'I barely know the man.'

'He thinks the same as you do. And he's convinced me. I suspect that we'll find that Yeremenko was the man who tried to grab Zechovská in the park, only he wasn't after a quick grope. He wanted to kidnap and kill her.'

'But Polstrelov wouldn't have told her what he'd done, surely?'

'Not in so many words, but she must know what sort of man he is and where his money comes from. She'd know he'd been doing something bad. And don't forget he must have been bloodstained after the killing.'

'So when she tells him she's been attacked she might not know what's behind it, but he will?'

'That's right. And bear in mind that by this stage Polstrelov's plan is coming unglued. I'll bet that he used Chigulin to get in to Ms Teslenko's flat, then made Chigulin watch so that Yeremenko would know exactly who had done this to his girlfriend. But when Chigulin phones Yeremenko, instead of Yeremenko coming hotfoot into a trap, he tells Chigulin to come to him, which also means that Polstrelov can't wipe out the one person whose testimony can convict him in court. So Polstrelov has annoyed a vicious hoodlum and now he doesn't know where he is. What he can't know is that Yeremenko knows where he lives and therefore where Zechovská is likely to be. Then it's just a matter of waiting his chance.'

'But how does he get in? Ms Zechovská must have been warned not to open the door.'

'We'll never know. But it wasn't that hard for me to get in, and I'm an amateur.'

'You broke in?'

'Certainly not. That would be highly improper. I just leaned on the door and my lock pick accidentally slipped into the lock.'

Valentin picked up his pear brandy but was too deep in thought to drink it.

'Are you going to cradle that like a girlie or drink it and have another?' Slonský asked him.

'Don't call me a girlie. A lesser friend could get very hurt by all these slurs on my sexuality.'

'We don't have sexuality at our age,' Slonský replied. 'We have beer.'

CHAPTER 23

'So when we brought Yeremenko in,' Jerneková asked at the next morning's team meeting, 'had he already killed Zechovská?'

'Yes, he had,' Slonský replied.

'He's a cool customer, I'll give him that. He must have thought we were going to question him about that, but we never said a word.'

'We wouldn't, would we?' Peiperová chipped in. 'We didn't know she was dead and we hadn't connected the attack in the park to the murder of Teslenko.'

It was Krob who raised the question that had disturbed Slonský's sleep that night. 'But that means that when Yeremenko met Darmant, he already knew that he had taken revenge.'

'Yes, but maybe he hadn't told Darmant yet.'

'So why has Darmant stayed in Prague?'

'He's got a funeral to attend, hasn't he? And he probably wants to know where this is going to stop. Whoever Polstrelov runs with may want their own revenge now.'

'You think we're in for a full-on gang war?' Navrátil demanded.

'I'm sure of it. We always were. I don't know Polstrelov from Adam, but if he acts against Darmant's daughter, every villain in Prague knows that's not going to be the end of the matter. If he talked to anyone about it, they'd talk him out of it unless a gang war is exactly what they want.'

'Then shouldn't we talk to Captain Grigar in Organised Crime?' asked Navrátil.

'Talking is going to work better than charades or interpretative dance,' Slonský conceded. 'Let's see what he can tell us.'

In theory, Slonský and Grigar should have got along very well together. Both dressed like throwbacks to a previous age, both were honest, lifelong policemen, both hated corruption and both liked a beer or two. In practice, they could barely tolerate each other. Slonský thought Grigar was pretty ineffective, his evidence being the continuing threat of organised crime, while Grigar thought Slonský was a disorganised maverick, which he based on the collected gossip of the Czech police service.

One habit that united them was a dislike of being behind a desk, so when Slonský suggested a meeting they soon agreed to meet in a café, ideally one where other police did not go. Navrátil tagged along because it was his case and Slonský needed a driver, added to which he had once again forgotten his wallet, which was, he said, in another coat. This was news to Navrátil, who did not know that Slonský had another coat. In two and a half years of working together Navrátil had never seen it.

Grigar was already in place when they arrived.

'Grigar is touchy about the amount of organised crime in Prague,' said Slonský out of the side of his mouth as they entered. 'We're going to have to be tactful. Follow my lead.'

Navrátil found it difficult to walk and stagger at the same time, but he gamely pressed on despite this remark.

'Captain Grigar! Thank you for giving up some of your valuable time to assist us,' said Slonský. 'You remember Lieutenant Navrátil.'

'Lieutenant now? Congratulations. Quite a meteoric rise.'

'I have two of them,' said Slonský. 'Peiperová is a lieutenant now too.'

'Quite a little promotion factory you have there.'

'Achievements get noticed,' Slonský said smugly, while biting his tongue to avoid any mention of Grigar's own lieutenant, currently serving six years for assisting criminals by leaking information to them in a case that Slonský had solved. 'Have you got a new lieutenant yet?' he asked artlessly.

'Yes, thank you.'

'Very good. It's terrible when your underlings let you down. I'm glad you've been allowed to replace him.'

'Can we get to the point, please?'

'Of course.'

Slonský invited Navrátil to expound all that they had discovered about Yeremenko and Polstrelov.

'Mean anything to you?' asked Slonský after Navrátil's recitation.

'Clearly we don't know Yeremenko and Polstrelov, either under those names or as — what was it?'

'Veremchuk and Polášek,' Navrátil told him.

'Whatever. They're probably too far down the food chain for us to know them by name. I'll ask the boys if the names mean anything to them.'

Slonský was puzzled. 'I thought Lieutenant Erben's replacement was a woman.'

'Lieutenant Voráčková. Yes, she's a woman.'

'So why do you say "Ask the boys"?'

Grigar shrugged. 'Force of habit, I suppose. Anyway she's fitted in very well. Definitely one of the boys — one of the team,' he corrected himself. 'But Darmant's mob is well known to us. If Yeremenko is one of theirs, then Polstrelov probably belongs to Klivánek's gang.'

'Sounds like a boy band,' sniffed Slonský.

'Klivánek and his guys are no boy band. Klivánek himself is Moravian. He had a nice little racket going there and would probably have stayed put if Darmant and a couple of other Prague groups hadn't tried to muscle in. Klivánek believes in getting your retaliation in before you've been hit. In no time one of the Prague mobs had vanished without trace and the other was so reduced that it was merged into Darmant's.'

'I suppose Darmant did nothing to prevent this robust approach to his competition,' Slonský remarked.

'Not a thing. Going on past form he probably hoped they'd batter each other to a standstill, then he could sweep in and wipe out both. It didn't work out that way. Klivánek isn't one for sharp suits and gold watches but he isn't the dimwit they took him for. Just a minute — have you got a photo of this fellow Yeremenko?'

Navrátil slid it across the table.

'Now it begins to make sense. I didn't have a name, but when Darmant is in town this guy is often in the car with him. We assumed he's some kind of local fixer. If Klivánek wanted to strike at Darmant, then showing he can hit right at one of his right-hand men would be entirely in character.'

'And does Klivánek want to strike at Darmant?'

'Slonský, all the time! But if our information is correct, the particular reason for this may be an incident about a month back. Klivánek has a thriving little protection racket around the men's clubs. He runs a booking agency that provides the dancers and you're encouraged to book through him and only through him. He tried to persuade a club called something like Fluffy Clouds to sign up with him.'

'Dreamy Clouds? That's where Kateryna Teslenko worked,' commented Navrátil.

'That's the dead woman, right? Yeremenko's bit of fluff?'

'I don't think he'd like that description,' growled Slonský.

'I'll apologise to him when he's behind bars, not before. Anyway, Dreamy Clouds said no, not too politely. Rumour has it that when two of Klivánek's men were collecting their so-called commission from their clubs, in cash of course, they were jumped by some of Darmant's people. You must remember the incident; a member of the public saw it and phoned for police and ambulance but by the time the ambulance got through the traffic to the Old Town the victims had been spirited away, so we're light on facts about that assault. She said one of the men was badly injured, coshed with an iron bar, and would have needed hospital treatment, but he's never turned up at any Prague hospital. My best guess is that they drove him to a friendly doctor in Moravia somewhere, and if he survived the journey that's where he's convalescing.'

'So if Klivánek wanted his revenge, the two obvious targets are the men who robbed him or a star dancer from Dreamy Clouds,' said Navrátil.

'And by great good fortune, the two coincide in Yeremenko, who may well have had something to do with the robbery and whose girlfriend worked at Dreamy Clouds,' Slonský suggested.

'If he knew that, Klivánek wouldn't look any further,' Grigar agreed.

'And would he do it himself or instruct an underling?'

'Klivánek is well able to do it himself, but he knows we're watching him. Much more likely to palm the job off to someone he trusts.'

'What about a man called Chigulin?' asked Navrátil.

'I don't know the name. Have you got a photo of him too?'

'Unfortunately not with me.'

'Can't help you, then. I'll ask about the name, of course. Anything else?'

'Just one thing,' Slonský said. 'What's the fascination with Teplice?'

Grigar looked alarmed. 'Teplice? Where does Teplice come into this?'

'When Teslenko was murdered, we think Yeremenko was in Teplice. Chigulin witnesses the murder — perhaps made to watch it — then Yeremenko tells him to get out of town as fast as possible and meet him in Teplice. That much I understand — it could have been anywhere, but that's where Yeremenko happened to be. But then we discover that Polstrelov's last known sighting was also in Teplice a few days later. I don't believe in coincidences. By the way, our station in Teplice can't find any of them.'

'Yes, well, Teplice isn't exactly our most efficient station.'

'Be that as it may, there's a question there.'

Grigar finished his coffee and bent towards them to lower his voice. 'What's Teplice famous for?'

'Big glass factory,' suggested Slonský.

'Thermal springs,' Navrátil added.

'Got it right there. It's a spa resort. Therefore it has casinos, and those casinos are doing very well. Being in the north-west of the country, it's easily accessible to Germans with lots of money. As a result both gangs are trying to get themselves a piece of the action. The snag is that the casino operators have put aside considerations of competition and they're resisting any outsiders. But you may be in luck. I've got one of my best men up there at the moment trying to keep track of what is going on and looking out for any familiar faces. If any of them have approached the casino managers again, he may know. His name is Havelka. If he knows anything I'll get him to contact you personally. Give me your direct line number.'

Navrátil wrote his on a page torn from his notebook.

'Give him mine too, lad,' said Slonský.

Grigar grinned. 'You don't know it, do you?'

'Why should I?' demanded Slonský. 'I never phone myself.'

When they returned to the office, Krob was in a high state of excitement.

'What is it, lad?' asked Slonský. 'You're not going to be a father again, are you?'

'It's a bit early for that,' Krob replied. 'I think I know where Chigulin is.'

'Then you're entitled to be excited,' agreed Slonský. 'Spill the beans.'

'When Yeremenko let us copy Chigulin's number off his phone, Hauzer noted his too,' said Krob.

'Why didn't Hauzer tell me this?' Slonský demanded.

'Because you've had him out of the office following someone ever since,' Jerneková told him.

'We'd better put a trace on that phone straightaway,' Slonský instructed.

'I already have,' said Krob, 'a few days ago. There's another number that calls regularly two or three times a day. Now, we can't find out who has it, because it's registered to a company, but it's the same company that owns Yeremenko's phone. It seems reasonable to me to suppose that Yeremenko gave it to Chigulin.'

'Top work!' Slonský said, beaming at the thought of a breakthrough. 'So where is Chigulin hiding out?'

'I got Spehar's technicians onto it and he says Chigulin is in Most.'

'Most? That's what, twenty-five kilometres from Teplice?'

'About that.'

'Within easy reach if he needs him but not likely to run into anyone he knows. Well, I suppose we'd better go to Most and see if we can find him. Now, if only we knew anyone who knows Most well.'

All eyes turned to fix on Jerneková.

'You can't make me! I spent twenty years of my life trying to get out of that godforsaken hole.'

'I would come with you,' Slonský said, 'but I can't drive at the moment and I daren't let you drive after the incident the other day.'

'What incident?' Peiperová interjected, causing Slonský to think once again how closed-mouthed Navrátil must be outside work if he hadn't mentioned it. In fact, Navrátil hadn't mentioned it because Peiperová had suggested a night at the movies that evening and one thing led to another which completely put any thought of police work out of his head.

'And Krob can't drive because of his shoulder, and Navrátil ought to stay here to mastermind the enquiry,' Slonský continued. 'So it looks like this is turning into a girls' weekend. Try to behave yourselves. I doubt our colleagues in Most have as much experience of drunken hen parties as we have in Prague.'

'How will this work, sir?' Peiperová asked.

'Krob will keep an eye on the phones with some help from Ricka or whoever else Technician First Class Spehar puts up for the job. When Chigulin rings we'll get a precise fix on him and you two will chase round there and nab him.'

'A fix is only accurate to within about fifty metres, sir,' Navrátil pointed out.

'Yes, but they've got a photo of him and I doubt he's going to ring from somewhere he's easily overheard. I have every confidence that these two will be up to the task. Unless, of course, you're suggesting they're not?'

Even if he had thought that — and he did not — Navrátil could see by the look on his wife's face that it would be a very dangerous proposition to put forward.

Jerneková was still scowling. 'If he's in Most on his own there's not many places he can go at night for entertainment. We may need to tour the clubs just in case he doesn't ring. In which event,' she said, 'we'll need to put it on expenses.'

'You bring me Chigulin and it'll be worth every crown.'

There was no doubt about it, thought Krob; Ricka was definitely different. He appeared to have built himself a small office cubicle out of eight computer monitors, each of which showed something different on their screen, and somehow he appeared to be able to watch all eight of them simultaneously.

'Still there,' Ricka mumbled, nodding in the general direction of screen 3. This was the screen that was devoted to tracking where Yeremenko's phone was. It had stayed in central Prague for some time, probably in the hotel where Darmant had taken over a couple of suites for his stay. They were extremely palatial, which is more than could be said for the front seat of Hauzer's car. The fact that Hauzer was uncommonly good at following people did not mean that he enjoyed doing it.

'What about the other phone?' Krob asked.

'Still switched off, I reckon.'

'So Yeremenko wouldn't be able to contact Chigulin, even if he wanted to.'

'Doesn't look like it. He has to wait until the pre-arranged time.'

'Good for us. It means that if we run Chigulin in, Yeremenko won't know until the time of the next planned call.'

It was going to be a long day. Slonský had instructed Peiperová and Jerneková to go home to pack a bag each and then drive to Teplice that evening so that they would be in place the following morning rather than risk them arriving too late.

On arrival Peiperová's plans revolved around getting something to eat and a hot bath. Jerneková favoured something to eat followed by using the expenses to the full. They compromised by going for a drink, and Jerneková knew exactly where they should go. She led the way to a bar that was as dark as a cave and about as well furnished. Having found a stool she proceeded to stroll up to the bar where she spent a full ten minutes chatting up the barman, a young man with a lot of stubble and a faded T-shirt commemorating a tour by a rock band that must have taken place when he was about eight years old.

'Friend of yours?' asked Peiperová when Jerneková finally returned.

'Goodness, you sound like my mother.'

'Just curious.'

'Not exactly a friend. He's my brother Jiří. Well, half-brother technically. Same dad, different mothers.'

'I'm sorry. I forgot your parents were divorced.'

'They weren't. Not until Mum heard that Jiří was on the way. That's when she turfed Dad out.'

'Do you ever see him?'

'No, he's right out of my life. Not so good with Mum either. She expects me always to take her side and frankly she can be a bit of a bitch.'

Peiperová was close to her parents, and knew Navrátil adored his mother. While she was aware that not every daughter gets on well with her mother, it was still quite a shock to meet someone who felt that way.

'You need to know,' Jerneková continued, 'that I've asked him to tag around with us in the morning.'

'Why?'

'Because there are places in this town where decent women don't go, and it wouldn't surprise me if Chigulin is holed up in one of them. Don't worry, I haven't told him what we're doing, or mentioned any names. I just asked if he could chaperone us. He's not due at work till six o'clock so he's happy to hang out with us.'

'Will he keep his mouth shut?'

'Jiří? Sure. First, because he doesn't know anything, and second, because he knows I'd fill him in if he didn't. I've done it before. Admittedly he was about eight at the time and I was going through a moody teenager phase — I know, hard to believe, isn't it? — but he won't forget it. And he quite likes his big sister. I bought him his first proper drink.'

'When was that?'

'Right after I'd filled him in. Fancy another?'

CHAPTER 24

The next morning, while Krob was keeping Ricka supplied with pots of yoghurt and cans of a particularly lurid energy drink, Peiperová and Jerneková were sitting in their car in a parking space outside an opticians' shop on Ulice Josefa Skupy with Jiří in the back. Jerneková had suggested this site as the best way to get quick access to roads in any direction they needed.

'What's the time?' Jerneková asked.

'Time you got a watch,' Peiperová replied.

'I've got a watch. I just forgot to wear it.'

'It's twenty past nine. Going on past precedent he'll probably ring around half past nine. Jiří, are you sure you're okay about this?'

'Helping out? Sure.'

'All we need you to do is to look for the man in that photo you're holding. Don't take it in with you, by the way. Don't get involved, don't confront him, don't be brave. He may be armed. If he isn't, he may be with other people who are armed. Understood?'

'Yes, ma'am.'

'You don't have to call me ma'am. Kristýna will be fine.'

'Okay, Kristýna. I'm Jiří.'

'I know. But thanks for the introduction.'

Peiperová's misgivings about involving Jerneková's half-brother were not entirely allayed, but she had to admit that she knew what Jerneková meant about places where women didn't go. It was not so much that they would be thrown out, but they would draw attention to themselves just by being there, which was the last thing she wanted.

Most was a fairly grubby northern industrial town. Peiperová came from Kladno, which was no oil painting either, so she understood how the place functioned. It was a man's world. They worked hard at tiring, sweaty jobs, watched television at home during the week and at the weekends they had some beers with their mates. Wives were only invited on special occasions. A few women would go out without men, but there were not too many places where they could be really comfortable. It was changing, but not quickly enough for her liking. It was not that she wanted to go out in a short dress and drink herself stupid, but she didn't want to be looked down upon if she did.

'What did you do for entertainment growing up here?' she asked.

Jerneková thought for a moment. 'Movies when we could afford it, if there was anything worth watching. Sat around and talked. Went swimming in the summer. Sniffed a bit of glue.'

'No, you didn't,' came a scornful voice from the back.

'No, I didn't actually sniff it. I didn't like the smell. How about you?'

'Much the same,' said Peiperová. 'Played tennis in summer. But we lived on a little farm so I wasn't right in the town. Once I'd gone home after school I didn't usually go back to town. It was only really Saturdays. A bunch of us used to get together and walk round the town centre.'

'Ever do any shoplifting?'

'Certainly not!'

'Not you, obviously. But your mates?'

'Not that I ever saw. I'd have made them put it all back. Wouldn't you?'

'Yes. Except once when Tereza stole some condoms. Probably best all round if she held on to them. Bit of a slag, Tereza was.'

'Lucie!'

'No, she's right,' Jiří confirmed. 'Still known for it.'

'I hope you're keeping away. God knows what you could catch,' his big sister told him.

'Don't worry. I'm not stupid.'

Peiperová's phone rang. It was Krob.

'He's talking. Get ready. I'll relay as soon as we've got a fix.'

Peiperová started the engine.

'South of you,' Krob said. 'City centre somewhere.'

'Right turn then,' Jerneková instructed.

'We're narrowing down. It's somewhere along Višňová.'

'Okay, I know it,' Jerneková replied. 'After the bus stop you need to turn left, then we'll have the park on our left side. When we run out of park, turn right.'

'He's hung up,' Krob said. 'I hope you're close enough to surprise him. Can you keep me posted? Stay safe, both of you.'

'We will,' Peiperová assured him. She drove quickly but without attracting notice following the directions that Jerneková had given.

'There's a couple of sports bars around here if I remember correctly. That's where I'd start looking. The first one does breakfast so we could go in. It won't be odd at this time of day. If he isn't in there I'll spin a yarn about being vegan so we don't get trapped.'

'They might do vegan food,' Peiperová pointed out.

'This is Most,' said her partner. 'You're lucky if they bother to cook the meat.'

Slonský was reading the newspaper while he waited for his guest to turn up.

'Sorry to keep you,' said Kristoň. 'My clients can be very demanding.'

'No problem,' said Slonský. 'I like to read the papers now and then to find out what criminals have been doing. It saves having to read the crime reports. There's certainly a lot of crime around. I'm surprised the police don't do something about it.' He ordered two coffees. 'I need to get a message to your client and I don't want to be too formal about it. Cards on the table, I'm a cop and he's a thoroughgoing villain so we can't really meet up face to face, but in this case we have a certain common interest that means communication and some information sharing might be a good idea.'

'You wouldn't expect me to comment on your characterisation of my client, I'm sure,' Kristoň replied.

'Of course not. Your hands are tied. But you've spent too long in our business not to know a baddie when you see one. We don't need to get hung up on that,' Slonský said cheerfully. 'The thing is, I want to reduce crime. If I can prevent it I'd rather do that than solve it. And if I can talk someone into not committing a crime, I'm up for that.'

'I'm not quite clear what this has to do with me,' said Kristoň guardedly.

'You will,' said Slonský. 'Forgive me for putting my phone on the table. I'm expecting an important call any minute.'

Jerneková stuffed her hands in the pockets of her blouson jacket to look tough and then realised she couldn't open the door. Fortunately Jiří had a hand free. Peiperová had gone to check for any back doors that Chigulin could use to escape.

As was customary in Czech bars, the owners did not waste a lot of money on lighting, so it took a moment or two for their eyes to adjust to the gloom. Since Jiří had no idea what to do in these circumstances he behaved entirely naturally and picked up a laminated menu.

'Hey, sis, they do pancakes,' he remarked.

Hearing another voice in a very sparsely populated establishment, a man at the bar turned to look at them.

'Look at the menu,' hissed Jerneková.

'Isn't that the man you're after?' Jiří whispered.

'Yes, but we need to be sure that Peiperová is in place. I'll just text her. If the waiter comes, order your pancakes.'

Jerneková busied herself with her phone. A reply came back almost instantaneously, causing Jiří to puzzle again how women were able to type so quickly. Smaller fingers, he guessed.

The waiter appeared, and Jiří ordered blueberry pancakes and a coffee.

'What are you having, sis?'

'I'll just have a coffee, thanks.'

'Sure? You're not stealing my pancakes like you used to.'

'I've got to go to work,' she explained to the waiter. As he left she tucked a banknote under the menu holder. 'You stay here. That'll cover the bill. Use the change to get home. Good to see you, Jiří. We should do this more often.'

'That'd be good. Thanks for the breakfast.'

Jerneková hitched her bag on her shoulder and opened the zip, reaching inside to put her hand on her gun. Her heart was pounding into her ribs, but she thought through what was going to happen and she was confident she had everything covered.

Chigulin was watching the news when he realised she was standing beside him. She held up her ID. 'Police, Mr Chigulin. You're under arrest.'

Chigulin did not move.

'Please keep your hands where I can see them. I am armed and this is your warning. If you try to escape I will shoot.'

Chigulin slowly turned. Suddenly he threw his coffee at her and lurched off his stool, racing for the front door. Jerneková produced her gun and raised it to eye height, but as Chigulin ran down the aisle Jiří kicked her chair over and Chigulin tripped over it, sprawling full-length on the floor. It was an old-style chair, solidly built, and it drew blood on one of his shins. As he struggled to get to his feet, Jiří flopped on top of him, while Jerneková ran up and cuffed Chigulin's hands behind his back.

'Did I do good, sis?' asked Jiří.

'I was just going to shoot, you mad idiot! I could have killed you.'

'You wouldn't do that, would you?'

'Not deliberately. But I'm not that good a shot. Do me a favour. Go round the back and tell Peiperová she can come in.'

'Okay. Don't let them take my pancakes away.'

Slonský's phone rang. He listened intently, barked 'Good work!' and smiled at Kristoň. 'That call changes things.'

'Does it?'

'Oh, yes. We had some circumstantial evidence but now we'll have hard evidence. So let me tell you what I think is going on. I don't believe for one minute that Darmant is staying here for his daughter's funeral. Her body is evidence in a criminal case. It won't be released for burial until my boss or the prosecutor signs it off, and that won't happen in the next few days. Besides, he could come back anytime if he needs to.'

'No comment.'

'Shall I tell you what I think? I think Darmant is trying to find the person who killed his daughter before I do so that he can deal with him. I think he has known all along who it was likely to be. Yeremenko couldn't reach the man responsible so he did to his girlfriend what had been done to his own — a reciprocal copycat killing. And Darmant knows that but isn't handing Yeremenko over to justice.'

'Permit me to point out that you had Yeremenko in custody.'

'Indeed we did, but he had already committed the murder. Staying in custody suited him quite well because the longer we kept him the more the body would decay and the harder it would be to say definitively when she died. And because we can't prove precisely when he returned to Prague that would make it difficult to convict him. So let me ask you a simple question, and don't prevaricate or you'll regret it. Does the name Denis Polstrelov mean anything to you? Or do you know Stanislav Polášek?'

'Off the record?'

'So far off the record it couldn't find its way back.'

'The name Polstrelov has been mentioned a few times over the last few days in my hearing. I won't say who mentioned it.'

'Of course not. It would be utterly unprofessional.'

'I don't know Polášek but I've heard of him. Quite a rough character I believe, with interests in casinos and nightclubs.'

'Would it surprise you if I told you that they're the same person?'

The way that Kristoň jumped illustrated that it was definitely a surprise.

'I didn't know that.' Kristoň looked down at his hands as if avoiding eye contact. 'I got the impression — I may be wrong of course — that this man Polstrelov had at one time been a protégé of Mr Darmant, or at least an associate. He was, I believe, based in Belarus where Mr Darmant was seeking to expand his business interests.'

'The fallen angel. That explains a lot.'

'I beg your pardon?'

'Something my assistant Navrátil explained to me once. Lucifer was once a top angel but he fell out with his boss and set up on his own account. Something like that, anyway. Theology isn't really my thing.'

'I can tell,' Kristoň smiled wryly.

'So let me posit that discussions in your hearing may have reflected a belief that this man Polstrelov killed Yeremenko's girlfriend to put the frighteners on Yeremenko and his local network. A sort of hors d'oeuvre before flat-out warfare, if you like. He made Chigulin watch, so that Chigulin could tell people who did it. The next step would have been to wipe out Chigulin, only Yeremenko managed to whisk him away into hiding.'

'No comment.'

'Only Chigulin isn't in hiding any longer.'

Kristoň jumped once more.

'And I'm not such a fool as to keep him in a city centre police station where a bunch of armed goons can try to spring him or silence him. In fact, it would be a good idea if you kept that little snippet of information to yourself for a day or two. It shows how much I trust you, Daniel, that I'm telling you this. But I need hardly point out that if you say anything to Darmant or Yeremenko they may not believe that you don't know where Chigulin is being held and they may try to persuade you to spill the beans. Which would be a great shame because you really don't have any beans to spill, do you?'

Kristoň mopped his face with a large handkerchief. 'This is putting me in a very difficult position,' he protested.

'Not if you keep your mouth shut. That way you get to decide when you want to open it. Much better than opening it now and finding Yeremenko wants to keep it open with pliers, don't you think?'

Kristoň fumbled with his coffee cup. His hands were shaking. 'You said you wanted me to pass a message.'

'Yes. I want you to persuade Darmant to give me Yeremenko. He has to pay for what he did to Polstrelov's girlfriend, Ms Zechovská. He won't hang. We don't do that now. And life imprisonment won't be that bad. Polstrelov won't be able to get him there. As things stand, he faces a life in hiding from the fallen angel anyway. He might as well be in a cosy jail. Three meals a day and your heating paid for by the state. Plenty of exercise so long as you take little steps. It sounds quite tempting. I might go there myself.'

'I doubt Mr Darmant will acquiesce.'

'Don't put yourself down, Daniel. You can be very persuasive.'

Kristoň shook his head. 'This smacks of the police taking sides,' he grumbled. 'It would be much easier to sell to Mr Darmant if Polstrelov was behind bars.'

'He will be,' Slonský replied. 'Trust me, he will be.'

CHAPTER 25

Despite his claim, Slonský still had no idea where Polstrelov was, and not much more of an idea how to flush him out. Nevertheless, he had Chigulin, or would have once the two officers returned from Most with him. Peiperová had been able to borrow a policeman from there to act as a prisoner escort on the promise of sending him back on the train with a good lunch inside him so he would be back before the end of his shift. This allowed Jerneková to sit in the front and both women to relax a little, partly because their colleague was one of those old school types who believes that someone in handcuffs must have done something or he would not have been arrested, and therefore any misdemeanour warranted a slap or a tap on the kneecap with a baton. Each time Chigulin shifted his position his guard would yank on his seatbelt, tell him to sit still and reinforce the instruction with a rap on the knee. As a result Chigulin endured a fairly uncomfortable journey back to Prague.

As they drove Jerneková received a call from Krob, who had been detailed to divert them away from police headquarters.

'Take him to Pankrác, please. Captain Slonský and Lieutenant Navrátil will meet you there.'

Jerneková relayed the instruction. 'Do you know where Pankrác is?' she asked.

'Yes, I've been a few times. It's more secure than Ruzyně Prison.'

Jerneková had never been to Pankrác, but like most Czechs she knew its reputation. Many people had been executed there in the past, and conditions were alleged to be quite grim, even for prisoners on remand. Those who were serving a sentence had guaranteed exercise sessions and could take part in so-called enrichment activities, though what could enrich a prison sentence was not obvious to her; those on remand were only expected to be there a few weeks so they got no such perks. Since Chigulin was neither on remand nor convicted, taking him to Pankrác was quite unusual, but not entirely unprecedented. There was a high security courtroom there which was used for hearings where it would be dangerous to take the prisoner out of the building.

In popular culture, every criminal in the Czech Republic was believed to be in Pankrác, and it was the obvious place for Slonský to send Chigulin, so Slonský's plan was to extract all the information he could and then either let him take his chance outside or, as he suspected Chigulin might prefer, transfer him to a rather nicer prison somewhere in the deep countryside. The difficulty there was the right of certain people like lawyers to demand information about their clients' whereabouts. Slonský would not put it past Darmant to send a lawyer to represent Chigulin and insist on a face-to-face interview.

Navrátil had been posted at the entrance to Pankrác to direct Peiperová to the parking area where Slonský was waiting along with two prison guards.

Chigulin was bundled out of the car and pushed against a wall while Jerneková retrieved her handcuffs and the Pankrác guards applied their own ones. Meanwhile Slonský cautioned Chigulin.

'You have the right to remain silent, though I will be very disappointed in you if you do. You have the right to legal representation once I have determined that there is no terrorism offence here, which will probably take me a while. It may harm your defence if you rely on something in court that you didn't mention when being questioned. It will certainly harm your good looks. What have I forgotten, Navrátil?'

'You have to tell him what he is being charged with or questioned about.'

'Oh, yes. You're going to be questioned about the murder of Kateryna Teslenko for starters, and I may think of something else later. All done, lads?'

'Yes, sir,' chorused the guards.

'Jolly good. Get him into the interview room then, and try to see he doesn't fall down those treacherous stairs more than once.'

Krob was compiling the folder of evidence to go to the public prosecutor. There was no relevant Czech history for Yeremenko, but he painstakingly read through the folder sent from Kyiv. Krob did not speak Ukrainian but he had the benefit of a translation that had been hastily prepared.

He was looking for similar fact evidence; that is, anything in Yeremenko's past that bolstered the case that he could be guilty here because he had done the same before. As Slonský had explained it, if someone has been strangled with a dog lead then the fact that Mr X previously tried to strangle someone with a dog lead may be suggestive. He could find no evidence of attacks on women, which surprised him, but perhaps the women had been too frightened to report them.

However, he found something that puzzled him. He dug out the original section in the Ukrainian report and laboriously copied it out. He needed to go back to the translator and make absolutely sure the original text said what she had put in her report.

Chigulin was obstinately sticking to his story. At each point, as Navrátil and Slonský challenged him, he might give way to admit, very reluctantly, information that did not show him in a good light.

'Let's return to the start,' Navrátil suggested. 'Why did you go to Ms Teslenko's flat on that Saturday?'

'I'd promised Yeremenko I would check that his girlfriend was okay. He had planned to come home that day but he was going to be a day or two longer. He didn't want to wake her up to tell her that on the phone so he wanted me to pass on the message so he could be reassured that she knew there hadn't been an accident.'

'So what time did you get there?'

'A little bit after four o'clock.'

'Wouldn't she normally still be asleep then?'

'You could never tell. I hadn't planned to get there until half-past four but the traffic wasn't too bad, so I parked my car and sat and waited.'

'And then?'

'I got out of my car and I walked to the block of flats. As I went in through the street door my arm was grabbed by someone and I felt a gun barrel in my back.'

'That was Polstrelov?'

'I didn't know that at the time, but, yes, I recognised him later.'

'When had you met him before?' snapped Slonský.

'Pardon?'

'How did you know this was Polstrelov? You must have met him before to know who he was. So where? When?'

'I don't know.'

'I mean, he's not going to get an invitation to any social events run by your gang, is he? He wouldn't go if you invited him. I'm just curious to know how your paths have crossed.'

'I don't think I'd met him. I think Yeremenko must have shown me a photo of him.'

'Ah, that would explain it,' Slonský agreed. 'Carry on, Lieutenant.'

Navrátil had learned by now to make a note of his train of thought when Slonský launched into an interruption. It could be some minutes before they were back on track. 'So Polstrelov grabbed your arm and threatened you. What next?'

'He said he'd heard that I was keeping an eye on Kateryna. He asked if that was all I was doing with her.'

'Implying that there was some sort of relationship going on behind Yeremenko's back?'

'Yes. But I would never do that! Oleg is my friend. He's been good to me. He's been keeping me safe now.'

'And here was I thinking he was a complete thug all along,' Slonský interrupted again, 'when he's been looking after a mate. We could all do with friends like that.'

'Yes, we could,' insisted Chigulin vehemently. 'I'm very lucky.'

'Not so lucky where Polstrelov is concerned though. Sorry, Navrátil, I interrupted.'

Navrátil held his tongue and took a breath before continuing. 'Polstrelov makes his suggestion. Did you deny it?'

'Too damn right I did! If I'd laid a finger on Kateryna, Yeremenko would have beaten the crap out of me, friend or no friend.'

'And her?' asked Slonský.

'Eh?'

'Well, it takes two. I'm asking if he'd have thumped her too.'

'I don't know. I suppose. But he loved her, so maybe not. Maybe he'd have given her the benefit of the doubt and assumed I'd forced her.'

'You see,' said Slonský, 'I'm just trying to get my head around how much you have to hate women to be able to do what Yeremenko did to Zechovská. I know you're loyal to your friend but you're painting a picture of a kindly man who helps old ladies across the road and always has treats in his pocket in case he meets a kitten.'

Chigulin spread his arms in a gesture of confusion. 'I can't tell you any different,' he said. 'Okay, we're not angels. But I won't say a word against Yeremenko. The way he treats other people isn't my concern. He's always been good to me.'

'Let's return to that moment after you denied any relationship with Ms Teslenko,' Navrátil said, a little more forcefully than usual. 'What happened then?'

'Polstrelov said he'd like to meet her. He told me to knock on the door and not to try any funny business because he'd be out of sight with his gun pointed at my head. The least hint to her that he was there and he'd decorate the wall with my brains.'

'And you believed him?' Slonský said.

'I always believe a threat,' Chigulin replied. 'In the circles I move in, people don't issue idle threats.'

'Very wise,' Slonský agreed. 'People like Polstrelov usually go through with their threats.'

'So you knocked on the door?' Navrátil asked.

'Yes. Kateryna had a spy hole in the door so she could see who was there. After a moment I heard a chain being unhooked and she opened the door.'

'What was she wearing?' Slonský demanded.

'What? Am I a fashion correspondent?'

'T-shirt and jeans? Dressing gown? Nothing at all?'

'T-shirt and leggings, I think. Her hair was wet so I guessed she'd had a shower.'

'And then?' persisted Navrátil.

'Polstrelov barged in. He pushed me in front of him and pointed the gun at us both.'

'He can't point one gun at two people,' Slonský pointed out.

'It felt like it to me!' Chigulin shouted. 'He'd wave it a bit, first at one then the other. And it was a narrow hallway. We were almost in line anyway. In fact, I think Kateryna tried to hide behind me.'

'Does the bathroom have a lock?' Slonský asked.

'I don't know. I suppose so. Don't they all?'

'I just wonder why Ms Teslenko didn't go back in the bathroom and lock the door.'

'You'll have to ask her that. Oh, no, you can't. She's dead. How the hell would I know why she didn't do that? And would it have made a difference? Those doors aren't exactly steel, you know.'

'Let's just get the sequence of events fixed once and for all,' suggested Navrátil. 'Polstrelov forced entry and threatened you both. What then?'

'He ordered us into the bedroom. He told Kateryna to sit on the bed with her hands on her head and not to move or make a noise. Then he told me to kneel by the radiator. When I did that, he tied my left wrist to the radiator with a cable tie and then he tied my wrists together with another one.' Chigulin held out his arm to display a cut on his wrist.

'It was obviously very tight,' said Slonský. 'He could have hurt you if he wasn't careful.'

'It did hurt,' Chigulin answered. 'It hurt like hell. And I couldn't get my legs out from beneath me because I couldn't raise my upper body enough. I got cramp in my legs.'

Slonský ostentatiously wrote on a piece of paper in front of him, reciting as he wrote. 'So that's murder, grievous bodily harm, and causing cramp in a witness's legs. I've amended the charge sheet.'

'You're not taking this seriously,' Chigulin protested.

Slonský's arm darted across the table and grabbed Chigulin's sweater. 'Believe me, I take murder very seriously. I'm just testing your evidence like the defence lawyer will. And I'm a teddy bear compared to them.'

Navrátil stood up. 'Shall we have a five-minute break? I'll get some coffee for us all. Captain, could we have a word outside?'

The translator confirmed what she had written, so now Krob was telephoning Dr Novák. The pathologist was unavailable, so Krob left a message on his answering machine, put his pencil down, and tried to make some sense of what he had heard. He had the strong feeling that it was significant, but he was not sure exactly what difference it made.

'Ready to resume?' asked Navrátil, remaining remarkably chirpy and patient in the face of some provocation.

Slonský leaned back in his chair and smiled as if the police allowed village idiots to sit in on interrogations now and again. 'Just to let you know,' he said to Chigulin, 'that I won't be saying very much for a while.'

'When we broke off,' Navrátil prompted, 'you were tied to the radiator and Ms Teslenko was sitting on the bed with her hands on her head.'

'Yes. He told her to strip and lie on the bed.'

'Did —' began Slonský, but stopped when Navrátil glared at him.

'Then what?'

'He put a piece of duct tape round her head and over her mouth.'

'Where did he get it from?' Slonský interrupted.

'His pocket, I suppose.'

'Only a roll of duct tape won't fit in a pocket.'

'He was still wearing his coat.'

'Ah, so he got it from his coat pocket. That's clearer.' Slonský wrote, 'Coat … pocket…' reciting as he did so.

'And then?' Navrátil prompted.

'He used another couple of cable ties to secure her wrists to the bedstead. He tried to do the same with her feet but the ties weren't long enough to reach to the end of the bed, so he forced her legs wide apart and strapped them to the sides instead.' Chigulin's mouth was dry. He looked in his cup but it was empty. 'Then he left the room and came back with a large knife from the kitchen. He knelt on the bed and rammed it into her stomach and began to cut.'

'I don't think we need to go through that whole process in detail,' said Navrátil.

'Don't we?' asked Slonský.

'Not for now.'

'Fine — it's your case.'

'We know what happened after that,' Navrátil said to Chigulin. 'Do you have any idea when she died?'

'I'd say almost immediately,' Chigulin responded. 'There was a lot of blood at first, but then it stopped pumping.'

'Why wasn't Polstrelov coated in blood?' Slonský asked.

'He took his coat and shirt off. I tried not to look but he told me he'd shoot me if I didn't watch.'

'So Ms Teslenko died in front of you. What then?' asked Navrátil.

'That was the worst bit. He cut her head off. I thought he was going to put it in my lap but he put it on the windowsill beside me.'

'And then?'

'He went for a wash. When he came back he said that he wanted Yeremenko to know that what he had done to his girl he could do to him too. I wasn't going to be killed because he wanted me to tell Yeremenko exactly what I'd seen. I had to do it as soon as he was gone. He said he'd untie me and we'd walk to the door and leave quietly. I was to stay in the hallway for ten minutes and make the call from there. If I tried to leave before that he'd be waiting outside in his car to shoot me. After ten minutes he would drive off.'

'And did he?' asked Slonský.

'I didn't see him when I got outside.'

'But you looked?'

'Too damn right I did.'

Navrátil closed his notebook but Slonský had one more question.

'He poured a lot of the blood around the flat. How did he collect it and when did he do that?'

'He fetched a bowl from the kitchen after the first cut. He poured some of the blood around as we were leaving.'

'Thank you,' said Slonský. 'No further questions.' He turned to Navrátil. 'Shall we get a bite to eat?'

Dr Novák had called Krob back and the two men had a conversation which perturbed Novák as much as it had Krob. The pathologist undertook to check his notes.

'You realise I won't be able to answer your question with one hundred per cent certainty? All my opinions are probabilities with a greater or lesser degree of conviction,' Novák said.

'I know that, doctor. It just strikes me as incongruous.'

'It's certainly odd, I'll grant that,' Novák replied. 'On the face of it, it can't be that way but let me be as definite as I can be.'

Slonský was disgusted. 'No wonder we have prison riots,' he said. 'Look at this food.'

'This is the staff canteen,' Navrátil pointed out. 'The prisoners don't eat here.'

'Just as well if this is what they'd get. What have you got there?'

'A mushroom omelette.'

'See? No meat. And people wonder why they set fire to their cells.'

'Prisoners might. Prison officers don't.'

'I'm not surprised. They wouldn't have the strength if they're living on this muck. I've half a mind to send for a takeaway.'

'I don't think they allow those firms to deliver in prisons. Anyway, we'll be done in an hour or so and then you can eat to your heart's content.'

'I think I saw a restaurant across the street,' mused Slonský. 'Any port in a storm.'

Slonský's mobile phone made an odd squeaking sound. 'Is this thing on the blink now?'

'It's a text.'

'A what?'

'A text message. Haven't you ever seen a text message?'

'Yes, but only when someone has opened it for me.'

Navrátil wiped his hands and pressed a couple of buttons before handing the phone to Slonský.

'Now people are writing piffle to me. Who sent this?'

'Dr Novák. It says so there, at the top.'

'Can you make sense of this message?'

'I can read what it says,' Navrátil replied. 'He wants us to ask Chigulin to draw on a plan exactly where Polstrelov was when he first stabbed his victim. Why he wants us to ask it, I couldn't begin to guess.'

'It's all those letters after his name. Too much education has turned his brain. But if that's what he wants, that's what we'll do. Straight after we've finished this.'

CHAPTER 26

Chigulin was puzzled by the request but complied. Navrátil took the drawings away and sent them to Dr Novák by some means that Slonský did not really understand. To his mind, phones were for making phone calls. The clue is in the name. He did not understand why you needed a phone that was also a camera or a fax machine. Now, if they had invented a phone that could cook waffles or warm a croissant, he would have invested in one of those.

'In America,' Navrátil had assured him, 'you can order a coffee by phone and pay for it by phone as well.'

'Really?' Slonský replied. 'Can you drink it by phone too?'

'Let's move on to what happened after you phoned Yeremenko,' Navrátil said to Chigulin.

'He told me to throw my phone away so I couldn't be traced, and drive to Teplice where he was. He said now that I'd passed on Polstrelov's message I was dead meat. I was to make sure I wasn't followed and to meet him by the railway station in Teplice,' Chigulin replied.

'And then?'

'He took me to a hotel and booked me in. He asked me to tell him what happened exactly, like I just told you, then he told me to get some sleep and he'd take care of things. He had one or two things to do but then he'd sort Polstrelov out. But I didn't know what he was going to do, I swear.'

'Let's move on to the day he killed Zechovská. Run us through that.'

'He asked me to go through it all in detail with him so I did. He said he was going to do to Zechovská exactly what

Polstrelov had done to Kateryna. Killing Polstrelov was too good for him, he said. The only snag was that he didn't know where she was living because she'd left her flat.'

'Hang on,' said Slonský. 'He'd already tried to grab her in the park but she got away.'

Chigulin looked shocked. 'I hadn't heard about that,' he said.

'So when did he take you to Most?' asked Navrátil.

'The day after I got to Teplice. He said the place was crawling with people who knew Polstrelov, and he didn't trust them not to tell. It was safer if I left the car there, because they'd be looking for that, and he'd drive me to Most and find me somewhere to stay till it all blew over.'

'So after his failed attempt to snatch Zechovská, what did he do then?'

'I don't know. I was in Most and he spent most of his time in Teplice. We talked a couple of times a day on the phone but I don't know what he was doing.'

'And yet Polstrelov turned up in Teplice. We know he used his bank card there. What made him go there?'

'I don't know for sure,' Chigulin replied, 'but Yeremenko said he was going to lure Polstrelov to Teplice so that he wouldn't be around Prague to protect Zechovská.'

'How did he know his phone number?' Slonský interrupted.

'There's always someone who can tell you. Polstrelov had been flashing business cards round the casinos trying to get them to join his mob. I guess Yeremenko got hold of one of them.'

'So he sent a message saying something like "Come to Teplice and we'll sort this out once and for all"?' Slonský suggested.

'Something like that, I guess.'

'And do you know how he found out Zechovská's hidey-hole?'

'No idea,' said Chigulin.

Someone had an idea, though. Peiperová had been thinking about that very question and an idea had come to her which she tested by going through the call logs for the emergency services. In the early hours of the day when Polstrelov's bank card was used in Teplice, there had been a fire at one of his casinos in Prague. The casino had closed at 4 a.m. and the fire had been detected at around 4.40. It was the opinion of the fire officers who attended that it had been a botched arson attempt. But what if the purpose was not to burn the place down, but to cause the owner to come to see how bad the damage was and then to follow him when he went back home?

Having done that, Yeremenko would want to complete his task before Polstrelov had the chance to move his girlfriend to some other safe house. If Polstrelov went to Teplice and found Yeremenko wasn't there, surely he would turn round and race back to Prague? Even if he kept to the speed limit he could drive from Teplice to Bubeneč in around an hour. The timing was really tight. The bank card had been used at 11:37. Assuming that it was either the first thing Polstrelov did when he arrived in Teplice, or the last thing he did when he left, he had either left Prague around 10:30 or returned by around 12:40. There must have been some risk that Polstrelov would return while Yeremenko was at his grisly work, but maybe Yeremenko didn't care? Perhaps he just wanted revenge; but he would not want Polstrelov to miss seeing what he did to Zechovská.

Peiperová badly wanted to talk her ideas over with Navrátil, but she knew he would be in Pankrác most of the day. It would have to wait until she saw him.

Slonský could not quite pinpoint the moment at which it occurred to him that his knee was not hurting any more. Was it the excitement of the case, or the deft surgery of Dr Stockner? Either way, it seemed to have done the trick, and he could not resist doing a little jig on the stairs just to test the feeling. It twinged very slightly, but nothing like as painfully as had previously been the case.

After six hours of questioning they were obliged to allow Chigulin a meal break, much to Slonský's disgust, so he and Navrátil had gone outside for some fresh air, a luxury denied to their prisoner, though the air around Pankrác was certainly not the freshest in Prague.

'What do you think, sir?' Navrátil asked.

'You're doing fine. Just keep pegging away at him and he'll give us what we need sometime.'

'We can use his eyewitness testimony to get a straightforward conviction for Polstrelov's killing of Teslenko, but by his own admission he wasn't there when Yeremenko killed Zechovská. Yeremenko left him in Teplice while he went to Prague to do the deed. Still, he gave Chigulin clear evidence of his intentions.'

'Yes, he did. He told him what he was going to do and how he was going to do it. We've got clear motive, and we've got a definite opportunity to do it when he lured Polstrelov to Teplice to leave his girlfriend undefended.'

'That leaves me uneasy,' Navrátil confessed. 'Why didn't Polstrelov get some of his men to guard her?'

'Maybe he didn't trust any of them with her. That's not unusual amongst gangsters with good-looking women. They reckon everyone must want to get with them.'

Slonský chuckled at a memory. 'There was a black marketeer back when I started out who tried to castrate one of his colleagues in the middle of a restaurant on Old Town Square for hankering after his girlfriend. We had to pin him to the floor and bang his arm on the tiles to get him to drop the razor. And she was as ugly as sin.'

'He obviously thought she was beautiful.'

'Maybe. Or maybe he just thought that her being the daughter of a Politburo member improved her looks. Anyway, we brought him here to Pankrác and about an hour later we got the instruction to take him home and say nothing about it. As if a restaurant full of diners weren't going to mention what they'd seen sometime. Though I suppose,' Slonský added pensively, 'anyone who could get a table there in those days was probably in with the Politburo themselves. Ah, happy days.'

'There's another problem,' Navrátil insisted. 'Why did Zechovská let Polstrelov in?'

'It's not something we can say in court,' Slonský replied, 'but I wouldn't make a big thing of that. I opened that front door with my little lock pick. It wasn't hard. If it had been, I'm pretty sure Yeremenko would just have smashed a window at the back and climbed in. The alarm wouldn't be on with her in the house, and one of the things about these folks with money is that they don't like being overlooked, so nobody would be able to see.'

'Right,' said Navrátil. 'One last burst, then I'll go back to the office to type it up and we'll get him to sign the statement tomorrow. Then all we've got to do is to find Yeremenko and Polstrelov.'

'Yeremenko won't be a problem. Hauzer is keeping an eye on him.'

'I thought Hauzer was watching Darmant?'

'He was. But when it became clear that Darmant was going to keep Kristoň with him we didn't need Hauzer there too, because I can get a report from Kristoň with a bit of pressure, so I switched him to watching Yeremenko. Not that it makes much difference, because the two of them have stayed in the hotel for days. Didn't I tell you?'

'No,' said Navrátil, 'you didn't. And it is my case.'

'It certainly is. And I certainly should have done. Put it down to the effects of the pain from my knee.'

'You don't seem to have much pain from your knee now.'

'I don't. But I did then. You know, lad, when we haul in Polstrelov I'm pretty sure I'll be able to give him a good kicking with no pain at all. If necessary, which we all hope it won't be, of course.'

After all that had gone before, Navrátil was a bit surprised when Chigulin said he would not sign a statement of any kind.

'I'm not stupid,' he said. 'As soon as those two see my signature on a statement I'll be on my way to the bottom of the Vltava with a concrete swimsuit.'

'But they'll be behind bars,' Navrátil argued.

'They've got plenty of people who'll do it for them.'

'We could give you witness protection.'

'Sorry, but I don't want to spend my life worrying that I might bump into someone I don't want to meet. The Czech Republic is a small place in the greater scheme of things.'

'We could send you back to Ukraine,' Slonský suggested.

'Where Darmant lives? He's got a third of the police force in his pocket.'

'Stop being difficult,' Slonský told him. 'There's bound to be somewhere. Australia maybe. Or you could loll around the Mediterranean on a yacht.'

'No,' said Chigulin. 'N-O. With a capital N. I'm not signing anything.'

'That's really disappointing,' Navrátil replied, 'after we've invested so much time in taking your statement.'

'We've got it on tape though, haven't we?' said Slonský.

'Yes.'

'Fine. Type it up anyway and I'll nip along the corridor here and get Felix Frolík to sign it for him.'

'Who's Felix Frolík?' asked Navrátil.

'One of the Czech Republic's finest forgers. He'll whip up a signature for Chigulin in no time. We'll lift it off some other document.'

'If this Frolík character is such a good forger, what's he doing in jail?' Chigulin wanted to know.

'He's a great forger, but unfortunately he's dyslexic. Didn't quite get the words right on a passport.'

'A dyslexic forger? You're having a laugh.'

'I hope you're not displaying a prejudice against someone with a disability? That might well be an offence.'

Navrátil held the door open and gestured to Slonský that he wanted to speak to him outside.

'Yes, Navrátil. What is it?'

'We cannot forge a signature on a witness statement, sir.'

'Of course we can't. There was a time, though…'

'Well, if we can't, why did you say it?'

'Because you know we can't do that, and I know we can't do that, but maybe Chigulin doesn't know that. Maybe where he comes from that's just what the police would do. Small advantages, lad; little things that might tip the balance our way.'

Navrátil sighed. 'We'll get finished and I'll type it up tonight. Maybe he'll have changed his mind after a night in here.'

'A word to the wise, my boy. Go home. You can type it up in the morning. Go home and put your feet up with one of those furniture catalogues you keep getting and a nice big glass of sparkling water. The statement will keep till the morning. Let him stew. We won't see him tomorrow just to rub it in. Give him forty-eight hours to think and sweat. After he's had a couple more prison meals the idea of a new life in a cave in the Balkans may appeal a lot more. It certainly would to me.'

The last session was a damp squib. Chigulin refused to say anything at all while the tape was running. Slonský disappeared for a few minutes to make a call, and an hour later one of the warders handed in a piece of paper.

'Ah, excellent. Thank you,' said Slonský. 'A kindly person at the Ministry of the Interior has certified that you may have links to an unfriendly government so we can hold you for up to five days without charge.' He passed the paper to Navrátil who read it carefully.

'What evidence was this based on?' he whispered.

'My word. What else do you need?'

'Sir, the Criminal Code distinctly says…'

'Oh, we all know you've got a law degree, Navrátil! Stop thinking like a lawyer and think like a policeman.' Slonský pushed his chair back and stood up. 'Well, that's me done for the night. I'm off for a nice cold beer. Anyone want to join me? Oh, sorry, Chigulin, you can't, can you? Never mind, enjoy your night in. It'll be the first of many. You may as well go too, Navrátil, unless you're going to summon another officer to sit in, because you can't interview a witness on your own.'

So saying, Slonský swept out of the door. 'Come along, lad,' he shouted from the corridor. 'You don't want to be locked in here. It's full of violent criminals.'

CHAPTER 27

Morning came. Slonský polished his shoes before work, chose one from his collection of ties (which ran to two), and strode off to work with a purposeful stride and a glint in his eye. Great things were going to happen today.

There was no time to waste, so he did not detour to the canteen to fetch a coffee on the way to his desk. He could always send Krob later. It would have to be later, because Krob was not at his desk. A pencilled note stuck to Slonský's blotter told him that Krob would be in as soon as he could, but he was going to meet Dr Novák as soon as the pathology department opened. It also told him what Krob and Novák were going to discuss.

'Well, that requires a bit of a think,' Slonský said to himself, and sat down to do just that.

Navrátil and Peiperová walked in. Both looked immaculate. Navrátil's hair was parted with a perfectly straight line and Peiperová had pinned hers in a bun from which no blonde hairs had escaped. Both had shirts so white they might have belonged to angels.

'Good morning,' said Slonský. 'Beautiful day.'

'It's bucketing down out there,' Peiperová answered.

'Yes, I wasn't giving a weather report. I was talking about this being the day we wrap up this whole ghastly business.'

'You think so?' said Navrátil.

'Well, it might take till tomorrow,' Slonský conceded. 'But we're on the march.'

'Seeing as it's my case,' said Navrátil with just a touch of asperity, 'would you like to explain it all to me?'

'You've heard it all,' said Slonský. 'What puzzles you?'

'Let's start with where Polstrelov is. Then there's how we're going to arrest Yeremenko quietly when he's in the hotel suite of a top foreign gangster? And finally how are we going to prove it was Yeremenko who killed Zechovská given we only have one highly suspect hearsay witness?'

Slonský looked at Navrátil quizzically. 'Sometimes, lad, you can be very negative. Why don't you go and get us all some coffee while I make a couple of phone calls, and then I'll explain it all to you once the others are here to chip in.'

'Are you sitting comfortably?' asked Slonský. 'Then I'll begin.'

'I'm not,' said Jerneková. 'I could do with a new chair.'

'Then indent for one after I've finished my particularly brilliant series of deductions and if you're very good then maybe Baby Jesus will bring you one on Christmas Eve.'

'That's me stuffed, then. Baby Jesus hasn't visited me for years.'

'Before you start, sir,' Peiperová interjected, 'I think I ought to tell you what I discovered yesterday, because it may have a bearing on your conclusions.'

'Of course. Let's hear it.'

'I was puzzled about how Yeremenko managed to find Zechovská. After all, we hadn't. You'll recall he tried to grab Zechovská in the park, but after that her boyfriend took her into hiding in his own place.'

'Yeremenko had an advantage over us there, though. He knew the identity of her boyfriend. If we'd known that you might have found her. Don't beat yourself up about it,' Slonský told her.

'It's clear from the pathology,' Peiperová doggedly continued, 'that Zechovská was killed some days after the attempted abduction, during the time when Yeremenko was in Teplice. I looked at the emergency call-out log and discovered that somebody started a fire at one of Polstrelov's casinos early on the morning we believe her to have been killed. I think Yeremenko started the fire, then followed Polstrelov home after he came to view the damage. Yeremenko then telephoned Polstrelov and somehow persuaded him to come to Teplice; but actually Yeremenko wasn't in Teplice. He was in Prague, and as soon as he saw Polstrelov leave he broke into his house and committed that awful murder.'

Slonský rubbed his chin in thought. 'Well done, lass. You make a good case there.'

'You agree with my line of thought, sir?'

'Certainly. One or two little details I might quibble about, but we'll come to those in a moment.'

Krob raised his hand.

'Not now, lad. I want to call you in at the right moment in the narrative.'

Krob nodded his acceptance.

'This is quite exciting,' Jerneková announced, taking a scoop of yoghurt on the end of a pickle. 'It's like one of those Agatha Christie stories where they all sit round waiting for Miss Poirot to tell them whodunnit. Except in them the murderer is in the room.'

Slonský sighed. 'There's no suspense here, lass. I may as well say now I agree with everything Peiperová just said except one little thing.'

'What's that, sir?' asked Peiperová.

'The one who did all that. You see, we don't need to track down Polstrelov, because he had nothing to do with it. We've got the murderer under lock and key. It was Chigulin.'

His words were greeted with a very gratifying buzz of consternation.

'How do you make that out, sir?' Navrátil asked.

'Chigulin can give us a very good eyewitness description because he did it. I don't think he masterminded it all from the beginning. His plans changed as he saw a way to grab himself a piece of the action — ideally, a very big piece if he could get the two big bosses locked up.'

Navratil took his notebook out. He obviously planned to probe this account for weak points.

'You saw the scene of the first murder and I didn't,' said Slonský, 'but when I looked at the photographs one thing jumped out at me. Teslenko's clothes on the chair.'

Navrátil said nothing as if he had nothing to say on their significance.

'Suppose someone breaks into your flat with a gun and orders you to undress. What do you do with your clothes?'

'Who the hell cares?' Jerneková replied. 'If I can't fight him off and I think he means it when he says he'll shoot me, I'd get them off as fast as I could.'

'Exactly. And you wouldn't fold them nicely. But when we questioned Chigulin about it he said that she was dressed when they arrived and was ordered to strip by Polstrelov. If Chigulin's story was true I can't imagine Polstrelov allowing her the time to fold her things neatly and put them on the chair. I think she was pretty well naked when he arrived, and whether he was a friend of her boyfriend's or not, she's not going to let him in. She might talk through the door but she'd dress before opening that door. I think Chigulin arrived earlier than he said, knowing that she would be asleep, and that somehow he'd got hold of a key — although, truth to tell, the locks on those *paneláky* don't take a lot of picking. And the chain wasn't on because he told her Yeremenko was coming home as originally planned.'

'But why would he do that to her?' Peiperová enquired.

'He's trying to behave like he thinks Polstrelov would behave because he wants to give the impression that Polstrelov did it. Yeremenko and Polstrelov are rivals. They don't spend time together. All Yeremenko knows is Polstrelov's reputation. So Chigulin tells Yeremenko what he would expect to hear — that Polstrelov is a sadist. I wouldn't mind betting that Chigulin has been egging Yeremenko on to deal with Polstrelov for a while and Yeremenko wouldn't. But he won't ignore this insult.'

'Surely Polstrelov's going to deny it. He may even have an alibi,' Krob suggested.

'Do you think Yeremenko is going to give Polstrelov a chance to say anything? You don't get to say much after a bullet to the back of the head. And anyway Yeremenko trusts Chigulin and he doesn't trust Polstrelov.'

'Where does Darmant fit into this?' Navrátil wanted to know.

'I don't know whether Chigulin knew that Teslenko was Darmant's daughter, but does it matter? If Yeremenko is convinced, then he'll convince Darmant. If anything, Darmant's presence makes it more likely that serious action will be taken against Polstrelov. Even if Yeremenko doesn't think he can take on Polstrelov, Darmant can bring a lot more steel. He isn't a man to take a backward step.'

'But do they really want a gang war?'

'No, but if it starts they'll want it to finish. Darmant must have a lot more behind him than Polstrelov and he can bring it all to bear for a while. But he can't risk Polstrelov hitting back when he withdraws his extra men, so he has to wipe him out.

Yeremenko was happy with the status quo. Presumably Darmant was too. Chigulin wasn't. Simple as that.'

'What about the blood by the radiator and the cable tie marks?' Krob asked.

'Chigulin's story needs some backup, and we're the patsies. We're going to find the blood that proves his account. You've got to admire his nerve — relying on the police to prove you right is a bit cheeky. He needs to make sure no other blood hits that bit of floor, then he scrapes his wrist to draw some blood. I'll be surprised if Novák tells us the cable tie marks are old enough to be contemporaneous with the crime. But we'll see.'

'Why does he mutilate her so horribly?' Peiperová wanted to know. 'He must have known her personally. How can you do that to someone you know?'

'Because it's the brutality, the horror of it, that will make Yeremenko mad.'

'There could be another answer,' mused Jerneková. 'Suppose he knew her too well. Suppose he's been playing with the boss's girl and she's pregnant. And suppose Yeremenko knows it can't be his baby. That's a good reason to remove the womb.'

Slonský considered this for a little while. 'You might be right. There are a lot of "supposes" in there. But it's worth asking Chigulin when we charge him. Now, Chigulin rings Yeremenko and tells him the cock and bull story he told us. Look at it from Yeremenko's point of view; he's going to be upset and he's going to want to hurt Polstrelov in return. But he's got to look after his mate. If Chigulin's story was true, he'd be at immediate risk. As soon as he's served his purpose by telling Yeremenko what has happened, Polstrelov would want to make sure Chigulin couldn't tell his story to us. So it makes perfect sense to tell Chigulin to get out of Prague and destroy all methods of tracing him. You see, Chigulin's story is very clever. There are bits we can check, and they'll ring true. There's a temptation to believe that because A, C and E are true, B and D must be too.'

'So it's all been pre-planned?' asked Navrátil.

'Up to this point. Or, more accurately, up to the point when Yeremenko tries to snatch Zechovská and fails. She's going to tell her boyfriend, and Polstrelov tells her to leave her own place and stay at his for a while until he can find out who is behind the attempt. But Polstrelov has no reason to think that Yeremenko is the culprit. Now, remember that Chigulin is in Teplice or Most. It doesn't really matter which. The point is that he isn't in Prague, so he doesn't know that Yeremenko has tried to abduct Zechovská. That was quite clear from his reaction yesterday when we mentioned it during the questioning. So far as Chigulin knows, Yeremenko hasn't taken revenge yet. If he doesn't Chigulin's masterplan goes off at half-cock; he needs Yeremenko to start that battle with Polstrelov. So if Yeremenko won't start a gang war, the other alternative is to get Polstrelov to do it.'

'Why didn't Yeremenko do anything else about the horrific killing of his girlfriend?' Jerneková wanted to know.

'Because he knows what will happen if he starts a fight with Polstrelov. There's an awful lot at stake, and much of what is at stake belongs to Darmant — who, of course, has his own reason for revenge. I'm guessing that when Yeremenko told Darmant what had happened Darmant told him to do nothing until he got there — and of course we've been watching them since they arrived so even if they had wanted to do something they'd have found it difficult. But we weren't watching Chigulin, because we had no idea where he had gone. Note that Yeremenko willingly handed over Chigulin's phone number.'

'Of course he did. He'd told Chigulin to throw it away,' said Navrátil.

'Yes, but we could still get information from the phone records. It would have been very easy for Yeremenko to tell us he didn't have the number but he didn't think it was of any importance. He'd swallowed Chigulin's story as the truth, just as we did at first.'

'But you didn't,' Peiperová observed.

'Not entirely. I didn't have a better idea then so my first thought was that Chigulin had misremembered things and that Yeremenko was the real villain here. We knew he had a criminal record back in Ukraine for violent offences, as did Polstrelov in Belarus, but we didn't know that about Chigulin. Until I asked, that is.'

'And you didn't tell me?' said Navrátil.

'I'm telling you now, aren't I? Chigulin doesn't exist. It's another pseudonym. We'll send Kyiv a photo and some fingerprints and see if they know who he really is. But it seems likely to me that if he left Ukraine in a hurry to come here under an assumed name, the chances are that he's a very naughty boy. Anyway, Chigulin needs to keep the ball rolling once he's set it in motion, so he decides to do the same to Zechovská as he did to Teslenko. Presumably he and Yeremenko have been talking about her when Chigulin was trying to spur him into retaliation, so he knows the name, but he doesn't know where she is. That, Peiperová, is where your brilliant deduction regarding the fire at the casino comes in. He followed Polstrelov exactly as you said, only it was Chigulin instead of Yeremenko. Chigulin is in Most by now, and Yeremenko is in Teplice. Chigulin doesn't have a car, but he can hire one in Most, or he can catch the train to Teplice — it's less than half an hour away — and pick up his own car. Needless to say, the idiots we pay to be police up North haven't been watching his car, thinking that our interest in it ended when he got there and they found it. How long the nincompoops would have left it before they realised that he was never going to pay for his parking and towed it away is anyone's guess.'

'That's why I left Most,' Jerneková claimed. 'I don't fit in there.'

'Anyway, if you compare these two pictures, you'll see that even though the car is in the same car park, it's at a slight angle to the white line in the second picture, whereas it was beautifully parked in the first. There's also streaky marks on the windscreen because he has used the wipers on the way back from Prague. Incidentally, our colleagues at Teplice have managed to find an image of the car being driven out at 01:05 that morning and it's back about eleven hours later.'

'During which time Chigulin drove to Prague, found the house, diverted Polstrelov away, killed Zechovská and drove back,' Navrátil recited.

'Yes. Remember that Polstrelov has no particular reason to hate Yeremenko, and Yeremenko doesn't know what is being done in his name. I'm going to guess that Chigulin phoned and suggested meeting up to carve up the Teplice business between the two gangs. He'd suggest a public meeting place so Polstrelov would be assured of his safety. And he'd stress the urgency — come today or the deal's off. So Chigulin sits round the corner and watches Polstrelov drive off. Even if he gets there, waits ten minutes and drives back he'll be gone for at least two hours. Of course there's a steel gate, but Chigulin climbs the fence. The door is less of a problem for him than it was for me — he's a hardened criminal and I'm a mere amateur — so he lets himself in and then does exactly the same thing again.'

'Just a moment,' Peiperová interrupted. 'If he does it again why does Dr Novák think they're two killers?'

'Bright girl!' said Slonský approvingly, then, remembering the list of things you weren't supposed to say these days he added lamely, 'if you don't mind being called a girl.'

'Take it,' said Jerneková to her lieutenant. 'I would.'

'You're absolutely right,' Slonský continued. 'Chigulin has to give the impression that they are two different people doing the killing, so he makes slight changes. He's more hesitant with the knife cut, he doesn't put the head facing the right way, but because of the story we've been spun we think that's logical because Yeremenko didn't see the first crime scene. He's working from a description he has been given, and some of the details weren't in there. Chigulin would mention the head on the windowsill, but might omit that she was facing into the room. But there's one key fact that Chigulin has overlooked. Krob, this is your big moment. Milk it for all it's worth, lad.'

Krob gave a wry smile. 'Yeremenko is left-handed. I found out yesterday from an old crime report in Ukraine. He was identified as the assailant in a knife crime precisely because he was left-handed, though he had fled before he was convicted. And in the photographs made from the video of the shooting of the Turkish courier in the police station you can see him aim with his left hand. So then I asked Dr Novák whether the second murder could have been committed by a left-hander, which is why Dr Novák asked for drawings from Chigulin to show how Polstrelov was kneeling when he committed the first crime. But with the furniture as it was in Zechovská's room, a left-hander would find it difficult to make the cuts we saw. He would prefer to work from the other side of the bed. Of course, it's not definite, but it's indicative.'

'And what it's indicative of,' said Slonský, 'is that Zechovská was probably killed by a right-hander, which would let Yeremenko off the hook.'

They all sat in silence for a moment or two, if you disregarded Slonský's rumbling stomach which reminded him it was time for his second breakfast.

'I think I might go and see if they've got any fresh pastries in the canteen,' he said.

'If they've got any of yesterday's they'll be half price,' Jerneková told him.

'So they will. I can have twice as many for my money.'

'What shall we do now?' called Navrátil to Slonský's retreating back.

'It's your case, not mine,' said Slonský. 'But I'm going to contact Darmant to tell him to go home. I suppose somebody ought to go to Pankrác and charge Chigulin. but since it's not my case I don't think I ought to make that call.'

Navrátil and Krob patiently went through it all with Chigulin who denied everything. Even when confronted with the forensic evidence he kept insisting there was some mistake. He was duly charged with the murders of Kateryna Teslenko and Paulina Zechovská.

'Would you like me to ask Yeremenko to find you a lawyer?' asked Navrátil.

'No!' screeched Chigulin.

Krob smiled. 'I can see that two and a half years of working with the Captain have started to rub off on you,' he said quietly.

Slonský spoke to Kristoň, who in turn spoke to Darmant. As a result, Slonský was invited to come to Mr Darmant's suite for coffee, or perhaps something a little stronger.

Darmant held up a decanter of brandy. 'But perhaps you're not allowed to drink on duty, Captain?'

'I could sip it now and not swallow until six o'clock,' said Slonský, 'but I suspect that would be an awful waste.'

Darmant poured three glasses. 'Your health!' he said.

'And yours,' Slonský replied. 'Needless to say, the little chat we're about to have never happened.'

'Of course. We understand.'

'Good. And when we've finished here I'm sure you'll want to return home on the earliest convenient plane. I would hate to have to take unpleasant measures against a grieving father.'

'That's very considerate of you.'

'As soon as your daughter's body is released by the prosecutor I'll contact you so we can arrange repatriation for burial outside the Czech Republic. A grave here would be very difficult for you since neither you nor Yeremenko will be frequent visitors here. I'm sure after the recent tragic events Mr Yeremenko would want to look for new business challenges in a place with fewer unpleasant memories for him.'

'Would you like me to send for him? He's just along the corridor.'

'No need. I think you will be suitably persuasive without my help.'

'You would expect me to observe, Captain, that all my businesses here are above board and pay their Czech taxes in full. And neither Yeremenko nor I have been charged with any offence here, let alone being convicted.'

'I'm sure that's all true, sir. And from the police's point of view, we don't want a concentration in one pair of hands, either yours or Polstrelov's. I have no plan to force a change of ownership. But I think that a change of personnel may calm the atmosphere a bit, don't you?'

Darmant sipped his brandy. 'Yeremenko can come back with me if you're satisfied he had nothing to do with this mess. Kristoň led me to believe that you wanted to question him.'

'It's not necessary now,' said Slonský, and proceeded to explain the case against Chigulin.

'Chigulin, eh? Otherwise known as Yuri Khramov. He kept the Yuri part of his name because he's too stupid to learn a new one. It's taken long enough to drum into him that Ukrainians spell it differently to Russians.'

'You know him, then?'

'Son of a long-time friend. I promised his father I'd give him a job. He's an unremarkable man, little presence, a man of no account. He thought he would be my number two just because his father had been. In the end I fobbed him off with a move here. I told him he would be a bigger fish if the pool was smaller. And this is how he repays me.'

'So he knew Teslenko was your daughter?'

'I'm sure he must have done. Yeremenko knew, after all.'

'So his calculation that if he could pin the blame on Polstrelov it would lead to severe retribution had a secure grounding.'

'If Polstrelov had done it, Polstrelov would have paid. Maybe not today, not tomorrow, but sometime. I am a patient man, Captain. And if he had gone to prison I would have had men waiting for him on the day of his release, however long the sentence. I'm glad that won't be necessary.'

Slonský drained his glass. 'Thank you for the drink. I need Chigulin to go to court and be convicted. Please don't attempt to interfere with that.'

Darmant offered his hand. 'I'll start packing now. You won't see me again, I hope.'

'I hope so too.'

EPILOGUE

Valentin placed a glass of schnapps alongside the beer. 'You'll need that after your triumph,' he said.

'A long day in court, but ultimately a happy one,' agreed Slonský.

'Through the door, turn the key, see you in a lifetime.'

'Depends how long the lifetime is.'

'You think he'll get parole?'

'I think he'll have a terrible accident in there. He'll slip on the soap, stab himself repeatedly with a kitchen knife, choke himself to death on a sock. I don't know how it'll be done, but Darmant will feel he's kept his part of the bargain by not wiping Chigulin out before now.'

'Anyway, that's not your concern. You've done your job.'

'No, it was Navrátil's case. As you heard when he stood up in the witness box.'

'He was very impressive.'

'Law graduate, you see. He knew what they wanted to hear and how they wanted it presented.'

'And you got your extra year.'

'Yes, I did. More to the point, my knee feels fine now, just as Dr Stockner said it would. I must make a point of going out to the open prison and giving Pepa Mach the kick in the ribs he missed out on due to my indisposition. By the way, did I ever pay you for that belt you bought me?'

'Of course you didn't.'

'Have you still got the receipt?'

Valentin dipped into his wallet and produced a piece of paper. 'As it happens…'

'That's good. It'll come in handy when you take it back to the shop. It seems to have shrunk.'

A NOTE TO THE READER

Dear Reader,

I started writing this book before the Russian invasion of Ukraine, and the action is set in 2008, so please do not suppose that present-day events have inspired or affected it.

Authors occasionally say that their characters have a habit of intruding themselves into stories whatever the writer planned. That was certainly true here. This book started with the intention that Slonský would be in hospital throughout so Navrátil would be in charge, but then Slonský got himself discharged and insisted on butting in.

Slonský had been taking a back seat while I was writing the adventures of Master Mercurius, but he was never forgotten, nor will he be now. He is still not quite ready to retire.

I took a trip to Prague to do some research for this book but I do not have an encyclopaedic knowledge of Prague nightclubs and escort agencies, so I will offer the disclaimer that any similarity of name with a real place is entirely coincidental. I have much more in common with Navrátil than with Slonský when it comes to that kind of thing.

Dr Novák would like me to point out that he was not actually wrong with his conclusions. He was deceived by someone who set out to do so, and he qualified his judgements, as he always does, with phrases like "It seems to me" and "On the balance of probabilities" which I may not always have recorded.

If you have enjoyed the Slonský stories please tell your friends, then maybe they will buy them too and I will be able to afford another research trip. Všechno nejlepší!

Graham Brack

Sapere Books is an exciting new publisher of brilliant fiction and popular history.

To find out more about our latest releases and our monthly bargain books visit our website:
saperebooks.com

Printed in Great Britain
by Amazon

39621617R00145